HER BEAUTY WAS HER CURSE

This is the story of Sara Hamilton, a woman whose dreamlike beauty led her into a nightmare of degradation, first at the hands of her unloving parents, then at the hands of men she could not resist.

Overwhelming in its naked truth, it is the story of a bright beginning that turned into a dark labyrinth of drugs, violence, and sexual debasement —the story of the glamorous world of international modeling, and of life on the other side of the law.

But above all, it is the story of how Sara Hamilton found her way out of the depths—the story of a born-again faith that changed her life from a heartrending tragedy to a soul-stirring triumph. . . .

LADY ON THE RUN

Lady
on
the
Run

Lucille Schirman

Ⓞ
A SIGNET BOOK
NEW AMERICAN LIBRARY
TIMES MIRROR

Except where otherwise indicated, the Scripture quotations in this book are taken from *The Living Bible*, Copyright 1971 by Tyndale House Publishers, Wheaton, Illinois. Used by permission.

Copyright © 1981 by Harvest House Publishers

Published by arrangement with Harvest House

SIGNET, SIGNET CLASSICS, MENTOR, PLUME, MERIDIAN AND NAL BOOKS *are published by The New American Library, Inc., 1633 Broadway, New York, New York 10019*

FIRST SIGNET PRINTING, OCTOBER, 1982

1 2 3 4 5 6 7 8 9

PRINTED IN THE UNITED STATES OF AMERICA

To Mildred
Who Showed Sara
The Way of Escape

ACKNOWLEDGMENTS

I would like to express my special appreciation to the following people:

Sara Hamilton (not her real name), for granting permission to use her story, though she knew full well the pain of telling it all.

Nancy Young and **Marjory More,** for sensitively critiquing and faithfully assisting in editing.

Marie Wolff, for constructive suggestions and encouragement.

Dr. Marylea Henderson, whose assistance in obtaining portions of this story was vital.

Irmgaard Carl, who arrived on the scene at a crucial time to spur me on.

Rex Page (not his real name) and those others, who for obvious reasons must remain anonymous, who relived the anguish of difficult memories to make this story more complete.

My parents, who for five years have listened to this story, encouraging, prodding, and generously assisting me to its completion.

To God, most of all, who is my Helper!

PREFACE

Several hundred school teachers and administrators were crowded into the auditorium, attending a convention. A hush fell over the audience as the program was about to begin. However, the master of ceremonies made no effort to get up. On the stage, next to him, I noticed he was as captivated as the audience by a young woman in search of a seat. She spotted one in the third row from the front, directly before the rostrum. As she walked down the aisle, she had the bearing of a queen, and the beauty of a Miss America.

Seated next to her was my traveling companion. Secretly, I hoped they'd become acquainted so I'd know something about this lovely creature.

To capture the audience's attention, as my turn came to speak, I asked, "Have you ever been so overcome by personal guilt, you could not shrug it off?" Some in the audience nodded in assent. But down in the third row, my friend turned to listen to the young woman's response. "Have I ever!" she whispered, then hesitating, she added, "If you knew what I've done, you wouldn't even be sitting here next to me."

As we traveled home, my companion said, "I believe there's a story there."

"Who is she? Is she a teacher? Where is she from?" I asked.

My interest had been stirred.

"Who was this woman who could catch the approving eye of an audience by simply walking down the aisle?" I wondered.

It appeared too remote to consider further. I filed it under "Ideas" and sent up a prayer.

Five days later, on Saturday, at four o'clock in the afternoon, a long distance call came.

"You don't know me, and I don't know you," the voice began. "We live a long ways apart. Last week I attended a convention. You were introduced as a writer. For the past five days, I've not been able to put out of my mind that I'm to tell you my story. I finally called an office in another city to inquire how to reach you. When I explained why I wanted your phone number, they gave it to me.

"I really believe I'm to tell you my story." She filled in a few details. "It's never been told before. It won't be easy. But if you want it, we'll need to go into seclusion. I'll arrange it."

This was the story I was waiting for. Based on actual incidents, this highly explosive dramatic account is almost unbelievable. The reader will be tempted to wonder, "Did this really happen?" Truth sometimes overpowers fantasy.

Fragments have been altered where necessary to protect both the innocent and the guilty, with details incorporated from the lives of others. All names and most cities have been changed.

Lucille Schirman
Santa Barbara, California
July 1981

TABLE OF CONTENTS

Part One

CHAPTER ONE

The Lurking Phantom

"YOU'RE nothing but a whore! My own daughter a whore! You're no good! No good!" Marc's clenched fist struck the table with full force.

Everyone scrambled to rescue cups of spilled coffee. Dishes rattled and the bouquet of fresh flowers toppled. Marc's voice boomed throughout the whole house, scaring them all.

When Marc inhaled in that special way of his, Sara knew it was a prelude to another name-calling episode . . . the one clue indicating that disaster was coming. It was strange, but the other members of the family at the breakfast table seemed not to notice his warning. But to Sara it was as obvious as a flashing signal light.

Wide-eyed and innocent-looking, Sara sat before her father, speechless. Shocked and numbed, she couldn't believe his new name for her. All his names hurt, but what a sting "whore" carried. Even if she had been guilty, there was no way to respond to this.

"I saw you encourage that young man who let you off in front of the house! You flaunted yourself at him!" Marc's voice thundered louder than ever this morning.

Sara stiffened. She saw Marc winding up for still another onslaught, red with rage.

"I can't stand the sight of you! You're a disgrace to the family!"

"Disgrace?" The word cut her to pieces. "From the beginning I've been the family scapegoat," she wanted to scream,

1

but didn't. "Why me?" It was a question she had often asked herself.

Pushed through school at an alarmingly fast rate, Sara at 18 was about to graduate at the top of her class from Cambridge University. Never had she been more anxious to get away from the domination of her parents. But not today. It was Saturday, the one day she usually helped out in the family-owned store.

Marc, having cleaned his breakfast plate, and ending the name-calling ritual, left the dining table. It was time for everyone to go to work. They all climbed into the family car. Sara shrugged off the family "outcast" image. Changing mental gears was a matter of survival, a game she played well.

Carlisle's Jewelry is a fashionable shop in the heart of downtown Cambridge, a suburb of Boston and the home of Harvard University. And Marc is obviously proud of his business.

Behind the jewelry counter, it's difficult to tell which of the three Carlisle sisters is the most beautiful. Stephanie and Sophia are extremely efficient and knowledgeable about their work, but inclined to be coldly businesslike. Sara, the youngest, in spite of all the verbal abuse thrown at her by her family, remains soft, vibrant, and warm.

From below the counter where she had replaced a tray of rings, Sara caught sight of a well-cut, custom-made suit. She lifted her head from the jewelry case and recognized the handsome face of the customer she had waited on two weeks earlier. She had really been impressed with Bruce Lane's distinguished manner as she assisted him in choosing a new watchband.

"Probably about 25," she guessed, "and an executive."

While measuring Bruce Lane's wrist for the number of links to fit the band, she had observed the absence of a wedding ring on his left hand. She felt relieved. She wanted an excuse to have him return. He suggested that he leave his watch for cleaning.

"It'll be ready two weeks from *today*," she had told him, hoping he would return on Saturday, when she was there. Now, almost too eagerly, she greeted him.

"Mr. Lane! A new watchband and a cleaning, wasn't it?"

Their eyes riveted on each other. Encouraged by her pleasant reception and excellent memory, he gallantly held out his claim check and a brochure.

"Please call me Bruce. But I don't know your name."

"I'm Sara, Bruce. Sara Carlisle."

"I'm really impressed that you'd remember my name, Sara. There's something special I want to ask you." He hesitated, then pointed to the brochure, studying her carefully to make sure she was attentive.

"I'm running for city council. Would you vote for me?"

"I'm sure you'll win without my vote, Bruce. I'd happily vote for you if I were old enough."

For two weeks Bruce had carefully planned his strategy to see this enchanting young woman again. As a lawyer he was usually in command of the situation, not helpless and clumsy, as he felt now.

He wished the circumstances were different. Things weren't going as he had planned.

"Sara, what I really meant to ask is will you go with me next Saturday, as my date, to a political campaign dinner?"

He knew that a hundred-dollar-per-person campaign dinner wasn't exactly conducive to winning her romantically.

At the counter they completed their arrangements as Sara's father looked on disapprovingly. She knew it would result in another bad scene at home, but decided it was worth it.

On the evening of the date, in Bruce's expensive sedan, Sara breathed the aroma of new leather upholstery and was impressed by the carefully matched hides. Driving inside the country club's majestic-looking gates, she was glad there was just enough daylight left for her to scan the parking lot.

Bruce was intently looking for a spot to park his Mercedes, but Sara was no help. Her eyes were on other things. A sweeping glance revealed a Rolls Royce here, a Bentley there, interspersed by fancy foreign sports cars and a few limousines with their chauffeurs milling about. She liked what she saw! Expensive cars and handsome men! In that order! They were her greatest weaknesses.

Entering the country-club lobby, Bruce watched as eyes focused on Sara. He knew that her charming personality and breathtaking beauty could be threats as well as assets to him. But he was willing to take any risks that might be involved.

Sara was a natural show-stealer without realizing it. From the very first, Bruce had been attracted to her for just that reason. Now, in front of the assembled dignitaries, he believed she was just the asset he needed to give his campaign a winning boost.

Moving from the lobby to the ballroom, Bruce's attention was diverted elsewhere on a campaign matter, leaving Sara to shift for herself. While not seeking it, she soon became the center of attention. It started when a suave, commanding voice greeted her.

"You must be Sara. I'm Monty Davis, Bruce's law partner."

Monty's clean-cut, distinguished features and slightly graying temples set him apart from most men. His pleasant personality took over as he began introducing her to one person after another while Sara took it all in.

Monty observed Sara's talent to project "You are the most important person here" to each person without ever using the words. He felt it himself. Watching her use this rare gift, he knew he wanted to get better acquainted and wished Bruce weren't his competition.

Anxious to come up with a quick icebreaker for himself, Monty fumbled to keep Sara's interest. He wondered how he, a fast-talking attorney, could suddenly feel at such a loss for words.

"This is the place to be tonight, Sara. I'm so glad Bruce brought you." He paused. "Sara Carlisle!" He said the name most reverently. "It's a lovely name. Sounds French. Where were you born, Sara?"

Here they were at a hundred-dollar-per-person fund-raising affair and she was being asked where she had been born! He had meant it as an opening for further conversation, but she shivered. The question had touched a most sensitive spot.

"Why can't I handle this simple subject like other people?" she wondered,

"Would you believe I came into this world in a sheik's tent?"

The calmness of her voice belied the tumult within. She hated her answer as much as the question.

Ears perked up with Sara's reply. She felt trapped.

The audience, utterly fascinated by Sara's innocent declaration, responded with a ripple of laughter. How clever they thought she was. Sara felt they were poking fun at her and they thought she was being evasive. She joined their laughter to cover her feelings.

"Come on, Sara!" Monty urged. "Where were you really born?"

Sara hesitated as her eyes quickly searched the room for Bruce. Where was he? This was his special night. She wanted to be with him. Monty interrupted her thoughts.

"Were you really born in a sheik's tent, Sara?"

The scene had quickly changed from serious politics to a partying mood. But right now Sara certainly didn't feel like this was a party. She would go along with the atmosphere of fun. She knew the question that would follow. Sara could see Monty preparing for it. The probing mind of this clever attorney was about to trap her into telling more, and she wasn't ready.

"Where was this sheik's tent, Sara?" Monty asked, as though the place really mattered.

To Sara the cute crinkle in the corners of Monty's eyes seemed to be saying, "Aha! Let's see you handle this one!"

"My sisters were born in Baghdad," she began, hoping to turn the spotlight off herself. "But I was born about a nine days' camel journey out of Rafha, in the Arabian Peninsula."

"Isn't that something!" A voice spoke for them all. "Imagine this gorgeous creature, who looks like a top-paid fashion model, coming from camel country in an isolated part of the world!"

"Where's Rafha, Sara?" someone asked, as though with only a little more information they would all know the place.

"There's only one way out of all this," she concluded. "Make a joke of it." Her eyes were talking even though she wasn't.

"You know about the land of flying carpets, Aladdin's Lamp, the Forty Thieves, and Ali Baba? That's where it all started for me!"

It sounded like a fairy tale, and they loved it! But Sara was wishing dinner would get under way. Finally she blurted out her feelings.

"This is a campaign dinner. I'm not running for an office. I can't even vote. I'm too young! What's going on here anyway, with you candidates questioning me when we're supposed to be questioning you?"

"This is marvelous, Sara." It was Bruce's voice at last. He had finally moved in to stand beside her.

"Some help you are," she thought. And then another voice chimed in.

"Does that make you an Arab, Sara?"

The question hit her like a bolt of lightning. The audience adored her spunk and even clapped at this added prodding. Finally she answered.

"No, even though I may look like one." Her voice bore no trace of the distress she felt. "My parents are European. They were traveling in Asia on business and didn't make it back to Europe in time for my arrival."

"Sara, whatever your background is, you're lovely enough to be a princess," Bruce told her.

That was the end of it as dinner was served. Between the shrimp cocktail and the prime rib, Bruce was in deep thought.

"With Sara at my side, this affair isn't as dull as I'd expected. Being only 25, I'm in for stiff competition from older more-experienced politicians, and I need all the help I can get. Sara is just the right mixture of shrewdness and loveliness to put me over the top. I've watched her charm women, while men seem overcome by her beauty. She's petite, she's gracious, she's beautiful, and she's sharp . . . all the things I've been hoping for in a wife. I didn't know I'd be conducting a double campaign—win the election while wooing Sara."

Later at home, Sara had trouble getting to sleep. The events of the evening flooded her mind.

"Bruce has such high hopes—all the way to the governor's mansion. I wonder if I'll be there with him. With graduation from the university only days away there's a new life awaiting me. Will it get me out of this house?

"Even if everyone at the dinner tonight seemed to find my past entertaining, it's been no fairyland for me to have been born under such conditions. No wonder they found it unbelievable. A sheik's tent, of all places! It's left an indelible stamp on my life. It might have been a lovely fairy story if it weren't for Mother.

"But that lurking phantom keeps shadowing my present. I wish I could put it to rest and get on with life."

CHAPTER TWO

Buried Alive!

MARC CARLISLE, Sara's father, was a dealer in precious stones. Traveling for an American company, he bought rubies, diamonds, emeralds, pearls, and other rare gems. This took the Carlisle family on the trade routes where these minerals are found. Marc didn't want to travel without his little family, and he took painstaking effort to keep them all together. He never would have seen them if they had stayed home. His pay was more than sufficient to cover the additional expenses it took to carry out this plan.

They called Brussels home, but Marc's work rarely brought him to the location of his company's European headquarters. Someone else saw to it that his merchandise reached there safely. His job was to obtain the uncut stones, then get them to a site from which they could be transported.

Strange and exotic places were common to the family. Marc's territory stretched from Turkey to India, some of the world's most rugged land. He even searched along the Persian Gulf and Arabian Sea for daring divers who would sell their pearls directly to him. This merchandise was far too valuable to entrust delivery to anyone else, so he personally escorted it to designated marketplaces. Locating and delivering these stones meant passing through dangerous and exciting regions of Southwest Asia.

When they arrived at Rafha, Arabia, Camile hoped they would stay there until her baby was born. But Marc's announcement shattered his wife's world.

"Camile, we're going to have to leave here right away. I've just received orders to deliver a shipment to Istanbul."

"Marc, now is not the time to go! I'm in no condition to travel. Even under the best circumstances, this trip isn't pleasant. How can we handle this with our two toddlers and my pregnancy? You know I'm due in about four weeks."

"Everything will work out just fine. Put your mind at rest. We've always made out well in all our travels, and I'm sure we'll get to Istanbul long before the baby arrives."

"Just like a man. He thinks this is nothing for me," Camile thought.

"While you're packing, you'll need to sew these stones into our clothing. You know how to do these things, Camile. We'll all wear Arabian clothing. It'll protect us from the sun and desert winds and make us acceptable to these people. I'll find a caravan heading to Jerusalem or Damascus."

Travel in the interior of Saudi Arabia in those days of 1935 was by camel caravan, and by automobile when there were roads for them. Sometimes in countries untouched by modern civilization, they used an oxcart. When they were near a port city in this part of the world, they would go by ship. But this could be worse than riding camels, and more hazardous, too. Some of the ships arriving in these ports looked like carry-overs from the days of Marco Polo. Waiting for one headed in the right direction could cause great delays, and this was not the time to wait.

Here in Rafha, the sea seemed as far away as Istanbul, Turkey. Almost in the middle of the Arabian peninsula, there were no airplanes coming or going. It was as though time had stood still since the days of Sinbad and the Arabian Nights. Camile thought Marc sometimes deliberately detoured from his itinerary just to see how far away from civilization he could get.

The sign over the building where they were housed said "hotel" in Arabic. It was a joke to Camile. No amount of money could buy comfort or improve the circumstances. Conveniences were simply not available.

"Couldn't we stay in a more-civilized part of the world until the baby comes, Marc?" Camile begged.

It was a bad situation, and Marc tried to console her.

"You know how good the pay is for this risky work. But things have always turned out all right for us. We'll take all the precautions we can," he said to reinforce his earlier prediction.

On the route with the camel caravan they had joined, Camile felt every sway of the camel, and it was torture! How she hated Marc for insisting on making this trip now. The pressure of the baby within her was unbearable.

"Stop the camels. I want off! I'm not going any farther!" she screamed. "You don't know what it's like. Do you want me to have the baby right here?"

But the caravan moved on. The leader was glad he

couldn't understand her language. He understood enough from the tone of her voice.

Five days out of Rafha, the old route was blocked by an unusually great number of Bedouin nomads. Such pandemonium could only mean trouble, and they had headed right into the middle of it. Marc dismounted his camel to listen to the excited exchange of feverish conversation. Being good with a number of languages, he was able to piece the story together.

These nomads were in the heat of a tribal dispute over territorial rights. Since sheep and goats were their main source of livelihood, pasture for them was no little thing. The water holes were bringing sickness to the animals from the accumulation of surfacing oil. Now the sheik of the opposing tribe had declared open war. Unless they surrendered their land by morning, it would be too late! The enemy, now nowhere in sight, was undoubtedly within close range.

Marc didn't want to upset Camile any more than she already was. He purposely left out the most important details in reporting his findings to her. The caravan leader refused to proceed any further and would not agree to Marc's argument to backtrack to avoid the possibility of a confrontation. Instead, he requested permission from the local Bedouin sheik for all in his caravan to remain overnight.

"You are welcome to spend the night. We expect the battle to begin at daybreak," the sheik told them. "You should be on your way by then."

Camile sensed the tenseness. Even the children were scared and crying. Before bedding down for the night in the tent shared with the sheik's family, Marc ordered Camile to begin transferring the precious stones from their clothing into seams in Sophia's and Stephanie's outfits.

"They're less apt to be discovered in the children's possession than ours. Best they don't know they're carrying these," Marc suggested.

"I don't understand your thinking, Marc," Camile told him. "Have you any idea what you're asking of the children? This must be five or six pounds for each of them to carry. They're bound to notice."

"I'll keep out a few gems to use in bartering, in case they're needed."

It wasn't a new experience for them to remain overnight with nomads, but never before had they been in a predica-

ment like this. An ominous cloud of doom hung over the
camp.

At bedtime the men of the camp appeared well-fortified.
But before morning they were caught off-guard as the attack
got under way. Marc felt totally helpless! Why hadn't he been
more insistent with the caravan leader to set up camp a mile
or so back instead of remaining here overnight? Too late
now! They were in the thick of it!

The Bedouins defended their pastureland until all in the
campsite were held captive. But it didn't stop there! Seizing
the screaming women and crying children, the rival tribes-
men dragged them off as Marc watched helplessly.

Camile could hardly make the quarter-mile trip from
camp. When they stopped, she was aghast and let out a
blood-curdling scream.

A freshly dug grave?

Shocked, she realized it was intended for her! Frantically
she tried to tell her captors she was not a Bedouin. It did no
good.

Back at the camp, Marc had no way of knowing the plight
of his family, but he sensed this was the time to use the bartering stones.

"Please listen!" His voice bore all the urgency he could
muster. "We are foreigners. Last night the sheik was kind to
us, allowing us to share his tent," he explained to the rival
sheik. "We aren't part of this tribe. We are dressed like your
people to make travel through your land easier. Please accept
these stones for the release of my wife and children and let
us go free. My wife is great with child and this could kill her.
You may have these valuable stones as exchange."

"If it is not already too late, we will release your family,"
the terrorist leader eagerly agreed. "We didn't know you were
foreigners. You have no part in this."

Hastily mounting their camels, Marc, a few men, and the
sheik, who was now in possession of four rare and precious
stones, raced the brief journey to the location of the women.
To Marc it seemed an eternity away.

At the grave site, a revolting, loathsome scene was tran-
spiring. Unmentionable horrors were being enacted. A
"burying alive" tribal rite was already under way. Intended as
an act of submission for the enemy, this abominable ceremony was more effective when performed against pregnant
women. Camile became the likely choice because of her advanced pregnancy.

Completely helpless, bound at ankles and wrists, Camile was thrown into the desert grave as her tiny daughters wildly screamed, "Mama! Mama!" at the top of their lungs. It was a pathetic scene, with screams turning to sobs.

At the first shovelfuls of dirt thrown on Camile, she went into shock. When Marc arrived at this horrifying scene a layer of earth already fully covered Camile. Marc didn't comprehend what had happened until the children, pointing and screaming, yelled, "Mama's in there!"

Furiously Marc scooped the dirt to uncover her, literally snatching her from the grave. Barely rescued before she smothered to death, Camile was unaware of his intervention. Back at the Bedouin sheik's tent where they brought her, another emergency suddenly faced them as Camile went into labor.

Sara was born within moments of this hideous incident. But Camile was left with the permanent scars and mars upon her memory of that terrible day in the desert. Her warped reasoning cost them all dearly. "If it hadn't been for Sara, this wouldn't have happened."

Camile could not be persuaded to continue the kind of traveling Marc's dangerous work required, and he wouldn't go without her. Back at his company headquarters in Brussels, they promoted him from a gem collector to a gem cutter, putting him in charge of their Paris operations, until he decided to go to America and get into business for himself.

CHAPTER THREE

Time to Move On

MARC CARLISLE had become so absorbed in his jewelry business that when Sara announced her choice of a career he was both shocked and exasperated with her. Camile and Marc fully expected her to go into the family jewelry business with them. In fact, they had taken it for granted. "Why can't you be satisfied working in the store?" Your sisters work there without complaining about it.

"I've taught all of you the value of a well-cut stone and how to identify good quality. Most of all, I've shown you how to close a deal with a customer! What else do you want out of life?" he asked, implying that there wasn't anything better than this. Sara had other ideas and wasn't about to be talked out of them.

"Why didn't you choose to be a nightclub performer or a model?" he went on sarcastically, suggesting that teaching was in the same category—all being unfit for a Carlisle.

What makes a glamorous, radiant, and admired woman like Sara choose to become a schoolteacher? The decision began when Sara was eight years old, right after the Carlisles moved to America.

Marc decided to strike out on his own in business. Arriving in New Jersey from Paris, Marc prudently studied the jewelry market. A week later he returned to their hotel quarters with an excitement they hadn't seen before. When they asked what he had been up to, he signaled for silence!

"Camile, I've learned that the city's best jewelry store is for sale. I believe the price is fair. The two of us could run it together. Tomorrow we'll use some of our savings from a few stones to close the deal and establish ourselves here in Trenton."

Marc had come to America with a king's fortune in valuable uncut diamonds, rubies, and emeralds. Instead of cash, they were his savings. From time to time he would sell one. Usually he borrowed against them because he didn't want to give up any. They were his treasure, and he meant to keep them!

The whole family beamed with delight at the prospect of settling down for a long stay. While Marc closed the deal, Camile went apartment hunting. Struggling with the language, coping with strange and seemingly unreasonable customs, and locating their belongings was a challenge to them all.

Later in the day Camile reported her success.

"I've found a nice six-room apartment in a five-story building. It has everything—three passenger elevators and a fourth elevator for freight. The garage is in the basement and groceries can be loaded right onto the elevator. A special chute in the kitchen takes the garbage away, and each floor has a mail chute for letters. They thought of everything."

Immediately they all wanted to see it. Marc hailed a taxi to take them exploring. For the first time they had all been included in the decision of choosing their new home.

What an exciting day! Marc bought a business, Camile located a modern apartment they all liked, and Trenton, New Jersey, became their home. It was almost too much when the next day Sophia, Stephanie, and Sara enrolled in the school nearest their new neighborhood, and father bought a car and passed his driving tests. So much was happening all at once!

When they left France, Sara hadn't yet completed the third grade, After only two days in an American school they transferred her into fourth grade, explaining that she was too advanced for third grade.

On one of Sara's first days in the fourth-grade class, the teacher, Mrs. Lowell, innocently asked a question that fit into the geography lesson.

"Who in our room was not born in America?"

Up came Sara's little hand. She felt her olive-toned skin turn red with embarrassment as she noticed that she was the only one volunteering.

"Where were you born, Sara?" Mrs. Lowell asked.

"Saudi Arabia, ma'am."

"Now, Sara, will you go to the map and point out this interesting place to us?"

Mrs. Lowell looked pleased. But the kids laughed! Moving to America was hard on a kid, especially when you spoke little English. Her fluent French was now a language barrier. And her European-style clothes caused the kids at school to make fun of her. How she spoke and dressed, and where she had been born, just didn't seem to fit. Important seeds were planted in Sara's mind while sitting in class that day!

"If I were the teacher," she said to herself in French, "I'd never embarrass kids by putting them on the spot. I would want them to feel comfortable, just as if the class were their home away from home. They would like it so much they'd rather be there than at home! And if I were the teacher, I'd show them I cared how they felt. That's the kind of teacher I want to be! Kids would be important to me, and they'd feel important to others, too."

That day the die was cast for Sara. She would become a teacher, and a good one, too! And would she love it! It was so exciting to think about!

About the same time, a temporary vision problem made it necessary for Sara to wear glasses. At school the kids called her "Four Eyes" and stood at the hallway mirror taking turns making faces and checking their appearance while wearing her glasses. Although she didn't wear them long, she didn't like being different!

In spite of this, Sara happily looked forward to school, never missing a day even though she got sick every morning. Camile insisted that Sara eat oatmeal for breakfast, with milk on it. It didn't agree with her stomach, so she threw up on the way. But even with the oatmeal episodes, school was an exciting and happy place when compared with the problems at home.

One evening at dinner, Marc announced that he had found a new apartment to suit them exactly. It was time to move again. Changing schools in midyear wasn't fun, but Marc seemed callous to these feelings.

When Marc and Camile decided to broaden their education by enrolling in night school, the girls were pleased. They wanted their parents to become more Americanized. All too soon they passed their tests while their heavy accents remained. The girls had quickly lost theirs and had expected that somehow this blight would magically be removed from their parents when they had completed the course. It embarrassed them when it didn't.

"The Carlisles are foreigners" was a phrase they often overheard.

When the Carlisle mailbox was stuffed with Chamber of Commerce brochures from every corner of the nation, they knew another move was in the making. Marc's wanderlust had him using every spare moment studying the literature carefully.

"Camile, I really should go on a buying trip. To make

more money, I need to become better acquainted with suppliers, examine the newest equipment used in jewelry-making, and study the latest jewelry fashions."

Camile eyed him suspiciously. With no place to call home very long, she had become neurotic. Prosperity made Marc restless.

"Maybe I ought to look over Waco, Texas, while I'm gone."

Marc's comment brought no audible response from Camile. Instead, she tried blocking it out by working like a dog! Repairing jewelry and stocking display cases kept her up past midnight. Then at home she prepared food for the next day. Work and gripe—that was Camile.

The idea of moving to Waco couldn't be dislodged from Marc's thinking. It started while they were still abroad. A business acquaintance planted the idea, describing Waco as "paradise." Every new city was paradise to Marc until he lived there awhile. Waco sounded too good to be true. The plan grew in his mind until he felt a compulsion to go there. The family tried to ignore his obsession with Texas, hoping it would go away.

During Marc's absence to Waco, Camile changed drastically, becoming more insecure and high-strung. Marc's restlessness was getting to her.

Since business was going well, Camile decided to have someone do the laundry, marketing, and some housekeeping. She hired a part-time housekeeper while Marc was away. Coming home from school to a cold, impersonal, unfeeling woman who gave secondhand orders didn't seem to disturb Sophia or Stephanie, but Sara felt uncomfortable with her in the house.

"When you get home from school, you take the mop or the dust rag and do your job, but you don't play. Those are your mother's orders!"

"Don't play!" That sounded like Mother. It was a constant series of negatives. There was plenty of food in the house, but little feeling.

When "Don't bring your friends here" was added to "Don't play," Sara felt new pressures. Next came "Don't talk back!" Who had talked back? Sara hadn't. But when she asked, "Am I supposed to be doing the ironing? I thought that was your job," the reply was "Don't ask reasons." More and more these phrases sounded like Mother. School was definitely a happier place.

When Marc returned from his trip, the family waited for news of his success. They were relieved when he said nothing, thinking his silence meant that he had put Waco out of his mind. No one asked him any questions for fear they would be stirring up trouble. But before the year in Trenton ended, Marc made the expected but unwanted proclamation. It seemed that all news, whether good or bad, was delivered during mealtimes.

"I've put the business on the market. When it's sold, we'll be moving to Waco. Then I'll have to return there to complete escrow. Camile, you will just have to carry on without me while I take care of these matters."

Everyone else sat at the table dumbfounded while Marc continued eating his dinner with a festive spirit. The impact of his announcement didn't faze him as he kept on sharing his idea of good news.

Camile's insecurity became more obvious with threats of "I'm going to jump out the window." Sara, moved deeply by her mother's depressions, begged her not to. Many nights Sara didn't close her eyes while imagining Camile's bedroom window sliding open and her mother jumping to her death. Camile made Marc sleep in another room "because he snores," she said.

Sometimes Sara got up during the night and quietly checked Mother's bedroom to see if she were still there. Although Camile often spoke of suicide, she never tried it.

Camile was changing in other ways too. Her voice began shattering their lives as she yelled at everyone in the family for any or no reason. The little affection she had once shown to some of the family disappeared. She became as indifferent to them as she had always been to Sara. The only thing she cared about was her work, and it appeared that this was about to disappear too. She was afraid she would not be needed in the next store.

Moving day arrived. Going to Texas was like going to another continent, except that this time they were going to have their own house. Marc bought a two-story brick house in Waco after selling the store for a good price. They loved the idea of their own home, but no one knew whether to be happy or scared about moving to Waco—no one but Marc, who still believed it was paradise.

CHAPTER FOUR

A Flaw in Paradise

THE LOADED moving van disappeared down the street and the Carlisles bade Trenton a final farewell. Since Marc had been to Waco before, he assumed responsibility for being the family tour guide. Reaching Waco's city limits, Marc gave his best sales pitch.

"Didn't I tell you it was paradise?" he asked before they had a chance to express themselves.

"We'll wait and see," was Camile's cautious response.

"I thought Texas was dry cowboy country. You didn't tell us it rained here a lot," was Stephanie's observation.

Their lovely new home had a fine view of a small lake. Tree-lined streets and well-kept neighboring homes with lush green lawns added greatly to the splendid area. Baylor University gave Waco a homey college-town touch.

Enrolling at Victory Hills School, Sara was assigned to Mrs. Ellwood's fifth-grade class. When Sara arrived home from her first day singing, Camile interrupted her happy tune. "What's wrong with you?" She had a way of robbing Sara of any joyous experience, but Sara's enthusiasm was hard to dampen.

"Mrs. Ellwood didn't seem to notice that I'm skinny or was born in a place the rest of the kids never heard about. When I was introduced to the class, they seemed glad I'd come."

Sara didn't add that Mrs. Ellwood didn't even seem to notice how ugly she felt about herself. As the days went by, Mrs. Ellwood's magical ability to stimulate loving relationships in the class produced miracles in Sara. These responses were bringing out the best in her, awarenesses she had never experienced before—self-confidence, self-sufficiency, and self-respect. She thrived on these new feelings, and even noticed how much better she felt about everyone else. And did she love Mrs. Ellwood!

"Imagine! Mrs. Ellwood thinks I'm bright, pretty, and very creative! Best of all when she tells me, 'Sara, you're becoming such a lovely person. I hope you'll continue to show warmth and concern for others. This quality will make you great!

Don't ever become less caring.' I feel happy and warm all over just thinking about it."

"So you're Mrs. Ellwood's favorite?" her sisters taunted.

She was sorry she had shared it. Everything she thought was beautiful they made ugly and absurd.

"That's all right," she told herself while choking back tears. "I don't have to be like them. I'll make it anyway, because Mrs. Ellwood believes in me and I won't let her down."

Mrs. Ellwood wasn't only an educator, but also a character-builder.

"It doesn't matter what job you're doing—give it all you've got! If it's sweeping, sweep better than anyone else. If it's cleaning the chalkboards, do it so you'll be proud of your work and can say to yourself, 'No one can clean chalkboards better than I.' If you think it's outstanding, so will I. Then life will have a good many things and bring other rewards.

"If you make a mistake, profit from it. Admit to yourself and anyone else that was hurt by it. Whatever you do, don't quit! It's only those who pick themselves up and try again who get ahead. Don't hold grudges. The person who says, 'I won't forget what you did' or 'I'll get even' is a bitter person and only hurts himself."

Every day these thoughts were reinforced in Sara as she filed them away.

In Waco a new housekeeper kept a watchful eye on things, but not on the garage. Sara just ached to play, so she made up stories at school with acting parts for her classmates. At home she sneaked her friends into the garage and they put on their little productions using old curtains for dividers. If she got caught, she would call it homework.

Make-believe helped her over many rough spots. She could get away from the don'ts, bickering, name-calling, and rejection by writing stories, poetry, and directing plays. Mrs. Ellwood helped her bind them together, and this inspired her even more. With a flashlight under the covers, she wrote at night. But mother caught her several times and said, "How dumb!"

When the fifth-grade teacher suggested that Sara be double-promoted, Camile wasted no time getting to school.

"You've made a terrible mistake, Mrs. Ellwood. There's just no way my Sara can skip a grade. It'll make her swell-headed. She's not smart enough to make it. And she's too little to go to junior high school."

Camile didn't want to listen. She wanted to do the talking.

Mrs. Ellwood was polite and listened attentively. But when Camile finished, she finally got a chance to speak. It was simple and to the point.

"Mrs. Carlisle, I am convinced that Sara can do the work or I wouldn't advise it. But why don't we let her decide what she wants to do?"

Cleverly Mrs. Ellwood had taken the decision out of Camile's hands and put it into Sara's. The next September, when she was only ten, she enrolled at Lake Shore Junior High School with students two years older then herself. Looking them over brought a real sense of loss.

"I didn't only skip a grade—I skipped some of my childhood."

Sara had come a long way from where she started—back in the sheik's tent. Was she thankful she had spent those months with Mrs. Ellwood, who had helped her not to feel so dumb, ugly, and foreign!

By now the whole family knew that Marc's business trips meant that another move was on the way. When he said he was going on a buying trip, he meant exactly what he said—to buy another store, although he implied it was jewelry he was going after. This time it was to Oklahoma.

"I've been working on an idea to open a chain of stores. We'll call them *Carlisle Jewelers and Gem Designers*. We'll incorporate. We could have them all across Oklahoma by selling franchises. There's oil money there and those rich people need a place to spend it."

"Why don't you work on having a chain of jewelry stores in Texas? There's oil money here too," Camile suggested.

But those familiar words "Time to move on" meant that too soon it was time to say "Good-bye, Waco" and sorrowfully leave new friends.

Soon after the Carlisles moved to Tulsa, Sara came home from school overcome by the honor bestowed upon her. Her class entered her in the "Best Personality" contest and she won. Camile wanted to make another trip to school to say, "There's got to be a mistake. My Sara isn't qualified." No one in the family ever congratulated her or mentioned it. It was as if it had never happened.

Near the end of seventh grade the principal called Sara to his office.

"Sara, your teachers suggest that you could move ahead to ninth grade. With your fine academic record and high test scores we know you're capable. We'd like to see you do it. If you feel uncomfortable there, you could return to your regular class with no embarrassment. You'd know in a day or two if you 'belonged.' Of course we realize you're very young for all this. How do you feel about it, Sara?"

She knew how she felt—eager. She thrived on challenges. When Mother didn't get upset, she enrolled in ninth grade.

Everyone's heart skipped a beat when Marc went on still another buying trip. They were becoming far too frequent to suit the family.

"We're moving to Cambridge, Massachusetts," he told them upon returning. "It's the home of Harvard and other universities."

Whatever happened to the chain store idea, they wondered?

When Halloween came, the three girls, who had never been trick-or-treating, talked it over. They were really too old, but felt it was their last chance. Sara was 13 and it was her first night out without either parent. Threats hovered over their heads like Cinderella at the ball.

"Be home by midnight or face painful consequences," Camile warned.

Five minutes after midnight, they returned. Mother refused to listen to any reason why they were late. Assuming that something evil had been going on, she demonstrated her authority as a strict mother. Sophia, the eldest, lay on the floor, face down. Mother, with one foot resting on Sophia's back, began beating, using a strap.

Sara couldn't stand to see anyone hit. Pulling Sophia out of the way, she quickly took her place, saying, "Beat me instead." And she did! Sara often tried to be a peacemaker. "Please don't be so hard on her," was a plea she often made for either of her sisters. More than once Sara had a clump of hair cut off as punishment for interfering. "That's to remind you not to get involved," Mother told her.

Camile always insisted on a sit-down dinner each evening in the dining room. The food was excellent, but the subjects of discussions weren't, though they had become more adult as the girls matured.

"Bankruptcy!" A solemnness like a funeral descended upon the room. Sara dropped her fork and shivers ran through her body. What did this ominous-sounding word mean? It had tones of an evil omen, she thought.

As soon as she could be excused from the table, she looked up the word in the dictionary. Father had just taken out a small loan from the bank. Was he having trouble repaying it? The profits from the business normally would pay off any extras, but his voice took on a sober tone as he began telling of a competitor who had just filed bankruptcy proceedings.

"The Jacobsons have lost their business. They were doing very well in their jewelry shop. In fact it was so good that they went into partnership with Blackman in the shoe business. They bought half-interest in his shoe shop next door to theirs. Blackman owed a lot of money and the bank foreclosed. Now the children's shoe shop is out of business and Jacobson can't pay his own bills plus those Blackman left. It's very bad! Very bad! They won't get a cent for their jewelry shop and they're losing their house and an extra car. Blackman was a thief to have taken the money for Jacobson's half of the business and not have used it to pay bills. They've gone from rich to poor overnight!"

Was father implying that his own finances were in jeopardy? Was he expressing his own fear of losing his shop? Were they going to starve?

"We won't have any shoes or clothes," Sara imagined. Sometimes Marc would say, "I don't like borrowing money." He used the same somber tones in telling the bankruptcy story. Sara lay awake nights until gradually she noticed signs of prosperity returning.

One evening the delightful aroma of fried chicken and corn on the cob brought them all to the dining table. Before anyone tasted the good food, Marc began expounding on one of his worn-out topics. Tears began dropping unashamedly onto Sara's plate, and she could hardly swallow her food. She cringed in embarrassment when Camile joined into the conversation and the two of them got louder and louder.

The subject was "the Jews." How she hated hearing them run them down as cheats and liars in business. Marc's voice cleared in the same way as when he got ready for one of his name-calling episodes on Sara.

"They're rotten," he said. It hurt her more to hear him use that expression on others than on herself.

Melissa, Sara's best friend, was a Jew. Melissa's Jewish family showed her more love than Sara ever got at home, and she loved them. The Goldmans, next door, were such kind people. Often Sara wished her family could be more like they were. Mrs. Goldman always welcomed Sara into her home with open arms, but Camile had a strict rule: "Don't bring any of your friends to this house!"

Mrs. Goldman often invited Sara to stay for dinner, but Camile's response was always the same.

"Why would they want you to come to dinner?"

The Carlisles never entertained anyone for meals, but finally Camile consented to let Sara accept Mrs. Goldman's invitation.

How different they were! The Goldmans' conversation was filled with lots of laughter—no loud talking or yelling at the table. No one was put down. Mrs. Goldman even got a lovely compliment from her husband at the end of the meal.

"That was a magnificent dinner, Mother."

At home, Marc's remarks were intended to ridicule Camile. "I'm glad I married into an uppity-up family who had a daughter that could cook," was the way Marc put it. Camile's sarcastic reply was, "I'm sure you are, because your family came from the bottom of the barrel."

After dinner with the Goldmans, Sara could hardly wait to ask Melissa, "Do you always have such good times at the table? Someday I want a home like yours. You must promise to visit me." Then both girls laughed at dreams that seemed so far away.

In the kitchen Mrs. Goldman gave Sara a big hug, just like a loving mother would do to her daughter. Sara tried not to let her tears show. She was both deeply touched and embarrassed. Her own mother had never held her in this way.

"I'm so glad you and Melissa are close friends. You are a lovely person, Sara. We want you to feel that you are part of our family. Please honor us by coming to dinner often."

Sara headed through the gate thinking, "The Goldmans really feel good about themselves." And she felt good about herself, too, until she walked into the house.

"Well, I suppose you're going to tell us you had a meal fit for a queen," Stephanie said sarcastically.

They wouldn't understand that it wasn't the food that was important. Sara said nothing. She lay awake a long time remembering how loved she had felt because the Goldmans were sincere. Up till now, Mrs. Ellwood was the only person who had ever given her these feelings.

"I'd like Melissa to be my maid of honor when I marry. I can't wait to tell her."

The next time they heard Melissa playing the piano next door it was decided that Sara should be given piano lessons. She enjoyed playing, but hated to practice. Soon she advanced enough to play Chopin. With no encouragement, she became bored and began playing music that Marc disliked.

When Marc lost his temper he was frightening. He was over six feet tall, and when he got angry he seemed monstrous. But Camile, less than five feet tall and only 90 pounds, could be his match in striking fears into hearts.

Sara's piano-playing had gotten Marc so upset that he lashed out, striking her.

"You're stupid! You're wasting our money playing nothing but junk. If you don't play right, forget it."

His roaring voice brought Camile. It always brought Camile, not to rescue, but to join in the act. Waving her arms, she screamed at Sara.

"Open the window! Listen to Melissa! Why can't you play like that?"

Melissa had taken lessons for 12 years, and she was comparing the two of them. Sara had been studying less than two years. The lessons stopped. It was time to move again.

Move, move, move! That was the Carlisles.

CHAPTER FIVE

Raised Eyebrows

CAMILE PUSHED Sara away from her as though repulsed by her touch.

"Is she really my mother?" Sara pondered. "Maybe they took the wrong baby out of the Arabian Desert and I'm really Arabian, not European."

Sara watched Sophia and Stephanie being hugged. She wanted to be part of these displays of affections too. "It's like Cinderella and her stepmother," she agonized, while being coldly excluded.

Details of Sara's birth had never been explained, and her own mother's conduct was impossible to comprehend. She was in the dark about so many things.

A surprise visit to America brought Grandmother Carlisle from Belgium just in time for Sara's fourteenth birthday. Grandmother was a beautiful woman, and when she told Sara she thought they looked alike, Sara was elated. Grandmother, petite, well-groomed, and shapely, was exceedingly attractive. The two of them were uniquely drawn to each other. To Sara it was a dream of a lifetime come true.

"Someone cares about me. She loves me! She's a blood relative! It matters to her that I was born. It's beautiful. How I wish I'd known her when I was little!"

Sara's fourteenth birthday passed without a trace of recognition. It was nothing new to her, but Grandmother Carlisle was obviously grieved.

"How strange there's no celebration," Grandmother declared. "No cake, no song, no cards or greetings, no candles and no gifts." But then she had thought it strange that there had been no indications of pleasure at her own arrival from Brussels, either.

Right from the beginning of her visit, it was obvious when Grandmother Carlisle was displeased with the sarcasm or innuendoes the family used on Sara. Her looks of displeasure were warnings that she was about to release her wrath upon the guilty. Several days passed before she let her feelings real-

24

ly show. Finally she decided that it was time to do more than raise an eyebrow. It was time for action!

Grandmother spoke French, which they all understood. Armed with evidence like a detective who has finished scrutinizing the facts, Grandmother began the rounds. It was all very private. First it was Marc. Then Camile. An air of suspense and silence hung over the house. Next was Sophia, then Stephanie. Each time it was the same—very secretive and very serious. Now it was Sara's turn.

"Soon after your arrival into this world your parents returned to Brussels, and your father told me privately of the circumstances surrounding your birth. Now I learn you've never been told the details, that it's a closed subject in this house. I cannot believe it! Have you never been told about the terrible experience your mother suffered?"

"I don't know what you are talking about, Grandmother."

"Sara, my dear, there is a reason for your mother going to pieces whenever anything is mentioned about the day you were born. The day I arrived I thought it strange that you were the only one who mentioned that it was your birthday. Later, when Sophia had a birthday, I thought it interesting that they honored her. Do they usually skip celebrating your birthday, Sara?"

"Oh, Grandmother, it is the worst day of the year for me! My mind is full of questions about my birth. 'Am I really a Carlisle?' I ask myself on those days. But it isn't limited to my birthday. When I saw how much you and I look alike, and you even mentioned it, I decided I must be a blood member of this family after all. The question crossing my mind most is, 'Did they take the wrong child out of the Arabian Desert?' Tell me honestly, Grandmother, am I an orphan they rescued and then felt like throwing back?"

Tenderly grandmother took Sara in her arms, hugging her as though it could make up for the lost years and many aches.

"Oh, my dear! It pains me that you've been treated like an orphan. It's a tragedy that this behavior has been allowed, and all so unnecessary. Let me try to help you understand what occurred at your birth.

"Your mother was buried alive because of a local predicament. She was pregnant with you when this happened, and you were not yet due. Fortunately, your father rescued her after he intervened with the leader of the skirmish. But

Camile held it against you, feeling that you were responsible for her bitter and horrible memories.

"Her anger should have been directed against Marc for exposing her to such hardships and dangers when she was so near to her time of delivery. But she knew that if she showed hostility toward him it might destroy their marriage. So she transferred all these bitter feelings against the baby who arrived under such unfortunate circumstances. You were the baby!

"It's tragic that she suffered being buried alive because of a tribal quarrel, but she lives! She is well! She carries no physical marks because of it. She had no lung trouble from breathing dirt. And your body wasn't harmed. The darling baby she gave birth to was well! But she blots out all the good and has forgotten to be thankful."

"Oh, Grandmother, I had no idea these things happened. How terrible for Mother to have to endure such suffering."

"This ghost of your mother's past should have been put to death and buried long ago. I'm ashamed of all of them for keeping it alive and inflicting it upon you, Sara. It has robbed all of you of a normal, healthy family relationship.

"I blame your father for not clearing things up. He has a weak streak when it comes to standing up to your mother. And your mother is strong-willed and very stubborn. She has many good qualities, but some are lost because of these ugly memories that she and your father have nourished all of these years. Marc is a big part of the problem, and even though he is my son, I am ashamed of him for it!"

A sense of relief came over Sara in knowing why she had been rejected all her life. It opened the eyes of her understanding to so many, many things. She was glad that Grandmother had told her. But knowing did not change the relationship between mother and daughter. Only Camile could do that. No matter how much Sara tried to bridge this gap, she was unable to close it. And Camile would go through life unwilling to face her wrong notions.

When Grandmother decided that she had stayed long enough, she made an almost-formal announcement of her farewell, and an unexpected speech.

"I had hoped to see some changes in this house while I was here. You all know what I mean. Your unwillingness disappoints me terribly. Outside of my good visits with dear Sara, this trip has been a disaster.

"This is a most unpleasant house! It hurts me to see such

callousness! Except for Sara, how cold you all are! Her heart is warm with love for you, but you smother it with your pitiable attitudes. I offered to take her out of all this, back to Brussels with me, but she would rather remain in this hostile, friendless, hate-filled house. I am ashamed to call the rest of you family! I leave with a heavy heart.

"Sara will probably remain the scapegoat this family needs. Somehow she has managed to acquire a warm personality and a happy-go-lucky disposition. Yes, she will survive all this even though she has been rejected as an animal sometimes rejects its young."

CHAPTER SIX

Rebel from Day One

A MYSTERIOUS breathing problem began attacking Sara each afternoon while walking home from school. The mile walk each way didn't appeal to the other kids, but any reason to get out of the house was special to her. It didn't matter—snow, sleet, ice, or rain—walking with school chums who felt good about themselves helped her feel better about herself. But now these attacks were so bad that she wondered if she could make it till graduation.

"Strange thing," she noticed. "These usually hit me on the way home but not on the way to school. And the symptoms are gone by morning. Evenings and weekends are the worst, but dinnertime is terrible."

The first indications of this trouble arrived as she was about to approach her father with a special speech she had memorized just for him. Fear of facing him gripped her, tying her stomach in knots.

"College!" he thundered. "Why do you want to go to college? No one in our family has ever been to college. We've made out very well without it. Besides, this is a family business we're in, and all of us are needed to make it what it should be. Why do you want to be different? Isn't this life good enough for you? It's an honorable way to make a living. You can be successful right here. Haven't you been well provided for? No! College isn't for you! You're too young. We'll not discuss it again."

"Wasn't it Father who had said, 'What this family needs is more ability to close a deal?' " Sara reflected. "I'll have to come up with a new approach to close this deal."

"You're too young!" he had said. Could she help it that she had been put into fourth grade when she was only a third-grader, and then skipped two other grades? Why hadn't anyone considered her facing this problem when she was being promoted?

"I'm not ready to face the world at 15 even if I'm almost ready to graduate from high school."

One evening Sara had great difficulty getting to the table

for dinner. Feebly she made a gesture to Marc, seated at the head of the table, then sank back into her own chair. The breathing problem was at its worst, and she waited for the labored breaths to ease before she spoke.

"Well, how's 'The Nose' tonight?" he greeted her rudely.

No one but Father ever called attention to her nose, but this was his way of being abusive to her. Sara squelched the impulse to leave the table. Anyway, she was too weak.

What did Marc find wrong with her nose, she wondered? She knew her nose better than he did. She had studied it carefully in the mirror because of his attention to it. It crushed her to have him imply that she was a freak.

"I hope you have a good day, Father," she said at last.

Being called "Father" did something to him. Sometimes Sara called him "Papa," which is what she had known him by before they moved from Europe. Once in awhile, when she felt really brave, it was "Pop." Calling him "Father" made her feel she had become more Americanized.

While relishing his put-down of her, he ignored her greeting. He intended for all of his names for her to hurt, and they did! Mother had her own list too, and her favorite one for Sara was "Rotten." Whenever Sara wanted something the family didn't approve of, they called her "Dumb" and "Stupid." It was all part of the daily routine. Compliments were a rarity in this house, but after intimidating Sara, Marc usually followed with a compliment to another member of the family. This was his way of making Sara the ugly duckling and someone else a lovely swan.

"And how's my pretty Sophia tonight? You made some good sales at the shop today."

It was hard not to be bitter about the way things were at home. Love and caring feelings for the whole family were wearing thin. She worked hard not to be resentful, but it was a never-ending battle now. Back in fifth grade she had made a vow not to be negative and fault-finding like the rest of her family.

The coldness she felt toward them was getting to her. She knew it was wrong. It was a battle without weapons, and she didn't know how to fight back. What was it she was fighting? Her parents? Her hurts? Her breathing problems? Or herself? With parental rejection, persecution, and guilt, who could handle all this? She needed help, but didn't know where to get it.

"I'm guilty because I resent my family; I'm not contributing to their business. I feel guilty because I'm sick and it's costing money for medical help. I feel guilty for wanting to leave home. I'm too young to make it on my own. And I'm guilty because I want a college education and Father says no!"

One day it rained very hard, and Sara returned from school with wet clothes and sniffles. When her cold turned into pneumonia, she was hospitalized. Fears about not surviving engrossed her thinking. Just when recovery seemed in sight, she relapsed. The breathing difficulties increased until she gasped for air. They told her to try breathing through her mouth instead of her nose.

"That's what I'm doing," she gasped. "It's the only way I'm managing to stay alive! I can't go on like this. Please give me some relief! Do something or I'm not going to make it."

The pneumonia cleared up, but the other problems didn't. At last it was suggested that Sara go to a nose specialist. Mother remembered a leading nose surgeon from Europe who had set up practice in Palm Beach, Florida. He was of their nationality, and that was good. Arrangements were completed for Camile and Sara to leave.

In Florida, Dr. Bouvier found that something was seriously wrong with her nose. To correct it they would surgically remove a blockage.

During the consultation prior to surgery, Dr. Bouvier asked if Sara had anything else she wanted to say before scheduling the operation. When he sensed she did, but was reluctant to speak in front of Camile, he cleverly maneuvered her to the examination room.

"Now, Sara, I'm here to help. Do you have something to tell me?"

"I'm glad you asked, doctor. Father is always making comments about my nose. It really crushed me when he nicknamed me 'The Nose.' Do you see anything wrong with the shape of my nose?"

"Sara, you've got one of the prettiest noses I've seen, but if it will make you happy, we can give you an even more glamorous one than you have now. We'll do a 'nose clip' as a bonus. It's called that because we clip only a fraction."

While Sara was still recovering, she got the thrill of her life. A commotion at the nurses' station could be heard all the way to her room. She wondered what was going on and got out of bed to see. Two carts, rumbling down the corridor, were loaded with bouquets of red roses.

"Who's the celebrity around here?" she asked as a nurse approached. "You are Sara."

The accompanying telegram read, "At a special honors assembly today you were the winner of THE MOST POPULAR GIRL contest. May this happy news cause you a speedy recovery. Hurry back for graduation. We all miss and love you." It was from the senior class.

"Ten dozen? For me? Wow! And all this happened with my old nose. I didn't need the nose clip job after all."

When Mother arrived later in the day, she took one look and said, "There's got to be some mistake." Sara felt the same.

With graduation just around the corner, Sara was getting excited, and thoughts of returning to school speeded her recovery. "I must ask Father again to let me go to college. His argument about my being only 15 is valid. And I'm too young to drive. What if the university won't enroll me because of my age? I know Pop won't let me go to an out-of-town college."

Then it hit her! If her parents used the excuse, "You're too young to go to college," she would answer, "Then I'm too young to work in the jewelry store, too." Yes, this would be her angle to close the deal.

Soon after arriving back home, she got up her courage.

"I've got to take advantage of my recovery condition. All too soon they'll be back to ignoring me."

During dinner Sara brought up the subject of college again.

"I should think you would be proud to have someone in this family go to college," she began. But Marc immediately interrupted her.

"You don't do what anybody else does. Your sisters are faithful in the jewelry store all week. You only work there on Saturdays. Why do you have to make trouble? But you want to go to college! Don't you know I'd have to take you every day? Black sheep! That's what you are!"

There were no buses running near their home in this Boston suburb. However, when Father said, "I'd have to take you every day," Sara knew he was weakening. That meant he was seriously considering it.

Finally Marc gave in, and Sara enrolled at Cambridge University. On icy days, when driving was difficult, he would swear at her.

"If you were old enough to drive I wouldn't be doing this.

You're no good. No good! You've been a rebel from earliest childhood."

She felt like she had just been shot full of holes—like an old blanket eaten by moths. She choked back tears, then bravely responded.

"Rebel? So you've found another name to add to you list. Tell me, Father, what are these rebellious things I've been doing all my life?"

Father couldn't name any.

"You know, Pop, I may yet become some of the names you've called me. I've been 'The Nose' but you stopped calling me that when I got a new nose. Then you called me 'Spotty.' That was from splotches on my skin. Was I ever embarrassed to go to classes. Nothing worse, I thought. It didn't even help when the doctor diagnosed the problem 'You have a temporary pigment deficiency,' he told me. Temporary? Forever was more like it!

"In high school you don't want to be different. Seeing my spots in the mirror and then others seing me spotted was too much. I felt like everyone was saying, 'Here comes old Spot.' It just killed me! I was 'Spotty' first thing in the morning and the last thing in the evening. Your usual greeting at supper made me sick.

" 'How's Spotty tonight?' you'd ask me. Who could eat after that? No wonder the next name given to me was 'Skinny!' "

"Then this morning," Sara continued, while Marc showed no reaction, "Rebel! I resent it!"

She had had it with all of them! Inside Marc's Continental, she pulled the plug on her emotions.

"My name's Sara," she screamed at him. It scared Marc and he swerved to miss a car.

"Good!" she thought. "I'm going to get a little respect around here!" Then she spoke firmly again.

"You'd never know my name was Sara in our family. Sara's a good name! Mother probably got it out of the Bible. Besides, Grandfather Lambert was a Presbyterian minister and he taught reverence for Bible names. There ought to be a little dignity with my name being Sara and Grandfather being a clergyman! But you act like I don't have any dignity. You make me out to be a nothing . . . like a zero with the edges rubbed out. Well, I've felt that way long enough! I'm not going to take it anymore!

"I've got feelings. I've got self-respect. If I turn out to be 'rotten' and a 'rebel,' you can all take the credit because you will have been responsible. I don't ever want to hear you call me 'Black Sheep,' 'Spotty,' or any of those other names again. Not ever!"

There! At last she'd talked back! She felt good! It was high time she stood up to them and commanded a little respect. But she wasn't quite finished.

"I'll expect this new treatment of me to begin at dinner tonight, Father."

CHAPTER SEVEN

Who Shook My Cage?

"DON'T STAND UP. They made a mistake!"

There she was again, up to her old trick. And Sara obediently sat there. Camile, sitting next to her, was greatly disturbed. Her Sara just couldn't graduate with the honor of being at the top of her class.

The graduating class was seated in the front rows during the outdoor ceremony, with their parents beside them.

"Sara Carlisle," the dean announced for the third time, "Bachelor of Arts degree, summa cum laude."

Finally Sara walked up on the stage, received her diploma, and returned to her seat.

"That's okay," she thought. "You've made it! Don't expect any celebrations from this family, or any congratulations, either. It's no different from your birthday. They ignore it, so why would they count this as any great accomplishment? It's a closed chapter."

Armed with a still-wet university diploma, a resume consisting of "jewelry salesperson in my father's store," and a petite five-foot-four-inch figure, she approached the Department of Education in Cambridge. Earlier in the year she had filed an application to teach fifth grade. She was told to return after she had earned her university degree.

The director of personnel asked her to be seated, but was convinced she was the one for the job before she had even crossed her pretty legs. The interview was simply routine. Only her age complicated matters.

"Eighteen? You're exceptionally young to become a teacher, Sara."

She wanted to do more than sell jewelry the rest of her life, and she had made it this far in spite of the family's discouragement. She wasn't about to let her age interfere now.

"We've not had anyone as young as you in a classroom situation before. Are you certain you can handle the job?"

"Mr. Stevens," she said, noticing his name neatly placed on his desk, "While sitting in fifth-grade class at nine years of age, I decided to be as good as the master teacher I had. The

34

idea has never left me. I'm a born teacher, and I'll be the best you've ever had."

"The school board will ask me how you managed to get through the university so early in life. Tell me, how did all this come about?"

"How can I explain why I worked so hard to be on top? Mr. Stevens, it's because I was always on the bottom at home. I had to succeed somewhere to keep from going under, so I did it at school, where it counted."

At home, she happily made the announcement of her assignment to a fifth-grade class to begin in January. Father showed his usual reaction, reminding her, "You're no good!"

"You know, Father, I'm not going to tell a child he's no good. It might make him want to prove I was right. Sometimes I feel like proving you're right about me by doing some of the things you've labeled me. It may yet backfire on you!"

A few days after she began teaching, Bruce Lane came to visit her in her classroom. It was nearly time for lunch, and Sara quickly dismissed her students. Bruce had walked into her life in the jewelry store while she was in the last term at the university. His maturity, intelligence, terrific looks, and fancy Mercedes car had all impressed her. He had the compulsion to make it—all the way to the governor's seat.

Succeeding in winning the election as city commissioner, Bruce was ready to celebrate. Camile was proud of him even though she had never been proud of Sara. At home Camile was hard at work, putting on the finest dinner, with candles, flowers, and best linens. It was the first company they had had in years. Bruce's future looked bright. Sara's future looked bright. Everything was going beautifully until a few days later, when Bruce returned to Sara's classroom.

"Sara, I've just received terrible news. I've got to report to the army! I had hoped we would be getting married very soon, but it'll have to wait."

Shattered by the interruption of the Korean conflict, Bruce set out for basic training. Immediately upon completion, he was sent directly to Korea.

Faithfully his letters came, averaging three a week, until the first of March. When her mail was returned to her, and she received no more from him, she thought he was dead. At home she added her salty tears to the pan of potatoes she peeled for dinner.

A new member was suddenly added to the Carlisle household. Grandfather Lambert was left alone after the death of

Grandmother, so Camile invited him to come live with the Carlisles. The girls hardly knew their grandparents on mother's side, and what they did know they didn't like. It was strict discipline in an unhappy house.

Grandfather, a retired Presbyterian minister, was a very difficult person. It was easy for Sara to understand why her mother acted the way she did as she watched him. Camile could only pass on what had been put into her. Sara chose to adopt a different life-style and move out. The sooner the better!

Locking the door earlier than usual at school, Sara took her marked newspaper to check out several apartments. With no success, she arrived home weary and disappointed.

"That's strange!" she thought, noticing a figure seated on the porch steps. "He must have become tired and stopped here to rest."

As she pulled into the driveway, the figure stood.

"It couldn't be! He walks like him, but he's dead! Anyway, he's too thin to be Bruce."

When she realized it was him, she stopped the car abruptly and raced across the yard.

"Oh, Bruce!" she said, falling into his arms. "I thought you were dead. Thank God, you're alive!"

"I wondered if I'd ever have you in my arms again, Sara. Waiting for this moment is what kept me alive in that awful prison camp. You're even more beautiful that I remembered. Oh, Sara! This was worth it all, just to hold you and know you're mine."

The Carlisle household was all ears and eyes, and Camile was already busy cooking a fancy dinner in his honor. She could almost hear wedding bells ringing. But nobody in the Carlisle house had ever discussed marriage sex, love or anything related to these feelings. Such subjects hadn't been mentioned in Mother's day, and there was nothing to pass on now. Communication in these areas was zero, and Sara had missed a lot of college sex-education sessions because she was rushed through, and certainly she got no help from home.

Grandfather Lambert took in everything that was going on and butted into family matters that didn't really concern him. It was nice to have him interested, but he was obnoxiously opinionated.

One day Grandfather noticed that Sara didn't have a diamond on her finger.

"Sara, why don't you get that beau of yours into the Carlisle Jewelry Store?"

She cringed at his interference, but secretly she had been thinking the same thing.

Right in the middle of everything, a calamity took place. It came about because everybody knew everybody else's business and interfered.

While Bruce waited in the living room for Sara to finish dressing for their date, Grandfather walked into the room and blew it all!

"Bruce, you decide right here and now if you are going to marry my granddaughter, or if you're just fooling around wasting time."

Grandfather's abruptness scared everyone, especially Bruce, who had become his unwilling target. That confrontation led to one of those "Dear John" letters—in reverse, since it was addressed "My Dearest Sara." Bruce's letter was honest, even kind, but she couldn't believe what she read.

I just can't stand the pressure, Sara. If your grandfather thinks I have to marry you right away, it's just too soon for me. I've come back from the war having been a prisoner, and am trying to adjust to a new life.

My law practice was dissolved, I lost the commissioner's job because I was drafted, and I need to begin over again. Something's missing in me, Sara. The drive I had to succeed is lacking. It was taken from me, like a thief, during the time I was abused, manhandled, and starved by the enemy.

I wish I could share all my feelings with you. I guess I'm afraid you'd reject me as a person. I care deeply for you, Sara, and have from the moment we first met in your father's store, but right now I'm in no position to become further involved.

At this point in my life I'm full of questions. When I left for Korea, I thought my value system was straight. My morals remain unchanged, but I'm very confused about myself. Since being a prisoner of the Communists, I find I've drastically changed. I'm not even sure I like myself as I've become. I was pressured, mistreated, reprogrammed, and all that goes with it. It hasn't washed out of my mind.

When your grandfather put on another pressure,

I found myself rebelling. I thought I was ready for marriage . . . to you, dear Sara. I was planning to ask you as soon as I got my law practice back into operation, but when the urgency of deciding right away was forced on me, I wanted to back off!

Can you see, Sara, I'm just not quite ready to step into marriage? Do you mind if we have a cooling-off period, to allow time for me to understand myself before taking on any new responsibilities?

Right now I'm really not the same guy you cared about before Korea. I'd like to postpone action to keep you from getting hurt. I'm sorry if this distresses you now, but give me more time. In the meanwhile, Sara, my care for you continues and I remain,

> Sincerely yours,
> Bruce

The world crumbled before Sara right there on those pieces of paper. It was the lawyer in him, not the lover, who wrote this letter. How it hurt! He had avoided using the word "love," replacing it with "care." Thoughts of suicide crept into her mind and she found herself nurturing them. Bruce was the first real love affair of her life, and now he was gone.

Unconsciously she began to take risks. They showed up in strange ways. Her bitter feelings toward Bruce and Grandfather were ruling her judgment.

The first in a long series of accidents was a broken finger. It happened in the school office with the mimeograph machine. Her finger caught between the rollers as she adjusted the paper. That hadn't quite healed when a sprained ankle put her on crutches. Then she closed the car door on her left hand. She had become accident-prone. During recuperation, she tried making new clothes for herself and accidentally ran the sewing-machine needle through her finger. It looked as if she was the one who had returned from war.

When the family planned what they thought was a good time, Sara spoiled it by becoming a "wet blanket." She wasn't entitled to a good time, and neither were they. This made her cranky. The family thought she had become odd. She didn't have to be odd, but she chose to be . . . to punish herself.

Self-inflicted pain and lashing out at others didn't ease her misery, but only added to it. Did the cycle have no end, she wondered? She resented Bruce and couldn't forgive him. "You could have ignored Grandfather's remark if you really wanted to," she wanted to tell him. And every time she looked at Grandfather she wanted to say, "You're the cause of it all. If only you hadn't butted in."

Sara was no weakling, but she felt weak now. It was no wonder that after only two-and-a-half months into the new school year she was forced to take a leave of absence. The nose problems were back! Another trip to Dr. Bouvier was scheduled. This time Camile rented a tiny apartment in Palm Beach while Sara was admitted to the hospital.

Things seemed to go badly from the very start. Dr. Bouvier failed to inform Sara that a new process using plaster of Paris to make a mold would temporarily shut off her breathing. He became very angry with her each time she sat up to breathe.

"How can we work on the mold when you keep sitting up?" he asked. "Hold your breath for a few seconds until we locate the place to make holes for your nostrils. It'll only take a moment."

The third time that Sara sat straight up, the doctor became thoroughly exasperated and exploded.

"Sara Carlisle! If you don't cooperate with me, I'm not going to operate! I've got to make a mold of your face."

"I can't. I'm scared. I can't breathe! I'm dying!"

Gasping for air only made the situation worse. She was getting no air at all up one side, and only a smidgen up the other. Fears of dying terrorized her. She was smothering to death! Finally they used straws for air vents, and the mold for the cast was finished and set aside. The doctor then broke the bones across both frontal sinuses and the bridge of her nose.

Although Sara had local anesthesia, she could feel and hear the hammering. Surgery lasted six hours while all the bones that had been broken were hammered into place. She wanted to scream, but no sound came.

"I'd rather have breathing problems than this," she thought. "Just let me die."

Fear compounded the aggravation. She felt the furious pounding of her heart, and the grating and grinding sensations were torture!

Back in her hospital room, after surgery, things began to return to normal. Curiosity got the best of her and she got out of bed to see what had been done.

"They've removed all the mirrors!" New panic seized her as she imagined the worst. Frantically she searched for a mirror.

"Aha! I knew it. They don't want me to see that they've ruined my face."

In the bathroom she noticed that the shiny floor tiles dimly reflected her movements. She couldn't see well standing up so she got down on her knees to study herself. The part of her face not covered by bandages was black. Later it would turn purple, then green and finally yellow. Some rainbow!

A nurse found her on the bathroom floor. Assuming that she had fainted she rang for help. When they learned that Sara was using the floor for a mirror, they didn't know whether to laugh or cry. She was scolded and told to stay in bed and ring if she needed to get up.

"But why were the mirrors removed?" she asked.

"Your mother took them down," she was told.

One week later, the doctor released her from the hospital, but told her she would need to remain in town for some time.

"Don't attempt to remove your bandages, and report to me at least every other day so I can check your progress."

Back in the one-room apartment with Mother, Sara faced the problem of being seen with her mask. If she wanted to eat she would have to be seen the way she was. Camile refused to cater food to her.

"But everyone will stare if I go out looking like this."

Hunger finally made the decision for her. When she suggested purchasing a heavy veil, Camile said, "They'll stare either way."

It was her nineteenth birthday when Dr. Bouvier gave her the good news.

"Sara, I believe you'll be able to return home in a week or so. The bandages can stay off. Be careful how you treat your nose. It's very fragile even though the bones are healing nicely."

Studying herself in the office mirror, she wondered, "Which is worse, being stared at with the bandages, or this terrible discoloration?" The color was in the greenish-yellow stage.

"If I have to stay in Palm Beach for more recovery, I might as well spend it on the beach," she decided. "Since no one else remembers that today is my birthday, I'll celebrate it by buying a bathing suit and beach blanket. It will be a present to myself."

Leaving Dr. Bouvier's office, the receptionist called out to her.

"Sara, the hospital just sent this mail over for you."

The large bundle reminded Sara of an earlier visit to the hospital.

"Four years ago I was a patient here," she told the receptionist. "Ten dozen roses arrived. I thought I had been forgotten. This is the nicest present since then, but the nicest of all was when Grandmother Carlisle came to visit from Europe and arrived on my birthday."

Wearing her new bathing suit under her dress and carrying a beach bag and her mail, she caught the bus. On the way to the beach she began sorting through the pile of envelopes. Spotting one with Stephanie's handwriting, she opened it first.

"The day of your surgery, Mama phoned. When she told Papa how you suffered, he cried."

"Papa cried?" She had never known her father to shed tears. It touched her so deeply that tears came to her eyes. Dabbing at them, she thought, "I'm glad he cared, and was sensitive to my troubles. I appreciate it more because his gentle side seldom shows."

Accidentally she bumped her still-fragile nose while wiping her eyes again. It felt like a bone popped out of place, and the pain was excruciating. Dr. Bouvier had warned her to be careful, but who would expect a few tears to result in this? Quickly she grabbed her things, stuffed the mail into her beach bag, pulled the cord for the bus to stop, and cried out to the driver.

"Stop the bus! I've just broken my nose!"

Off the bus, she frantically looked up and down the street, desperate for help. Spotting a furniture store a few feet away, she hurried into it. When an upset salesman noticed she was about to sit down on a chair by the door, he yelled to her.

"Don't sit there! Sit on this desk instead. That one's $500. What happened?" he asked, noticing her bleeding green-and-yellow nose.

"I had nose surgery recently. I was on my way to the beach. Something's terribly wrong. A bone jumped out of place. Please call Dr. Francis Bouvier. Ask him to meet me at the hospital. It's urgent! And would you please get me a taxi?"

After the salesman completed both calls, he assisted her into the taxi.

At the emergency ward, the staff assisting her were amazed to see their patient clad in a lovely swimming suit.

"It's my birthday and I was on my way to the beach for therapy," she explained.

In surgery, the three hours to repair the damage was interrupted when complications set in. Dr. Bouvier became so nervous while he operated that he forgot he had put his glasses on a stool.

"Everything's gone wrong," he cried out, exasperated. "Why didn't you listen to my warning, Sara? Now I've sat on my glasses and can't see!"

Part Two

CHAPTER EIGHT

Whistles and a Nightmare

RECOVERY was slow, and Sara would need to remain in Palm Beach under the watchful eye of the doctor for several more weeks. She decided to try the beach again. The bus ride there and back helped passed the time. Down on the beach in her new bathing suit she was really an eye-stopper, looking exactly right in every place except her nose. The warm sand and gentle breezes helped her forget the surgery, pain, bruises, and being jilted by Bruce.

"Palm Beach might be a good place to live," she mused. "No wonder people from the North swarm here for the winter."

On her third trip to the beach she heard a whistle, and she knew that her bathing suit and its contents were being noticed—perhaps even admired. Lots of guys had whistled at her in her life, and it was natural to ignore them. Besides, what kind of guys would whistle at a girl with a black-and-blue face? (It had been greenish-yellow earlier, but now it had turned to black-and-blue.)

Relaxing and sunbathing on her blanket, she could sense that the whistler was still looking her way, but she continued ignoring him. In a few minutes she heard a friendly, deep voice.

"I'm Gary Cole. Mind if I join you?"

The whistler sat down on a corner of her blanket, and Sara looked him over.

"Wow!" she thought. "The first fellow to come along since Bruce, and he wants to sit by me?"

He was as handsome as a movie star. She guessed that the surgery didn't show as much as she thought. Sara wondered, "Is he blind or weird?" But he asked the right questions and listened attentively. What a proper Southern gentleman he seemed to be! His tall frame, handsome face, deep blue eyes, and light-brown hair all caught her eye. Added to these were his charming manner, friendly deep voice, and pleasing Southern accent. Sara graded him A+. When it was time for her to catch the bus home, Gary offered to drive her.

"Beautiful car!" she told him as she got in. To herself she said, "And what a handsome man to go with it!" Palm Beach was a mecca for the wealthy, and he seemed to fit in.

That evening as Camile and Sara sat on the porch, Gary Cole joined them. Even Camile was impressed by his looks, manners, expensive car, and fashionable clothes. He looked like he had just stepped from a James Bond movie. Wearing a cream-colored sports jacket, powder-blue trousers, silk shirt with ascot to match his jacket, and white shoes, it was almost too much. He began his conversation with sincere concern.

"Sara, I just had to drop by to see how you're doing. I live only three blocks from here."

When Gary got ready to leave, Camile invited him to come "anytime." From then on Gary gave Sara lots of attention, but to get away from Camile they went to the beach. Things were really going well. Gary had a Cadillac Eldorado and looked like a corporate executive for an international firm, and Sara was improving. But her mind was working overtime.

"What's going on here with 'Miss Ugly' and this good-looking guy? It's like a romance in a fairy tale—the tall, handsome prince and his ugly duckling in a wild romantic fling leading to a lovely swan ending."

All Sara knew about Gary was their times on the beach, the front porch, his Cadillac, his Southern accent, and his good looks—hardly grounds for an engagement. But Sara was swept off her feet. Methodical, precise, and well-disciplined Sara took less time to consider becoming engaged than she did to study expensive cars. She had spent more time picking the college she finally attended than the man she was going to marry.

Sara talked with Mother about it, and she talked to Gary, and she concluded that he was a very nice person and "it's all right to be engaged!" This was better than a fairy tale, because Mother gave her blessing.

After the decision was made, Sara felt as frightened as she had with the plaster cast before surgery. There was so much she didn't know.

Gary was excited about Sara going to his home for dinner and meeting his mother. Shocked by what she saw, Sara picked at her food. Just thinking of that untidy kitchen gave her enough doubts about what she had gotten herself into. The unclean house, with clutter in every room, bugs in the kitchen, and two cats sniffing here and there (and eating off regular dishes) made her realize that she had made a mistake. Gary's mother looked neat and clean and was very hospitable and kind, but the house! Then she looked at Gary, and that dispelled her doubts and melted her heart.

The doctor finally gave his release for Sara to go home. As she got away from the beach she faced things more realistically. Walking through the door at home in Cambridge, a flood of mixed feelings swept over her. Back came the memories of a broken romance with Bruce a few weeks earlier. How different things seemed at home, away from Gary and the beach! Was this beach romance with Gary a rebound situation, she wondered? The idea that she might have made a terrible mistake was quickly pushed aside as she returned to teaching.

On the first day back in the classroom she realized that this is where she belonged. The students, happy to have her back, asked all about her trip to Palm Beach. Arriving at home from work that day, she spotted three letters from Gary and hurriedly opened them.

"Oh, my!" she moaned. "He can't write as well as my fifth graders. I thought he looked the part of a corporate executive."

Gary's grammar was atrocious and his sentences didn't tell anything. She had expected to get better acquainted with Gary through the mail, but his letters turned her off. "I wonder, was I ever really turned on?"

A combination of feelings overtook her: embarrassment, humiliation, disappointment, and dismay. Tears welled up, and she threw herself on the bed.

"How could I have been so taken by his car, his looks, and his Southern manners and accent? What a fool I've been to be swept off my feet like this! Now what do I do about it?"

She was shaken to the very foundations by her sense of

honesty and loyalty, and now she was ready to betray herself. A struggle generated within her. Then she recalled Bruce's request—"Could we have a cooling-off period to check things out?" She had resented this, but now understood what he had meant and how he must have felt.

"I can't do to Gary what Bruce did to me. I just can't. I've got to have more time."

But Camile didn't. Hurriedly she sent an announcement to the newspaper stating that her daughter was going to be married to this man from Florida. Camile did the whole thing—pictures and all. Sara pleaded with her.

"Mom, I can't marry him. It's not going to work. It's not that he's beneath me, but he's too different. I don't consider myself better, just mismatched. He's not educated. I don't know why I got engaged. He's not the one for me!"

"Sara, you are going to go through with it. I don't care what you say! He'll be good for you."

"Mom, it's not going to work. We don't have anything in common. I honestly don't know why I fell for him. The whole thing is crazy. I don't know him! He's a stranger. And I don't know his family."

It was January when she had met Gary and February when they became engaged, and Mother had set the wedding for June. They had agreed not to see each other until the wedding, "because we both need to save money."

Back in the bedroom, Sara continued weighing matters.

"I've promised Gary I'll marry him, and I can't break a promise. My parents taught us 'Never break a promise. And don't walk out on a promise even if it kills you. Don't make one you can't keep, and keep the one you make.' But look at me! I can't eat, and I feel like I've developed an ulcer. It's not what I'm eating; it's what's eating me!

"What I need is a new start—to go somewhere and begin a new life. I've had modeling offers, and it shouldn't be hard to switch. But if I leave my teaching position I would be breaking my contract, and that's breaking my word. I would never be able to teach again because I couldn't use this job as a reference. Breaking a teaching contract would ruin my future. No one would hire me. I would just have to start over again in a new profession.

"I could get a job in a jewelry store, but I would need a reference. The only one I have is from the family business, and I wouldn't want them to know where I had run to. No, the jewelry business is out.

"How could I be smart enough to graduate at the top of the class and be so stupid in choosing a husband? Talking it over with my parents is out. It's the same as 'talking back,' or being disobedient. I feel trapped. I can't verbalize my torment, for then the torture becomes greater."

Sara's nonverbal dialogue alternated between accusing and excusing herself.

When Sophia began dating seriously, it looked like the solution to Sara's problem. The timing was perfect. The Carlisle "old-country" tradition expected the oldest girl to marry first. Sara would gladly step aside and postpone her wedding to maintain family custom.

One evening Sophia made her important announcement to the family.

"Sara, you're not going to get married first because Thomas and I have just become engaged and . . ."

"Oh, Sophia!" Sara interrupted. "I'm so happy for you! Of course your wedding should precede mine. I'll help in any way I can."

"I have the answer," Mother broke in, looking unusually smug. "There will be a double wedding. You will have matching dresses. We'll have a huge church wedding, plus a sit-down dinner for 500 people."

There went Sara's perfect solution! It hadn't lasted five minutes. Well, she would have to come up with something else.

"Five hundred people?" Sara asked, picturing the family feverishly trying to come up with 500 names when she thought they would have difficulty in naming 25 friends.

Sara kept her thoughts to herself, but wondered, "You never invite anyone in for dinner. Why would you want to have them in for a fancy wedding dinner? Who are you trying to impress?" She had enough troubles of her own without getting smart with Mother.

Sophia's engagement pleased everyone. Her fiance, Thomas McDuff, was of Scottish descent, and that made him all right. Over a hundred years had passed since this branch of the Carlisles had left Scotland to settle in Belgium, but when it came to tradition, the Scottish blood was still strong. The Carlisle girls had been told, "Inheritances are only given if you marry into the right nationality." Gary Cole was fine for a husband for Sara, but he was a Southerner whose European ancestry was nondescript.

"You have nothing to say about things," they told Sara frequently as the flurry of wedding preparations proceeded. "Stephanie will be maid of honor for both of you. If you weren't marrying an outsider we might listen to your ideas. Your wedding gowns have already been ordered from Lord and Taylor in New York—custom-made of ivory satin, with seed pearls and a long, long train. It's very high society."

"Don't order a wedding dress for me. I won't wear it. I'm not going to marry Gary. I can't go through with it," Sara insisted.

"All girls feel that way at times before marriage," her mother explained. "The wedding plans have been announced. I know what is best for you. You have nothing to say. Nothing! These are my final words!"

"Mom, I can't go through with it. I'm not going to make it. I don't want to marry him. Cancel my wedding."

At school Sara felt strong and capable, but at home she felt desperate and defenseless against her mother, who took charge of everybody and everything. Mother was a manipulator! That's what was wrong!

The best place to be was school. It was a refuge from this turmoil.

In June Gary arrived as scheduled for the wedding.

"Hi, Sara! How are you?" he asked.

Sara choked at his impersonal greeting.

"Is this the way lovers greet each other before a wedding?" she wondered.

"What a nightmare!"

CHAPTER NINE

You're Going Through with It!

IT WAS ALMOST as if Gary and Sara had never met. All the little ulcers seemed to be jumping up and down on her big ones. But on the surface Sara was warm and charming, magnificently hiding her real feelings.

"Well, maybe I can go through with it. He's striking looking. People will have that to talk about if nothing else. When they put our pictures in the paper, my friends will say, 'Look at the terrifically handsome man Sara married.' And I must say we really do make a good-looking couple," she thought, studying him during dinner.

"How dumb!" Sara scolded herself. "Why doesn't someone in this family call me 'Stupid' now?" But nobody did. She still believed she needed permission to break her binding promise to Gary.

"This time you're paying dearly for your weakness for fancy cars and good-looking men. Look what's it's done for you," she reminded herself.

Never had the Carlisle house had so much activity and excitement. Friends and strangers coming and going broke Mother's rule, "Don't bring your friends to his house." It didn't even bother her. In fact, Mother was in the height of her glory. She had even hired an enclosed truck to deliver the wedding party to church.

"Truck! What do you mean you hired a truck?" Stephanie asked.

"You can all dress at home instead of at church. By standing up in the truck bed, you'll not wrinkle your wedding clothes," Mother explained. The floor of the truck bed will have a clean sheet to keep your long gowns from getting soiled. You'll hang onto the railing inside the truck while being delivered to the church," she said, proud of her idea.

Mother thought of everything—everything except how Sara felt. It was Camile's day and she loved every minute of it.

Meanwhile Sara was having reckless thoughts. The morning of the wedding she peeked out the bedroom door to see

what was going on. She had come up with an escape plot.
Her heart pounded violently.

"I wonder why I didn't think of doing this last night when
it was dark. I could have made a clean getaway then."

With activity everywhere in the house, no one seemed
aware of her absence. Nervousness brought on a dry tongue
and moist hands as she visualized her daring flight.

While Gary carried their luggage out to the car, she hurried to the window to watch.

"It's now or never. I've got to call a cab without arousing
suspicion. I'll tell them to have the door open, motor running,
and be ready for a fast getaway. If I can't phone, I'll hide in
the closet and wait it out till they've gone to rehearse. They'll
think I've gone on ahead and won't look for me."

A desperate woman was trying to come up with a desperate solution. Running out on Gary wasn't a new thought, but
it was the last moment and she wanted out. Then she remembered the depths of despair she had sunk to when Bruce
walked out of her life.

"I can't do the same thing to Gary. He's the innocent party
in this."

It wasn't like Sara to hurt others. It was easier to take the
hurt herself—like the times she had offered to take beatings
for her sisters.

"My family would never let me through the door again if I
ran out now." She hesitated. "But why come back?" Sadly
Sara knew that family ties were binding in spite of difficulties
in their relationships. She left the window and made a vow to
herself.

"I'll make this marriage work. And it will be a good one
because I can't stand failure! So let's get on with the joyous
event."

The wedding took place as scheduled. Two strangers drove
off in Gary's beautiful car. On the honeymoon in Canada
they would get acquainted and try to fill each other's needs.
Sara wasn't up to it, but she believed that openness was es-
sential between them.

"How open shall I be?" she wondered as they passed
through New Hampshire into Maine. She realized that she
had become apprehensive. Her conversation seemed foolish
. . . just the way she felt. Did Gary feel the same, she wondered? "Better not ask," she decided.

"Well, we did it! There's no way out now," she was thinking. It was funnier than a movie. She wanted to explode with

laughter. The whole thing was a comic strip. How had this situation thickened to include marriage anyway? She had been caged by a set of values of her parents and her own making. But now the cage contained Gary as well.

From somewhere deep inside her a churning, bubbling effervescence was forming. Like a cork about to pop on a bottle of champagne, it was nearly to the bursting point. She could contain it no longer. It didn't matter what Gary thought—it had to escape. A combination of fear, tensions, aggravations, and everything she had repressed within her for weeks was about to go!

Beginning as a little chuckle, then progressing to a ripple, and then by degrees growing until it was irrepressible, she threw back her head and let it come. First she laughed with her mouth closed, then open, then closed. Finally she doubled over in uncontrollable, buoyant hilarity, letting it last as long as possible. Relinquishing all the pent-up feeling brought an almost-instant inner healing. Even the ulcers seemed to go.

Gary had no idea what had brought on this unexplained behavior. No one had said anything. But oh, was it catching! He laughed along with her, then, unable to see the highway clearly, pulled over.

"I don't know what's so funny, Sara, but who could keep from laughing when you're having such a good time?"

"Gary," she said when she finally got control of herself again, "I'm not laughing at you. I'm laughing at myself and it's just too funny for words. Believe me, it's a marvelous tonic of prewedding jitters and postwedding fears."

Sara's natural, happy-go-lucky exuberance helped them both to adapt. Being at their best kept the gaps in their new relationships from showing. On the honeymoon, Gary's physical expressions were more than ample, but Sara hoped his conversational abilities would improve in the days ahead.

Back in Cambridge after the honeymoon, they packed Sara's things for the move to Palm Beach, where Gary worked with the Corps of Engineers as a surveyor for the federal government.

In the car, on the way to Florida, Sara began facing what she had suspected but avoided during their honeymoon. Their interests were miles apart, and she had known it from his letters. Gary wasn't on the same wavelength. Sara couldn't find a common ground on which to communicate. No matter what subject she brought up, the responses were the same—nearly zero. How come she hadn't noticed this in Gary when they spent all those hours on the beach? Could she have been so blinded by appearances that she didn't notice his inability to communicate orally?

"I'm not going to begin a conversation for the next hundred miles or so. I'll just see what happens. This is a test."

She checked the mileage indicator. Mile after mile passed as the silence deepened. At last they spotted three donkeys with their long, sad faces hanging over a fence. Gary laughed.

"Relatives of yours?" he asked, breaking the long silence.

"Yes," Sara replied congenially with a trace of laughter, ". . . on my husband's side."

They both had another good laugh. Sara eyed the mileage indicator again.

"Seventy miles! So this is what I can expect. There's a big job ahead of me." Her tensions eased. "He's happy. He doesn't need more. I'm the one who needs help. Well, I'll just make Gary a special project. I'll enlarge his interest level. Right now it seems limited to his Geiger counter equipment and his surveying.

Arriving in Palm Beach, Gary announced that he had rented a tiny apartment.

"It's just temporary, Sara, until we can find something suitable."

She had been afraid to ask about housing earlier for fear he would say they were going to stay with his family. Just thinking about that unkept house he had called home made her squeamish.

"It's awfully tiny!" Sara exclaimed when they got inside. It wasn't long before Sara wondered, "What do I do with the rest of the day? Just how long does it take to clean a studio apartment?"

Each day she looked forward to Gary's return from work. She tried in every way to please him and have a harmonious relationship. Since his work took him out of town and sometimes out of state, he was often gone anywhere from a few days to several weeks.

"Gary, could I go along?" she asked. "I don't want to stay cooped up in this tiny place with nothing to do. I wouldn't be any bother to you."

"Sara, it won't work. Some places I'm assigned to are out in the boondocks. We use a small mobile home as our office and one end has a double-decker bunk. My partner wouldn't put up with a woman going along. It's no place for you.

Sometimes we survey a future dam site or land to be re-claimed from the swamp or sea. It's impossible. I don't like being away from you so much either, but that's my job."

How she missed the excitement of work and people! Gary's fears about her going back to work and earning as much as he did brought insecure feelings, and he already had enough of those. They showed up with his Cadillac and striking wardrobe—his status symbols. Palm Beach was a city of splashy things, and he wanted to fit.

"If you don't want me to teach, how about my getting a job at a jeweler's? Worth Avenue has some marvelous jewelry shops. There's Tiffany's and Cartier's. I'm well-qualified to work there. I really must have something to do, Gary. You're gone so much."

Finally Gary gave in, and Sara applied for a school-teaching job and was hired. Teaching helped some, but being alone in that tiny apartment smothered her.

"What kind of marriage is this? How can I work on having a harmonious relationship and common interests with Gary when I'm by myself? And where can I go to make friends when he's not with me? It's not much different when Gary is here or away except that we have an active sex life. I want more from marriage than this."

"Gary, don't you think we've set aside enough money now to make a down payment on a house?" she asked the next time he was home.

To Sara's delight, Gary agreed. On a hill, they found one they could afford, and soon moved in. The nearest neighbors were two blocks away. Lying alone in bed at night, Sara was upset hearing dogs barking and racing onto the porch and through the neighborhood.

The house had lots of windows, but no air conditioner. With the expense of buying new furnishings, they couldn't af-ford one, Gary said. Strange thing! He could run an expensive car with an air conditioner, but they couldn't afford one for the house. Either the windows had to remain open or she would die of heat. The screens offered little security from prowlers. Now Sara had a new companion: fear joined lone-liness, and they were bad company.

Frustration and discouragement over Gary's lack of using more than two or three words at a time was taking its toll. Things had gone on long enough to expect a change. She had run out of teaching strategies. She couldn't make him over.

Why couldn't she accept him as he was? She was more like Camile than she realized—manipulative.

Although Gary didn't get home often, it was long enough for Sara to become pregnant. During the first pregnancy she suffered a miscarriage during the third month. With two more pregnancies and two more miscarriages, she was at a low ebb physically and mentally. It was a struggle to get going in the morning, and she was missing too many days of work. She asked the doctor about it.

"You're anemic. If you want a child, you'll have to stay in bed during the full term of pregnancy or suffer another miscarriage. I'll put you on a nutritional program to supplement your deficiencies."

The fourth time Sara became pregnant, Gary insisted that she quit her job, hire a housekeeper, and go to bed. She had become too weak to care for the house and do the cooking. It was frustrating to allow someone else in her kitchen.

When new physical problems developed in relation to her pregnancy, she wanted Camile. As this desire surfaced, she was amazed. Then she wondered, "Would Mother care enough to come to help?"

"Mom, I've called because I'm having big problems. I need you. I'm pregnant. I've had three miscarriages and I want this baby. I know we've had problems, but Mom, I want you with me now. It's an S.O.S."

"If your father lets me come, I'll be there."

Camile's favorable response brought a new life to Sara. Camile had never wanted Sara, but now that Sara needed her, Camile responded. Even with the imperfections of their relationship, it helped to have Camile there. Anxious months ended in a difficult delivery. Chad was born and it was worth it all.

Gary's loving reaction to Chad made Sara's heart leap. She forgot about the gap in their relationship.

"Is 'normal' having things the way I hope they'll be, or the way things really are?" she wondered.

New illnesses assaulted Sara's body and with them more S.O.S.'s to Camile. Sara didn't realize that illnesses can be attention-getters and may be self-inflicted from depression, stress, or guilt. She was starved for companionship and would do almost anything for it.

Sinus attacks, bronchial problems turning into pneumonia, then an appendectomy, and later the flu—all took a big toll. The flu took a big toll. The flu was so bad that some thought it was her death warrant. Each time Camile responded. Father began coming along with Camile when the distress signals were received.

"You are always ill. Your mother has to come and it costs so much. She leaves the business all because of you."

"All because of you!" "It's all your fault." "You're always sick!" "You always have to have someone."

These accusations pestered Sara's mind as one guilt added to another. She tried to repress them by denying they existed. They were working against her and warping her, and she was suffering from self-pity. Then the old record of how this had started was replayed. She had married against her better judgment. The family pressured her into it. Yet she had made the final choice. They were tormenting thoughts.

When Gary was home, things weren't any better than when he was away. She accepted him physically, but not mentally. It didn't help her conscience any, but he was the only one around to inflict, so she tried tormenting him with guilt. "Why should I suffer these feelings alone?" was her reasoning. But Gary didn't feel guilty. This made her angry, so she lashed out at him still more.

Unable to forgive herself for making a mess of her marriage added more guilts, and one heaped on another until she had made a prison for herself.

The sign on the guilt cage read "OCCUPIED." It was always something, and that pen was a busy place. She wanted Gary in it with her, but he refused! It was agony being there alone.

One day Sara's father talked of moving. What a familiar subject! But this time it was different: Marc included Sara in his moving plans.

"We're moving to California! Why don't you and Gary go too?"

It was a great way out of her prison, and she wanted OUT!

CHAPTER TEN

Let Him Go!

"WE'VE DECIDED to retire in California. We want you to come along. You and Gary can make new lives for yourselves there. We can be together and look after you. Gary doesn't look after you the way he should. He's always away with his work. Get him to move to California with us."

This was the best offer Sara had heard in a long while.

"Oh, thank God! I'm going to get away from this lonely place and be where there are people again. I don't want to be by myself anymore."

Gary didn't want to go. He put on the brakes! Sara hadn't counted on that. They argued—their first big fight. In desperation, Sara threatened Gary with the only weapon she knew how to use.

"You're never here. You neglect me. What's the sense of being married to you? I'm not staying here alone any longer."

It accomplished her purpose, making him feel guilty. That's what she wanted! When Sara saw how she had hurt him with those words, she was sorry and felt guilty again. Gary, afraid of losing Sara and Chad, agreed to move. Marc and Camile headed for California first. Sara and Gary put their house up for sale and prepared to follow.

Marc bought two lots in La Habra Heights, a suburb of Los Angeles. He would build his house on the lot facing the hills. The other lot, for Gary and Sara's house, was across the street, facing the ocean.

"If you give me the money from your Palm Beach house, and $100 a month mortgage payment for 20 years, the house will be yours. I'll build the house. My labor will be a gift to you," Marc said proudly.

It came to $6,000 down payment plus $24,000 mortgage payments to Marc, making $30,000 with no interest. Gary and Sara would pay their own taxes and assessments. It was a lovely deal, so a verbal agreement was made. Since it was family, no one felt it necessary to draw up papers.

Was Marc outdoing himself in an effort to make up for the past? Never had Sara seen him more eager to please her.

56

Family relationships were at their best. At last things were bright and lovely, just as Sara had described them to Melissa in her childhood—a pretty house and lots of care.

Before the house was finished, Gary and Sara began working in the new yard, planting palm and citrus trees. Hopes for warm relationships, new friends, candlelight dinners, and outdoor cooking on the patio were all bright prospects. Sara was ready for them all. Friendly neighbors were already inviting them over for barbecues, and the house wasn't even finished yet! Little Chad, now nearly three years old, would grow up in the perfect setting.

During the construction of the two houses, they all lived together in an apartment. Marc worked on the buildings nearly every day, but Gary was no help and felt left out of things. He missed his previous job and couldn't seem to work up courage to try something else. His lack of confidence showed clearly, and both he and Sara were embarrassed by it.

One day while Gary was searching for the right job to match his abilities, he went to a drugstore for coffee. At the counter he studied want ads. Aware that someone had sat down next to him, he finally looked up. What he saw blew his mind. Quickly he paid his bill and left.

When he got home, Gary's behavior shocked everyone. No one had ever seen him explode and go to pieces like this. He couldn't explain his irrational behavior. Sara always counted on Gary to be in control of his emotions. Why was he so upset? It scared them all. Was he having an attack of some kind? After several minutes he became coherent.

"A black man sat down beside me! No one does that in Florida!"

All this because a black man sat down beside him? No one could understand his prejudice or his continuous outbursts about it. Florida was still segregated, and Gary could not cope with the integration.

"Gary, try telling me why you feel so strongly about this," she said, hoping for some clue that would bring an end to his problem.

"We were taught at school and at home never to associate with blacks. They weren't to sit by us, nor were we to sit by them. It just isn't accepted and I can't take it!" was all he would say.

"How can you be so biased about people with whom you've had no contact? It's stupid, boy!" was Marc's reaction to the issue.

Gary stiffened at this implication. His problem had become so magnified in his thinking that he was actually fearful of going out to look for work. Sara understood his lack of confidence. Gary couldn't seem to function in a world where blacks and whites competed for the same jobs.

Finally Sara asked Marc to speak to Gary about it. He was blunt and unsympathetic, and the matter only grew further out of proportion.

"Go back to Florida, boy! That's where you belong—with those Southerners." That was Father's solution to Gary's intolerance and continuing outbursts.

"I can get my old job back, Sara. Let's return to Florida."

Then Marc did a complete about-face.

"You can make it here, Gary. There's lots of good money in the coin-operated laundry business. Let's look over the possibilities of your managing a chain of them." His enthusiasm was backed up with a generous offer. "I'll get you started. I'll finance the venture."

With no risk to Gary, you'd think he would have been interested, but Gary didn't respond to Marc's enthusiasm. He was depressed and full of conflicts. He didn't seem to fit into the California scene. Gary's insensitivity to his father-in-law's helpfulness caused Marc to turn on Sara. His words scalded.

"Sara, why did you marry this stupid man? Why? He hasn't got a brain. He can't even think for himself. I've begged him not to go back into his old work because it took him away from you so much. He doesn't even know what's good for him."

For too long Gary had been sitting around looking pathetic. Sara was tired of his inability to make a decision. They had moved into their new house and it was high time that money began flowing in instead of out. Sara was thinking ugly thoughts and couldn't keep them bottled up any longer. Harsh words flew from her stony heart, cutting Gary to the core.

"Gary, you are the most stupid person I've ever known. Why did I ever marry anybody as stupid as you! Why don't you just get out of here? Move back to Florida! You certainly don't fit in here!"

"What have I done? When my parents talk to me like that it kills me," Sara reflected. "Too late now, I can't take it back."

Gary, far less used to hearing such things, walked away quietly, leaving only the echo of her harsh words.

"I guess I've just been waiting for a chance to dump him.

And this is it! For seven years I've covered up from myself what just came tumbling out. It's the beginning of the end. I didn't mean to hurt Gary with these terrible words. Now I'm as guilty as the others of name-calling and insults."

Camile arrived in the kitchen to size up the situation and exploded.

"You don't need him! He's no good for you anyway. Let him go! When you're sick I come to take care of you. What is he? He's no husband to you. He's no good! Let him go!"

It was the second time Camile said, "let him go!" that Sara grabbed it. This was the exact confirmation and permission she needed. Why hadn't they said this to her seven years ago, when she begged for it?

When Gary returned, sparks were flying in all directions, and most of them descended onto him, whose only mistake was being mismatched in marriage. Getting bolder, Sara repeated her stabbing words.

"Gary, why don't you go back to Florida where you belong? You know you don't belong out here."

There it was! Sara punishing Gary again, when it was her nagging to move west that had brought him here in the first place. Now she was telling him it was a mistake in his judgment. He was the one who hadn't wanted to come!

Talk about coldness! Sara became like a sheet of ice. Without fighting or arguing, Gary began packing. Quietly he pleaded with her.

"I don't want to leave you or Chad. I love you, Sara, and I care so deeply about you. I know I haven't been the husband you've needed, but we belong together. We've had a good life even with differences in our personalities and interests. I know you're much better educated than I, but we've gotten along well together. We've never fought. You've put meaning into my life that was never there before I met you.

"We've got a good thing, Sara. Don't push me out of your life like this! Please! Sara, I'm begging you to go back to Florida with me. It's best. We don't belong here."

Sara didn't seem to notice that these were more words than Gary usually spoke at one time. For him they were his finest and most eloquent words, and not easy to deliver. But his nice words came too late. She had already made up her mind. Her response conveyed no feeling for him.

"Maybe *you* don't belong here, Gary Cole, but I do! I'm staying. This is it, Gary. It's good-bye."

Gary hugged and held little Chad as though his heart were

breaking. Even when Sara saw tears in Gary's eyes, she would not allow herself to become emotional for fear that she would give in. She walked out to car with him. Tenderly he held her, then gave her one last kiss. It was over. Farewell!

As his car disappeared around the corner, she expected a great sense of relief to descend on her. Taking Chad's hand, the two of them headed into the house, where she faced her conscience.

"That's it! Face it, Sara Cole. You've just blown one fairly good marriage. It was a better marriage than your parents have had. This is what you wanted. Don't waste time regretting what's happened. Start making a new life for yourself," she said over and over.

"You just hate admitting it to yourself, Sara Cole! But there was nothing really wrong with this fellow who was your husband. Gary never did anything out of line. There just wasn't anything going for you. You married a complete stranger, and seven years later you're still strangers."

A noise at the back door interrupted her guilty conscience. Camile arrived, hands on hips, spelling trouble for Sara.

"You stupid girl!"

"Aha," Sara thought. "Gary's barely out of sight and you're back to name-calling. His influence kept you in line."

"You're not going to get a divorce, Sara! No one in this family has ever gotten a divorce. No way are you going to be the first one!"

"Whoa, Mom. Remember, it was your advice to me that I let him go. And remember, Pop kept telling me how stupid Gary was! So why do you care if it's over? Why are you here now trying to get me to patch things up with Gary after he's gone? You told me to send him away. It's over! And with your permission and blessing, remember? You ordered me to do it."

But Camile wasn't about to accept any guilt for her part in all this. Suddenly it occurred to her this was the perfect opportunity to dump Sara from the family forever! At last she had the excuse she'd been looking for. Memories detonated inside her, fanning fires of hatred she'd nurtured since Sara's birth. The words gushed from her.

"I've hated you since the day I was forced to make that trip through the desert against my will. What a weight you were within me. With each sway of the camel I hated you even more and you weren't even born. It was hard enough to make that trip with two other children. How I detested the idea of a third arriving at that time!

"Then the humiliation and discomfort of being dragged through the desert to that death scene! You were responsible for it all!

"As the first shovels of dirt were thrown on me I wanted to scream, 'Why can't you die alone? Why do you have to take me with you?' Now I'm going to pay you back! No one else will know why. They'll all believe it was because you have broken an unbreakable moral standard. You're divorcing Gary. That's reason enough for ending the family tie with you. You are guilty! And I'll punish you as I've been punished all these years!

"You have embarrassed me and humiliated me," Camille went on. "I will see that no one in this family has anything to do with you. We'll not be coming to your house again. Ever! Nobody! Not even your father!

"You have ruined our family name! I am ashamed of you! I disown you as a daughter from this day on."

"So that's the way you want it, Mom," Sara responded. "By my concluding this marriage to Gary, you conclude our relationship as mother and daughter."

Camile meant it. Nothing would change her mind. It was unforgivable of Sara to break up her home and it was Camile's perfect excuse.

With her hands still on her hips, she walked out. But the wreckage her words left would be picked up for years. Sara watched Camile cross the street, and through her tears managed a feeble laugh.

"Mom wouldn't be caught dead wearing an apron any place but in her own kitchen. She's so upset with me she forgot she had it on.

"I'm just getting back what I did to Gary. It's the law of retribution. You reap what you sow. I tossed Gary back after seven years of marriage labeling him both UNWANTED AND REJECTED. Because I hurt him I'm being hurt. Now I'm unwanted and rejected, too. It's what I deserve.

"If only it didn't have to affect Chad. He's innocent. Now he's lost both his father and his grandparents. Too many broken lives from this."

CHAPTER ELEVEN

Marry Me! I've Only Got Six Months to Live!

"NOW THAT Gary's out of my life, what do I do? He's left an empty place that must be filled, and quickly. If it remains void very long, it could bring on depression. I've seen what this does to others. It's not for me!"

On the surface, Sara appeared to have adjusted to her new circumstances. But oh, did she feel it! Was Gary hurt by her treatment of him as she was of Camile's treatment of her, she wondered?

When the La Habra School District informed her they had no openings for teachers, Sara was undaunted. The 25-minute drive to the Whittier School District was more productive. She asked the receptionist for an application. In a few minutes the Director of Personnel, Mr. Rand, ushered her into his office. During the interview he asked why she thought they should hire her.

"Mr. Rand, I consider myself to be a top-notch teacher in every way. I was born to teach."

Sara believed in herself and didn't care if it sounded vain to say it. Her love for teaching hadn't diminished. Who else was around to toot her horn?

"If I were sitting in Mr. Rand's chair and someone presented these credentials and had my attitude I'd hire him." And in a few days Mr. Rand called.

"Mrs. Cole, you've been assigned to a fifth-grade class at a new school in Whittier Hills. Your temporary teaching contract is ready for you to sign. When your teaching credential arrives from the department of education, we'll remove the 'temporary' designation."

Hillside Elementary School is in a distinctly upper-class neighborhood. Bradley Owens, her principal, was warm and friendly and told her what he expected.

"Mrs. Cole, we believe in making house calls on parents. This new community is interested in maintaining the highest educational standards. The parents and our board of education want to establish a close-knit relationship between teachers, parents, and pupils. Get the parents of your students on your team right away and make house calls."

When she learned of a day-care center within walking distance of Hillside School, she enrolled Chad and began making house calls on the parents of students assigned to her class.

A few days after the first Parent Teachers Association meeting, Bradley Owens called her into his office.

"You've made a tremendous hit in this community, Mrs. Cole. The parents are really impressed. You've done a great public relations job. I hope other teachers catch your enthusiasm."

On the way home, Sara's spirits were soaring. Things were looking up and she was doing what she was best at—teaching.

It was hard on Chad to be up so early, but driving to school gave them an opportunity to be together that was special. Living away from the school district had its advantages—the staff at school didn't know about her marriage disaster.

"I know how teachers react to another teacher who can't make it in marriage. They believe if you can't cut it at home you can't cut it as a teacher, either. The less they know about my personal life the better."

Two months later Sara decided that teaching hadn't completely filled the vacuum in her life. Although she missed Gary less and was getting over the break in family relations, something was lacking.

"Maybe I need to be busier. I've got too much time to think. Now that the divorce is final, I need something more to help me forget it."

Friendly neighbors accepted her without Gary and invited her to coffee times and patio suppers, and to use their swimming pools. Even Fran, a neighbor several houses away, asked, "Sara, do you ever need a baby-sitter? Chad is a darling boy and I'd love to take care of him."

This was the solution that Sara needed in order to take evening classes twice a week at Fullerton State College. An advanced degree would add to her earnings and fill out her schedule. When the next term began, she enrolled for Tuesday and Thursday evening classes.

Gary faithfully sent support payments for Chad. Now that she had a salary, there was enough money to fix up the house. A year earlier, temporary window coverings had been hung. Gary had held off on ordering drapes and wall-to-wall carpeting because he didn't have a job. Now Chad, still a toddler, frequently stumbled over the uneven floor surfaces where she had placed scattered rugs. It was time to make improvements.

"An interior-decorating job is just the life I need to give me a feeling of accomplishment. Then I can invite my new friends over for pleasant dinners."

This new motivation added a spurt of excitement to her life. Leaving school earlier than usual one afternoon, Sara headed for Benson's Interior Decorating Shop on Whittier Boulevard before picking up Chad from the child-care center. She had noticed that the shop had her kind of taste. But did her taste match her bank account? she wondered.

Throwing her fears aside, she drove into their parking lot. A sign, "Reserved for S. Benson," was posted in front of the white Continental Mark V, parked next to her car. The luxury car reassured her that she was right about their having good taste. A tall, friendly salesman met her. Sara's weakness took charge.

"He's just got to be the best-looking fellow I've ever seen."

What a pushover Sara was when it came to handsome men! While she explained the purpose of her visit, she paused here and there to admire various pieces of furniture she really couldn't afford. The salesman complimented her on her good taste. His manner was very reassuring.

"I'm Steve Benson. I'd be delighted to come to your home with samples of fabrics and carpeting. I'll measure your windows and floors and give you prices. There's no obligation to buy."

It impressed her that the owner of a big store would personally come. They arranged a time for the house call, and she left to pick up Chad, feeling really inspired and excited.

"What am I thinking of? Is it the interior decorating or the interior decorator?"

When Steve Benson drove into her driveway and got out, Sara's heart leaped. "Get hold of yourself," she ordered. "This is business, not romance."

While he measured the windows for drapes and the floors for carpeting, Sara made coffee. This was not time for mugs. It was an occasion for the silver tray, best china, linen napkins, and silver coffeepot. Adding a plate of cookies to the tray, she carried it into the living room, and placed it on the coffee table. When Steve sat down to talk business, she handed him a napkin and poured coffee. It was Steve's turn to be impressed.

"How thoughtful of you to do this. People buy coffee tables and seldom use them as they were intended. It's a gracious way way of being hospitable. You have a lovely home. Do you live here alone, Mrs. Cole?"

Steve directed the conversation away from business and centered it on her, but it was a natural question and Sara didn't consider him improper. Instead she thought, "Here is a man who knows how to communicate! How refreshing!"

Steve Benson knew how to ask the right questions to show interest in her and concern for her problems. His suggestions were helpful without seeming pushy. Very diplomatically he prodded her about herself.

"This is a beautiful residential area, Mrs. Cole." He stood at the window. "Wonderful view. A swag treatment on this window would lend itself to enhancing the scene. Have you lived here long?"

After more conversation Sara thought, "What a warm, caring person. How responsive and conversant he is!"

Everything about Steve appealed to her—his suggestions for improving the house, his apparent intellect, and his eloquent speech, which to Sara flowed like a gentle stream. His pleasant personality and handsomeness, mixed with owning a successful business, all left Sara greatly awed. She was gullible. When a big, fancy car was added to the other assets, plus the fact that he wasn't married, she came up with all the right qualities needed in the formula for togetherness.

When Steve followed up with phone calls, took her to interesting places, and introduced her to people of refinement, she felt, "Well, here is someone who cares what happens to me." Since her family didn't, it was nice to have the attention of someone who was smooth and articulate.

"This is what I've been missing," she thought; "a man who can carry on an intelligent conversation and enjoys doing it."

Not once did Steve share anything about his past. His life before he arrived in Whittier seemed nonexistent. If he was postponing telling her about it, she could wait.

"Maybe it's better that I not know. I might be turned off by it."

A year went by, and she still didn't know any more. Sara had to admit that there was some strange things about Steve that she didn't want to face. Once he threatened to commit suicide and later bought a gun. Something was wrong and she knew it.

"What am I doing dating a man who wants to kill himself? What does he need a gun for?" These questions baffled her, but she sidestepped them by rationalizing. "Oh, well, I'm making lots of nice friends and going out. So what if he has a problem with himself? As long as he doesn't inflict it on me or someone else, I refuse to let it be a threat to me. He has a bright, keen mind and is wonderful company most of the time."

One day as she left school to pick up Chad, she passed Benson's Interior Decorator Shop and noticed big signs across the display window. *MOVING SALE.*

"Moving? I wonder why he hasn't told me about this? Oh, well!"

Nothing was mentioned as they continued dating, but Sara felt a little more uptight each time they were together. Before getting out of Steve's car one evening, he reached for her. Thinking she was going to get a good-night kiss, she responded. Instead, he grabbed her by the neck with a stranglehold while saying, "I love you, I love you, I love you."

After she regained her senses and breath, she said, "Hold on, there! Don't get carried away by this thing."

Perhaps he had meant it in fun, but it seemed to Sara to have a twinge of sadism. A few days later he did it again. Her courage rose. She plainly ordered, "Don't do that again! I don't like it!" Steve became very upset. She dropped the subject, hoping the problem would not show up again.

One noon he came by the school to take her to lunch. In the restaurant she noticed how serious he had become.

"Sara, we're going to get married."

"No, Steve. We are not. I don't plan to marry you. We've had good times together and I really enjoy your keen mind and being with you. But marriage? It's not for us—not to each other."

"Listen, Sara! I have something serious to tell you. I've been going to a doctor for several weeks. I have a very serious heart condition.

"Yesterday I returned to the doctor for another checkup. He told me I have as much as six months at the most, and probably less.

" 'Give up your business,' the doctor told me. 'Don't even bother to sell it. Just enjoy the little time you have left without concerning yourself with business matters. Walk out on it and don't go back,' he said.

"Now I've managed to sell most of my inventory to a competitor. Maybe you noticed the GOING OUT OF BUSINESS signs. I wanted a realtor to handle the sale, but it was too much of an ordeal for me with this condition, so I chose the easiest way out.

"Marry me, Sara! We'll only have each other briefly, but we'll make our days full of love and good sharing.

"You know I've not been myself for some time. I've talked of suicide. This heart-condition news really threw me off balance. And yesterday's visit with the doctor was like getting a death notice.

"Does this explain why my behavior has been so beastly these last weeks? I'm sorry for the way I've acted. Even now I'm being completely selfish. But I can't stand the thought of going through these last days without you belonging to me. You're in my constant thoughts, Sara. I need you so very much! I've never loved anyone as I do you.

"If we got married this weekend, you wouldn't need to make elaborate plans. I know how you feel about breaking your work contract, and I won't ask you to give up teaching unless you want to.

"Could I pick you up Friday, and we'll go to the little chapel near my store? I'll make arrangements and do anything else to help."

Sara's mind whirled. "Steve is dying? How terrible!"

"I need more time, Steve. I need to think through what you've been telling me. I'm not one for making snap decisions on important matters. Let's talk about it after school at my house. My students are waiting. I've got to get back right away."

In the classroom with her students, other things besides teaching were crowding Sara's mind. She resorted to a practice that she knew other teachers used, but she considered it lazy and unethical, training herself to avoid it. Passing out "busywork" papers without properly motivating and stimulating her students was against her principles. But she needed thinking-time now.

"These papers should keep them busy at least 20 minutes without my help," she decided. Scanning the room to be sure that every student knew what to do, she sat down at her desk and sighed heavily. Making a decision as big as marrying Steve required soul-searching, and it was painful.

Maybe Steve's strange behavior with the gun and his threats of suicide were due to the doctor's "this-is-terminal" notice. Occasionally she had seen Steve slump over in pain. Mentioning it to him brought only a casual "It's nothing" statement. What relief she had felt when he came out of the attacks! She cared for him, maybe even loved him, yet she was afraid. Her feelings were so mixed up that she couldn't sort them out.

"Well, Steve is available and no one else is," Sara concluded. "Being useful and needed—those are good feelings. Being used is one of the worst feelings of all. If only I could be sure Steve doesn't have that in mind.

"When Gary asked me to marry him, I probably said yes because I had been jilted by Bruce. I certainly don't want to say yes to Steve because I abandoned Gary, or because my family has abandoned me. If I say yes there's got to be a reason."

CHAPTER TWELVE

He Needs Me

THE DISMISSAL bell rang and Sara left the classroom as eagerly as the students. Usually she stayed to get ready for the next day, and some students would linger, hoping for the intimacy of being with her when the others were gone. But not today. She had other plans.

"Everybody out!" she called to the stragglers. "I must lock up now!"

As she pulled into her driveway, she noticed her parents working in their yard. To avoid her, they made a hasty exit indoors. Then she saw her mother drive away. It grieved her to have them behave this way, acting like she was poison.

"It's the best show on the block, Sara," some neighbors told her.

Just the same, it hurt. Since they had cut the communications, the only way her parents had of knowing what was going on was to watch through their front window. Drapes moved slightly when Steve's car drove up. Sara knew she was being talked about.

Steve arrived, calling out, "Let's go to the store for steaks. My treat, Sara, barbecued on your patio."

At the store, Steve selected meat. As Sara picked out lettuce she accidentally brushed against another customer. "Sorry," she said. Then she discovered that it was her own mother!

"That fellow you're going with is a bad character!" Camile told her bluntly.

Just at that moment Steve arrived, placing his packages in Sara's shopping cart. He pretended not to have heard Camile's remark.

"Mother, this is Steve Benson; Steve, Mrs. Carlisle."

Steve knew he had arrived at an awkward time, and he backed off.

"It's nice to have met you, Mrs. Carlisle. Excuse me. Sara, I'll get in line at the checkout counter."

While Steve barbecued steaks, Sara fixed salad and baked potatoes. The phone rang. It was Camile.

"If you ever marry him . . ." she began.

"Aha! That's it! Mother butting in again," Sara told herself. She didn't even wait to find out what Camile had in mind.

"Good!" Sara told her mother. "You don't want me to marry him—I'll marry him."

Camile's response to Sara was to hang up! Camile never held long phone conversations.

"Don't hold grudges," Sara remembered that Mrs. Ellwood taught her in fifth grade. "Don't pay back. The person who says 'I won't forget what you did' is a bitter person and only hurts himself. Sara's thoughts teeter-tottered. "Mom didn't mind calling Gary stupid and wanting me to think the same. She didn't mind hurting Gary. It's the divorce she minds and my thinking of marrying again. That's against family principles.

"So she's ashamed of me, is she? Well, all right. Let her be. I'll make it worth her while. I'll marry Steve."

Part of Sara's guilt told her she had no right to be happy.

"You've done wrong. Punish yourself." Marrying Steve was that punishment. She didn't really want to marry him, but taking care of him in his dying days would be punishment enough for her part in dumping Gary. Since guilt requires payment, this would pay off the debt in full! The account would be settled once and for all! And it would all be over in six months instead of having to pay over a lifetime. Steve would be dead and that would be that. Paid in full!

She was unable to foresee how these actions would all backfire on her. Sara could hardly wait to tell Steve the decision she had reached.

"Steve," she began with a joyous tone in her voice, "I've decided to marry you."

"Oh, Sara! You've made me the happiest man alive," he said, taking her in his arms.

"I'll take good care of you, Steve—such good care that we may even lick this thing and add years to your life."

At seven o'clock the next morning the doorbell rang. Sara was getting Chad his breakfast and hurrying to be ready to leave for school by 7:15.

"Now who do you suppose that is, Chad? It's so early."

"Mom! What a surprise! Come in and have coffee with me." Sara ignored the latest problem that existed between them.

Camile entered the room just far enough for the door to

close. This wasn't about to be a "forgive, forget, and makeup" visit. She had come armed with information like a private investigator. This was the first time she had been inside the house since she had disowned Sara, but she pretended not to notice the new furnishings.

Chad, hearing his grandmother's voice, jubilantly ran into the living room, hoping for a hug. She pushed him aside with the same coldness she used on Sara. He left the room crushed and crying.

"Sara, I've found out Steven Benson owes money all over town. He's a dishonest person and a thief."

"Mother, where did you get your information?"

"I have my sources," was the limit of Camile's reply.

"I wish you cared as much about me as you do Steve's reputation, Mother. I'll be going on a honeymoon with Steve on Friday after school.

"I see it's useless for me to continue this conversation. Don't tell me afterward, Sara, that you didn't know better."

That night Sara phoned Fran, her neighbor and friend, to arrange for Chad to be cared for while she and Steve honeymooned in Palm Springs.

Between now and Friday there was much to do—shopping for a trousseau, changing to a Thursday hair appointment, and packing.

At three o'clock Friday afternoon she dismissed her students, calling "Everybody out" to hurry them along. She rushed Chad to Fran's, then greeted Steve, who was waiting in his car in front of the house. While she changed into her new wedding suit, he parked her car in the garage and loaded her luggage into his trunk. Sara wondered if her parents were watching.

Suddenly memories of an earlier wedding-honeymoon hit her. This was a repeat, except that the other time she wanted to run from the wedding. Steve's conversation brought her back to reality.

"First thing when we return from Palm Springs I'll change my will. You'll get everything. Then I want to buy you a nice sports car—something for running errands. And I have a wedding present you'll really like.

"Remember the pieces of furniture you admired the first time we met? When the inventory of furniture was made up to sell out, I omitted some items from the list and saved those pieces for you.

They'll be delivered next week. We'll make this house our

masterpiece of creativity. It'll be an interior decorator's dream—a showpiece for *Better Homes and Gardens*. It will keep our minds off the short time we'll have together."

Steve lived in a condominium apartment, but the "no children" rule meant that Sara wouldn't be moving in with him. The sensible thing for them all was to have him move into Sara's house.

At the small wedding chapel, she walked down the aisle to the altar.

"It wasn't much different last time," she sighed to herself.

"There's one thing I know for certain. It's only for six months. That isn't very long. I can make it."

CHAPTER THIRTEEN

Nobody Will Know How You Died

THE INTIMATE setting was perfect in every way. It was a dream come true. Even the words were right. Sara had first heard compliments like this at Melissa's house, when Mr. Goldman spoke them to Mrs. Goldman. Although she was only 14 at the time, they had left an indelible impression.

"Lovely dinner, Sara. You always do things so graciously. Candlelight, best linens, china, and sterling silver! And this spinach souffle has got to be the most delicious I ever tasted. The entire meal is magnificent. I call this 'living it up.' It's been a good year, Sara."

It was their first wedding anniversary, and Sara was seven months pregnant. Looking across the table at Steve, Sara spoke kindly, but her thoughts were troubled.

"You've done all right yourself, Steve Benson. Not one trip to the doctor in a whole year. Not one attack, and you look better than ever. You've had a miraculous recovery. That is something to celebrate."

Even before the second week of their marriage, Sara strongly suspected that Steve's declaration "I've only got six months to live" might be a lie.

Now, one year later, she wondered what made him do it. Had he been so desperate to marry her? Did he think it was the only way to get her?

Their honeymoon had been all it should be. He had kept his promise to buy her a car, a Mercedes 450 SL coupe. It fit nicely in the garage, but did it fit into their budget? she had wondered.

"Finances will be my department while I'm still able," he had told her. And why not? It was his money he was spending.

In spite of the apparent serenity, shadows of uncertainty still hovered overhead. The gnawing thought "How will I ever make it?" raced through her mind frequently these days. She wished her mother hadn't warned her about Steve being a dishonest person and a thief, even if it were true. It was bad enough to learn that he had lied to her about dying.

Having been forewarned and ignoring the notice made her feel more than guilty. She was stupid—just what they had called her at home when she was their scapegoat.

"How could I have been so gullible?" she often asked herself. "Too late now to back off. I'm in it up to the top of my guilt cage."

"Strange thing! Neither Steve nor I have ever mentioned the matter of his 'terminal illness,' though we both know what a hoax it has been."

It remained a closed subject, behind a locked closet door, like a skeleton. Sara knew better than to question Steve about how he felt. Once she asked the name of his doctor, "in case he's needed." Checking it out, she learned that the only Dr. Bradley Finch for miles around was a veterinarian. "No point in pushing Steve into more lies," she decided.

Steve's contacts with big-name investment people and his far-out dreams kept Sara uptight. What was going on in the den, with private little meetings and subdued voices belonging to men with big, fancy cars? The mystery of this man who was her husband became greater each day.

It was her own conduct that baffled her. She hadn't really wanted Steve as a husband. And now she was going to have his child. Maybe it was the way Steve treated Chad that gave her the idea. They had talked it over and agreed they both wanted a child of their own. As Steve brushed away Chad's tears, held him on his lap, and cuddled him, he showed his capacity to be loving and kind. These were big plus marks in favor of having their own child.

After Stacy's birth things seemed to go better. Steve wanted more family togetherness. That was good! The four of them constituted a close-knit family. Sometimes he just declared a holiday for no reason and they would all get into the car for a drive, then eat out and walk on the beach. Steve was lighthearted and fun, and he loved a nice family outing. Chad wanted to stay close to him and Steve responded affectionately.

Beginning to relax, Sara felt that life was the sweetest it had ever been. She had a loving husband and two beautiful children, and everyone was in excellent health. The house was the decorator's dream that Steve had promised. He had even added a swimming pool. Maybe the lies Steve had told could be put into the past and overlooked. With all these indications of a good life, why should she look for trouble?

Sara hated lying, and it was hard to forget, but she was trying.

After a leave of absence for Stacy's birth, Sara decided to go back to work. Steve's lavish spending with no visible income was disturbing. Suspicions about his financial affairs brought uneasiness about the children's and her future. With special facilities for infants at the child-care center, Sara felt at peace. During lunch hour she could run over to see Chad and Stacy.

When Stacy was a year old, Sara returned to complete her work for the advanced college degree she wanted. It was insurance on her future and would add greater financial security. Steve enjoyed baby-sitting on Tuesday and Thursday evenings while Sara attended classes.

Sara couldn't know that all hell was about to break loose in what had seemed a tranquil home. One evening she returned from work, scooted Chad to his room to play, and put Stacy into her playpen. In the kitchen she began dinner. Steve arrived home earlier than usual, complaining of a terrible headache.

"I spent the morning in Keith Byrd's office. We've been working together on some investments. I felt a bit draggy so Keith offered me a pill 'to fix me up,' he said. Something in my head exploded. I've had this terrible headache ever since. That's why I'm home early."

"What was the pill, Steve?"

His eyes appeared peculiarly glassy and his mouth was set.

"I don't know. Keith didn't say and I didn't ask. He told me it was something that would give me a lift. It did, all right. It lifted my brain right out of my head.

"I was going to buy some property today, but you didn't have any money so I didn't buy it."

"What do you mean, Steve, 'because I didn't have any money?' "

What kind of rationalizing was this? Where had all the money he had been spending come from? His $600 suits, $150 shoes, $25 neckties, and custom-made shirts all fit the picture of a successful businessman or a racketeer. Which was he? Sara still knew so little about him.

Priding herself on behing honest and reliable, she couldn't stand anything shady or underhanded. If there were the least twinge of dishonesty, she wanted nothing to do with it. But here she was, living with a person she knew was deceptive with her.

That night Sara slipped into bed later than usual. Carefully she crawled in so as not to disturb him, but he wasn't asleep. He drew her to him and she responded affectionately, then enthusiastically to his lovemaking. Later, when she was nearly asleep, he suddenly and without warning kicked her out of bed.

"What's come over him?" she wondered as she started to get up from the floor. "This is crazy." Before she got to her feet he grabbed her around the neck and dragged her across the room. Violently he seized her hair, then banged her head against the wall. This continued for about 15 thuds. Then, as suddenly as he started, he stopped and said, "I love you," leaving her crumpled on the floor.

Steve got back into bed. When all was quiet again, Sara heard "click, click, click." Here was his gun again! Why did he have it under his pillow? What was he doing spinning the chamber? What had happened to him? Something had changed him into a monster. Her heart beat furiously. She didn't know anything about demons, and was afraid to find out.

Was it that "pep pill" that had turned Steve into a fiend? It had all started at that time. When she was sure he was asleep, she crawled in again and clung to the edge of her side of the bed.

The next morning as she looked at him, a new uneasiness gripped her. His eyes, usually warm, were a cold, steel blue, so piercing and intense that it made her shudder. While she was fixing eggs he came up behind her, put his arms around her waist, and announced, "I am Lucifer." Then he laughed! It wasn't the laugh of the man she knew! Someone else down in there was laughing for him—an intruder!

"What did you say?" she asked, shaken by this bizarre behavior.

"My name is Terror. I bring terror into the lives of those I choose," the voice answered.

"Have you had any more of Keith's pills?" she asked. "What's Keith's last name?"

"No, I don't have any of Keith Byrd's pills."

"I think we ought to go to a doctor. I know a good one. Let me call his office now, Steve."

"No, I'm not going to a doctor. I'm starting another project today and it's time for me to leave."

The next night Sara studied for final exams after Steve went to bed. When she slipped in, trying her best not to disturb him, he grabbed her around the neck and cried out, "I love, I love you, I love you," while nearly choking her to death.

From then on it became a nightly ritual. He would pull Sara out of bed, hit her head against either the floor or the wall, and repeat over and over, "I love you, I love you, I love you. There's no one I love as much as you." Back in bed all seemed quiet until he suddenly began spinning the chamber of the gun, causing the "click, click, click" sounds.

How could a man who could be so sweet to the children and to Sara turn into something so evil? This wasn't the same man who enjoyed family togetherness. With no excuse other than that pill, he had changed. His actions were becoming more frightening each day. He swore he hadn't had any more pills, but what else could be behind his strange actions?

Chances of Sara surviving were getting slimmer and slimmer. Between the stranglings, beatings, and gun clickings, Sara's nerves were disintegrating. If she had had a choice between the wall or the floor beatings, she would have chosen the floor, since it was thickly padded by heavy carpeting.

This strange sequence of events all began with carpeting. Steve had selected it for her. Now here she was with her head on it, being beaten almost to the point of death. Something needed to be done, and fast. But what? There was no one to help. She was all alone with this problem.

"How much of this are you going to tolerate before you do something?" she asked herself, knowing there would be no reply. "Are you taking this from Steve as part of the punishment you still deserve for the shabby treatment you gave Gary? How long before that debt is finally paid up, anyway? How does one go about getting the bill marked 'paid in full'?

"If you leave him, where will you go? Whose house is this, anyway? If anyone's leaving, he's the one! How will you get him out? And the children—what about their safety?"

Thinking about these questions was punishment in itself. Afraid to stay and afraid to leave, Sara remained. What a mess she was in! Steve's unnatural and frightening voice threatened vengeance when she spoke of leaving to get a divorce.

"I'll kill you in a secret way if you file for divorce. There's a place in the back of your head I'll press and nobody will know how you died."

Steve claimed this gruesome knowledge about this spot on the cranium from having once worked in a mortuary.

One moment he was threatening her life and the next moment he had her on the floor, kissing her feet, telling her how much he loved her.

If Sara thought she had had a time of peace in her life before all this, it was removed in a fraction of time, supplanted by terror and confusion.

CHAPTER FOURTEEN

Invasion by an Unseen Presence

TERRIFIED SCREAMS ruptured the peaceful Saturday morning. Icicles of fear pierced Sara's heart.

"That's Chad! What on earth is wrong?"

She raced to the room where he had only a moment earlier been peacefully at play with his dog, Penny. Now she found him clutching Penny in the middle of the floor.

"Chad, what's wrong?" she gasped.

"Mama, I'm scared! The doorknob just turned," he sobbed hysterically. "But there's nobody there! Just an awful smell! See Penny? He knows there's something too."

Chad was right. Penny's hair bristled all the way to his tail. His body was rigid.

Before all these strange things began happening, they had gone to the pet store to buy a dog. It was Steve's idea that the dog be a Boston terrier. Sara had complained about the price.

"One hundred dollars is too much for a pet. Can't we find a good house dog for $25 or $30? Why not try the dog pound?"

But Steve insisted on buying *this* dog, and now she was glad they had him. Chad had been begging for one, and Steve agreed that every boy needs a dog.

"Boston terriers are alert, quick, and small enough to keep indoors, and they make good pets."

On the way home from the pet store they argued about the price. To change the subject, Steve questioned Chad.

"What are you going to name him?"

"I'm going to call him Penny 'cause Mom doesn't think he's worth much," he announced. It was one of the last good laughs they had.

Penny was a good housedog and watchdog. After Steve had taken the pill that Keith Byrd offered, Penny was immediately aware of a strange presence in the house. He seemed to observe it before anyone else did. His ears would perk up and his body would twitch to a strange kind of attention each time one of these attacks of "the wind with the foul smell" drifted into a room where he was. He never growled or

79

barked at these odd happenings, yet watched intently as the doorknob turned with no one on either side, as if he saw something the rest of them didn't. Then he would sniff the air.

Sara frequently got up and jerked the door open to see who was there, hurrying as fast as she could, trying to catch the thing in the act of turning the knob. She never succeeded. Nothing was visible on either side of the door, but the unmistakable odor was its telltale sign of intrusion.

"It's weird! If I show I'm afraid, I'll upset the children. They've already become highstrung by this."

Sometimes this nauseous and loathsome odor drifted into a room where Sara was at work and seemed to hover directly over her. Quickly she stopped whatever she was doing to examine the source of the smell by sniffing. Never did she find its origin or anything tangible, but only the displacement of good air—replaced with a sickening, foul-smelling scent. She watched curtains, drapes, and tablecloths move with no window or door open.

When Steve told her his name was "Terror" he was right. How eerie that "the wind from the wilderness" seemed totally separate from Steve, yet had arrived simultaneous with his strange behavior.

Neighbors were beginning to ask questions about peculiar things they witnessed—Steve's voice, now loud and strange, his odd behavior, and ominous happenings in the house at all hours.

Sue and Jack Worth, Sara's next-door neighbors, were caring people, offering assistance. One afternoon they met Sara in the driveway.

"Hi, Sara. We've really been worried about you. We just don't think it's safe for you here anymore," Jack told her. His brow was furrowed. "Who is this guy you're living with? He's not the same fellow you married over three years ago. What's happened to him, Sara?"

"I really appreciate your concern, Jack. I honestly don't know what's happened to Steve. I'm just having to play it by ear."

"Sara, we're genuinely concerned not only about you, but your children, too," Sue added. You're welcome at our place, day or night."

Sara made no effort to explain the depraved entity dwelling inside her husband. How do you explain that "a strange power, like a great wind from the wilderness" has taken possession of Steve and the house?

It was too difficult and embarrassing to explain that a foul-smelling and invisible being drifted from room to room spreading fear, hate, terror, and turmoil, invading and occupying every corner of the house. Drifting here and there at will, it sometimes lingered momentarily and sometimes remained several minutes before passing elsewhere or dissipating.

When Sara considered getting help from a psychiatrist for herself, she feared that her own sanity instead of Steve's would be questioned, so she dismissed the idea. It was just too humiliating to share any of these unbelievable happenings even with the closest of friends.

Steve Benson's looks and actions didn't match. This strikingly handsome 32-year-old man, dressed in $600 suits, could bring women to a standstill for another look. He certainly didn't appear to be possessed by a demon. Yet the diabolical phenomenon dwelling inside Sara's husband was beyond comprehension.

One night, hovering directly over her bed, the evil intruder overstepped his bounds. Sara woke suddenly and sat bolt upright. Instinctively she knew that something was radically different. She checked the clock—it was one o'clock exactly. The odor was unmistakable and lingered much longer than usual. Up till now the bedroom had seemed off-limits to it.

In the dimness of the room, lit by a ray of light from the street lamp, she examined Steve. He was asleep, but something was definitely wrong. What was it? She could not substantiate her conviction, so she got up, walked around to his side of the double bed, and bent over him. He looked so peaceful, but his breathing was heavier than usual. To listen better she kneeled. Something was different. But what?

Slipping into the master bathroom, she closed the door carefully, turned on the light, and sat down on the closed cover of the commode.

"Why do I have this heavy, heavy feeling of something being so dreadfully wrong in there? It's as though the evil one put a hex on Steve while it hovered above him."

Out of the corner of her eye she caught a glimpse in the mirror of the medicine cabinet door slightly ajar. Being a strict door-closer, she instinctively got up to close it. But it was Steve's side that was open, and curiosity stopped her. She opened it all the way. A few days earlier she had wiped out the shelves on both Steve's and her side of the medicine cabinet. Like a magnet she was drawn to a bottle with no label.

"Three capsules! What are these? Why is there no label? Something is definitely amiss here. Has Keith been supplying Steve with those "brain blower" pills? Are these what are responsible for the monstrous things happening in this house?"

Compelled to recheck Steve, she kneeled beside him again, carefully listening to his breathing.

"I'm afraid to shake him. If I'm mistaken about his condition he might turn on me and cause a scene of terror again. It's heavier than before. Is it my imagination because of the pills I found?" Sara's heartbeat quickened. "No! I'm not mistaken!"

She rushed from the room to the den. With trembling hands she dialed the number for the sheriff's station.

"This is urgent. I want to speak to someone who knows about drugs."

While waiting she thought, "There's probably only a skeleton crew on duty and no one knows about drugs." It seemed to take forever before someone responded.

"My husband is in an unusually heavy sleep and I believe it's because he's been taking some kind of drug. His irrational behavior has threatened the lives of my children and myself. Right now his breaths are labored and spaced abnormally far apart.

"I discovered an unmarked bottle just now with three capsules remaining. I believe these may be more of the same pills which caused some kind of explosion in his head the first time he took one. Since that first pill, his behavior has been irrational and terrorizing. I believe he's suffering from an overdose right now. Would you be able to analyze them immediately to determine if they are responsible for this condition?"

When the officer on duty told her she would have to bring the capsules to the station herself, she explained that she was afraid to leave the children in the house alone with Steve. Finally she agreed to his suggestion.

"Okay, I'll be down as quickly as I can. If I don't get help, we may all be dead before another day ends."

With thumping heart and trembling hands, it was difficult to get into her clothes. As last she grabbed her car keys, handbag, and the bottle of pills, and headed for the sheriff's station.

An officer escorted her into the laboratory and emptied one of the capsules into a vial. He examined it without expressing an opinion.

"It will take a few hours before we can accurately ascertain the contents of this particular substance."

"A few hours? We could all be dead by then. Can't you be more explicit than that?"

"It's a guess without proper analysis, but my opinion—and it's only an opinion at this stage—is that it's either PCP or acid, and your husband should be treated at an emergency hospital right away."

"Officer, he's a big, powerful man and wouldn't submit to me under any circumstances. I can't go home alone. And without help he could die. He's threatened to kill me, and tried more than once to do it since he took the first pill. Won't you send officers with me?"

By 4:30 that morning Steve was in the hospital, connected to breathing equipment, with Sara beside his bed. The quantity of drugs he had taken was enough to kill three men. At the first signs of daylight coming through the hospital window, Sara's thoughts were mixed.

"He's alive. I ought to be glad. I guess I really am. I fought to keep him alive. I wouldn't have done otherwise."

She picked up the bedside telephone to call for a substitute teacher. A recording took her message. Then she phoned Fran to take the children until she could free herself.

"If only Mother cared enough to help. I could sure use family with me now."

After a few hours Steve's coma began to subside. When he responded to the probes the doctors made on his body, the breathing machine was turned off. He was breathing for himself. It was a good sign. Sara went home to shower and check on the children. How could she prepare Chad for whatever might be in store? And there was Stacy, still too small to know what was going on, although she had definitely been affected by the fears and tensions around her.

Back at the hospital, Steve had been moved to another room. His hands and feet were strapped to bedposts by special bands. Several tubes were connected to his body. When Sara walked in, she found him asleep. Moving a chair nearby, she listened to his breathing. It was not labored as it had been at one o'clock, when her suspicions were aroused. A nurse explained that the bands were for his own safety.

Steve's eyes opened and he began studying the room. With

tubes in his nostrils and throat, he was unable to speak, so he gestured with his head and eyes for them to be removed. Sara sensed a growing anger rising in him and called for the doctor to remove the restraints.

With hate-filled eyes, he screamed curses in spite of the tubes obstructing his speech. In a wild rage he summoned all his strength. The nylon bands snapped, one by one, like strings on a package. Next he flung the tubes from his arm, mouth, and nose (plus a catheter) to the floor in one motion. Only moments earlier he had been near death, and now he was a hulk of superhuman strength.

The doctor's and Sara's eyes were riveted to this wild scene. It was as if they were watching a television screen. They stood transfixed for what seemed a timeless moment. Steve made an effort to stand. In that instant the doctor leaped from the room in a gigantic step, to summon help.

Meanwhile, Sara watched as Steve grabbed the metal bed and ripped it apart with nothing but his hands. The room was a bedlam of commotion as first two men tried to subdue him and failed. Then two more arrived. Finally five were holding down this fiend. This was no human being they were holding down. It was a demon of PCP. Three others placed new restraints on Steve.

In the hours of awakening from a near-death trip, when any normal man would be too weak to even lift a hand, it took eight men to repress him. Sara knew that this was not merely a case of mental illness, but that something else was occupying Steve's body and making it his abode. Had it pushed Steve out to make room for itself, she wondered?

Five days later Steve returned home—or rather his body did. Steve did not seem to be the occupant. All the mannerisms associated with him were lost. The eyes looked out and claimed that which belonged to Steve, but it wasn't Steve who claimed them. His head was held differently. His walk, unlike the one he had had previously, did not have the lilt that had enhanced his appearance.

The voice, now owned by another being—an evil monster—was filled with hatred. An altogether different set of decibels, ranging from loud to extremely loud, was not that of the man Sara had lived with. The tone range and pitch belonged to another being, who used Steve's body and threatened to burn, stab, choke, and commit murder, mayhem, and rape.

This time when Sara asked the body of Steve, "Who are

you?" she received still another reply. "I am Deceit. That's my name."

"I already know that." Lying was nothing new, but these lies were. Lies, lies, and more lies, most of which were targeted against Sara.

With the home in shambles and "the thing" in control of her husband's body, there was only one place in the house offering sanctuary. Sara was grateful for the seclusion that her bedroom afforded. "The thing" had not entered it since one o'clock the morning she had awakened sensing "the wind with the foul-smelling scent." There was no explanation as to why it had not invaded this room along with all the others. Steve, not desiring entry into it, never set foot inside the bedroom after coming home from the hospital. Instead, the den became his private domain while the master bedroom became hers.

CHAPTER FIFTEEN

Drowned by a Garden Hose

ONE MORNING about four, the phone awakened Sara. The impostor's voice oozed sickeningly from it. The words were vile.

"Everybody's dead. You're next. They're all burned up. When you step out of the bedroom door, that's it!"

The fiend had gone more berserk than ever. Where was he? Frantically Sara dialed the sheriff's station. She was afraid to leave her room to see if the children were still alive. There was a feeling of safety in the bedroom. The emergency operator asked the address.

"Please don't make me come to the door when they arrive. I've been threatened over the phone and told my children are dead and I'm next. If I check to see if it's true, I may be killed. He said I'd get it when I opened the bedroom door. Have the deputies let themselves into the house. The key is located inside the clothespole pipe nearest the back door."

Sara dropped to her knees in desperation to call out an S.O.S. to God—something she had not done before. There wasn't anyone else to help.

"Oh, God, I don't know who else to ask. I feel helpless. I've not been exactly on speaking terms with You. I'm not up to promising anything in exchange for Your help. Right now I need You without any strings attached. Please see me through this and protect my children if they're still alive."

When she heard deputies calling to her, she shouted back.

"Please see if my children are alive."

In a moment, they responded. "You can come out now. Your children are peacefully asleep."

"Is my husband here? Since he went berserk, he's slept in the den."

The sofa bed hadn't been opened. Where was he? And where was this disaster he spoke of? Was it only in his mind or was he just torturing her? Sara calmed down and plugged in the coffeepot. The deputies joined her at the kitchen table while she tried sorting out what had happened.

"I know things look strange to you, but imagine getting a

86

phone call in the middle of the night telling you everyone is dead and you're next!"

She spotted a figure in the doorway, and shivered. He looked like he had just come from the pit of hell.

"S-S-Steve!" His name stuck in her throat.

He glared at her with piercing eyes, then fired questions so fast she could not answer one before he asked another. He cut her answers to pieces. The presence of the deputies did not restrain his ugly manner.

At first Sara tried to form answers, but quickly realized that his questions were framed to discredit the truth—to make her seem scatterbrained to the deputies. They looked at one another, then signaled that it was time to cut out.

"It's just a family quarrel," Sara heard one of them say as they left.

Steve went to the den as though nothing unusual had happened. Sara went back to bed to try to get a little more sleep.

"If only I could sleep in," she thought when it was time to get up. "But it's Saturday. This is the day I'm supposed to graduate. It's taken three years of hard work to earn this, and I'm not going to let last night's episodes spoil it."

Each Saturday at 10:30, Sara had a standing appointment at the beauty shop. In less than four hours she was due to go through the graduation line. It was hard to get her mind on what needed to be done.

"I can't go looking like this. I've got to get my hair fixed. I'm afraid to leave the children at Fran's. Steve might take them. Well, they'll just have to go with me."

On the way to the beauty appointment, Sara tried to explain the situation and busy schedule to Chad.

"Daddy isn't well and can't take care of you today. You and Stacy can sit on the lawn at the university while I graduate. It's a big job, Honey, because you'll have to watch Stacy and keep her happy and quiet. Do you think you can do it? You won't be able to leave her to play."

"I can do it, Mommie. I'll take good care of her and we'll be quiet."

As she sat under the dryer at the beauty shop, Sara mentally ran through the sequence of things to do.

"Make lunch as soon as we get home. Put cap and gown into car to wear after I arrive on campus. Fix snacks for the children to keep them happy and quiet while I'm in the commencement exercise.

"It's important for me to go through that line. And the

children need to feel needed. Right now we need each other more than ever."

Rushing home, everything went smoothly until it was time to leave again. They were totally unprepared for what happened next. Heading out to the car after a quick bite of lunch, she checked her watch.

"Good. A few minutes to spare," she sighed.

Sara helped the children into the car. As she turned, she was surprised to see Steve standing behind her with a garden hose running at full force, even though he hated yardwork.

Without warning, Steve grabbed Sara by the throat with one hand and rammed the hose into her mouth with the other. She struggled to free herself, but was powerless. As she gulped down water, she tried desperately to push the hose out of her mouth with her tongue.

Sara was drowning—by a garden hose! What a terrible way to go. Somehow she finally broke his hold on her and ran into the street. Oblivious to cars, she ran panic-stricken, gasping for air. The water in her was making the same sloshing sounds one hears while shaking a hot-water bottle. She felt she was waddling in slow motion, making no progress. The water weighed her down.

"Help! He's crazy! Absolutely crazy!" she screamed to a family in their yard. "Please help me, He's trying to kill me. Help!"

Before anyone could respond, Steve caught up and grabbed her arm.

"I'll kill you right here, Sara, if you make another sound. I don't care if I have to do it right here in front of the neighbors," he hissed.

The neighbors stood transfixed, not realizing the seriousness of the situation. *Another incident ended with no known dead.*

Steve disappeared. Back at home she blotted herself dry. No time to change clothes now. Her hair was wet, but the graduation cap and gown might cover the worst damage. She dashed into the car and drove off. The children seemed unaware of what had happened, since the car was facing away from the incident.

Arriving at the college campus, she reviewed last-minute instructions with Chad again, then got into her cap and gown.

"You'll be proud of us, Mommie. Don't worry," he said trying to sound like a man.

"Do a good job taking care of Stacy while I'm busy, and

the three of us will got out for a special treat when this is over. We'll eat out and have hamburgers, French fries, and milk shakes. This is a special day and we're going to celebrate."

While rehearsing for graduation earlier in the week, Sara had learned that she could cut out of line after she had received her diploma without being noticed. Being near the beginning of the alphabet had its advantages.

While speeches were being given, Sara was mentally tuned out. She was here primarily because attendance was required to receive her degree. She could allow her mind to wander until her name was called.

"How come I graduated from college with highest honors and can earn an advanced degree, but can't make a decent choice when it comes to husbands? The only decisions I make are wrong ones. I operate my life like an unthinking computer that's been incompetently programmed. Usually a person falls over a rock once, but not a second time. I fall over the same one a dozen times.

"If this is such a special day, why am I thinking of the past? I ought to be thinking of a bright future. It's pretty late in the day to come up with something, but I'm capable. The most special thing I can think of is to wash Steve out of my hair. For good. And why not?

"His six months were up a long time ago! Why hasn't he died? Why haven't I left him? I won't function properly again until he's out of my life and his threats leave with him.

" 'If you leave me I'll kill you,' he says. I'm sick of hearing it. 'If you divorce me I'll kill both you and the kids.' It can't be any worse than it is. Today I almost drowned. How dumb to take any more. If I do, I deserve whatever I get!

"There's a way out of this mess without killing or getting killed. What I need is a new sense of authority. I might as well take the chance. I can do it! And I will! That will be my graduation present to myself. I'll do it at the next encounter with Steve. Living in the high-risk area is nothing new to me!"

CHAPTER SIXTEEN

We'll Blow You to Kingdom Come

EAGER AND excited by a new feeling of bravery, Sara was ready and waiting to take on Steve. When he threatened Chad with one of his scare tactics, she knew the time had come to take command.

"If you ever lay a hand on either Stacy or Chad, I will kill you with my bare hands," she barked. The new sense of authority she asserted both scared and pleased her, but she disliked the threat.

Using the word "kill" in this house had become as common as saying "hello" or "good-bye." Its use must be terminated immediately, she decided before it is forever too late!

For an instant she felt like reneging, then charged ahead full speed.

"I'm not afraid of you anymore, Steve. I'm not afraid to divorce you. So don't come up with any old or new threats, because they won't work.

"I want you out of this house *now!*" she went on, pointing to the door. "You, your deceit, your 'wind from the wilderness' with all the scare tactics you've gotten your kicks from—take them with you and don't ever return! Do you understand? Get out and stay out!"

It was the schoolteacher coming out in her. Just saying the words gave Sara a brave image. They sounded like her mother's words, and she hated the mannerism, but the boldness pleased her. And it worked!

Steve left immediately. No arguments, no threats—in fact he left almost meekly. Why hadn't she used this authority to speak up earlier?

The next day a locksmith installed heavy-duty deadlock bolts inside the frames on both the front and back doors. He changed the doorknob locks and dropped a bar into the bottom rails of the sliding-glass doors. If Steve tried to return, it wouldn't be easy to get in.

What relief with Steve gone! Even Penny was different.

With no traces of "the wind from the wilderness" and no doorknobs turning mysteriously, life seemed worth living again. Sara was thinking less about Steve every day.

About a week after Steve's departure, Sara rose as usual at 5:30, put on the coffee, and stepped out the front door to get the paper. On the driveway where it had fallen, she unrolled it, then caught sight of a white Continental parked down the street.

"No, it can't be," she thought in disbelief. "He wouldn't sneak into the neighborhood. He'd just boldly pull into the driveway" She dismissed the idea and went inside.

Promptly at 7:15 she opened her attaché case and placed the corrected students' paper inside.

"Time to go to school," she called to the children, then unbolted the new lock and stepped from the kitchen into the garage. Her blood ran cold! The attaché case fell to the floor. A big noose struck her in the face, then swayed gently to and fro.

"Is this meant for me?" she gasped.

There was no question in her mind that Steve was behind this. That car parked down the block had been his. When the locks were changed, she had not thought about the garage.

Where is he now?" she wondered. Just then the noose swayed again. She looked up and her fear changed to rage. He had perched himself in the rafters.

"So you're back! You look ridiculous up there, Steve. Get down this instant! And put that gun away!" she ordered.

The noose scared her, but it was the sight of him that produced boldness. He began yelling obscenities at her. Here she thought she was in charge, and suddenly the strength she had regained with his leaving dissolved. She pushed the children through the kitchen door, hurried inside, and rebolted the door behind her. She dialed the number of the sheriff's station. She knew it by heart.

"How many more trips will they need to make?" she wondered while waiting for them. Shouts at the back door a few minutes later gave her courage to join the deputies in the garage.

"Come down peacefully or we'll blow you to kingdom come! Throw down your weapons—NOW!" they ordered.

Steve was waving his gun while swinging the noose. What was on his mind, anyway? Had he planned to kill her with the gun and hang himself? Or was it the other way around?

Forcibly they brought Steve down, then handcuffed him.

The menacing monster crumpled into a pathetic and beaten man. In spite of all he had done to her, Sara's heart went out to him in an indescribable compassion—like the times her mother hit her sisters. The deputies led him away.

With Steve in jail, Sara should have felt relieved. But after school she had a compulsion to check on him. It was a feeling of pity. In the jail parking lot she locked the car, then looked up at the barred windows on the second floor. Suddenly she caught a glimpse of Steve. Meekly he raised his hand in a gesture of recognition. There had been a time when she thought she loved this man.

Back in fifth grade, the decision "not to be cold, but compassionate," had become a way of life she could not easily alter.

"I've suffered a million deaths at Steve's hands. Still, I don't feel like celebrating his being in jail even if I know that's where he belongs."

Behind bars he appeared gentle and innocent. The desire for revenge left her.

All too soon she learned of his release on bail. Two days later, as she turned onto her street, she saw two sheriff's cars parked in front of her house. "What surprise awaits me now?" she wondered.

"We know all about you, Mrs. Benson," a woman deputy greeted her at the door. "Your husband called us. We know you have a gun in the house and are planning to use it to kill yourself and your children. Don't make a scene. Just quietly direct us to it."

"I need a moment please," she told the woman deputy who accompanied her to the bedroom. It didn't matter what the deputy thought. She dropped beside the bed and on her knees silently prayed.

"Oh God, here I am again. If You really exist, help me right now. I don't know what to say to these people. I feel trapped. Please give me direction." Then she rose and returned to the other deputies.

"I've been teaching school all day. You believe I'm irrational because my husband says so. If I were irrational, there's no way I could teach. I'd like to call my principal. He can vouch for me."

The woman deputy nodded.

"Brad, please help me. When I arrived home a few minutes ago, I was met by deputies. Steve told them I'm the one who's sick. You know the story. Would you talk to Deputy Ellis? I need your reinforcement."

The only ones who knew of her domestic problems at work were the principal and the secretary. She never discussed her family situation with others, and the front office knew only because of her absences.

Sara handed the phone to the woman deputy, who identified herself to the principal.

"Deputy, Mrs. Benson is a most reliable teacher, highly regarded by the school and community. It is her husband who is the problem."

The deputies were finally satisfied about Sara and left. Exhausted and weak by this latest episode, Sara wilted. At last she regained her composure with the help of a self-lecture.

"Do not give yourself or that vile creature the satisfaction of collapsing in hysteria. You've held together this long. You can make it."

A little later she heard a gentle tap, tap, tap at the back window. Thinking it was a neighbor, she was about to call "come in" when she looked out. There stood her enemy—this culprit who only moments earlier had brought such chaos into her life. Now he gently beckoned for her attention. Noticing the return of softness in Steve's face caused her to once again be moved by compassion. She unbolted the door but locked his entry.

"Sara, I'm really sorry about the trouble I've caused you. I was provoked because you were responsible for my going to jail. But I'm over that now. I've come with good news. I've rented space in a warehouse and am making fiberglass caskets and upholstering the interiors. It's really a different kind of interior decorating, isn't it?" When Sara nodded he continued.

"I already have orders from mortuaries. With a 500 percent profit on them I'll be able to pay the bills I owe. Together, Sara, we can get back the things I've taken from you. I'll be able to repay your friends and you. I want to make up for the past.

"A crew is at work in the warehouse now, and I'd like to show you the project. It's a very good business venture. I'm sure you'll approve of it. I'm not asking to move back here—just for you to examine the potential and see if you want to help out."

"If it's honest work and will help pay the bills, that's fine, Steve. But count me out. I've already got a full-time job."

His persuasive argument continued as she studied his face.

It definitely was softer—more like his old self. And he said he wanted to make his wrongs right. That's the first time she had heard him say that. And his voice! Other voices had been doing the speaking, but now he was talking, using his own vocal range. This sounded like the old Steve. Had some exorcism taken place? Finally she agreed to go with him.

While Steve showed her around in the warehouse, Sara's mind whirled. "So this is what he's been doing. Is this a bona fide business project? Is he contemplating putting me into one of them? Is that what he had in mind in bringing me here? Have I fallen into a trap? He once worked for a mortuary. Why did I give in to him to come? I thought I had put him out of my life. What am I doing letting him back in?" Then she addressed Steve.

"I'm appalled by all the coffins you've made."

"See this material, Sara. Examine this completed casket. See the fine detailing? Once the pleating is finished, a little glue holds it in place. I've designed the caskets myself, and we mold them using fiberglass.

"I really want to repay your friends, Marilyn and Howard Mears, who loaned me $10,000 to get this business on its feet. They think I've cheated them, but their money was used to buy materials. Since you aren't going to college anymore, Sara, you could do the pleating and gluing and the children could play here while we work."

"I'll think about it, Steve," Sara said reluctantly.

"The profit is terrific, Sara, and with your help we'd get out of debt."

Sara knew she would give in for the sake of repaying the Mears'. They had loaned Steve money because of her friendship with them. Paying off this debt to them was worth the sacrifice of her time and energies. It was true that she would have more time now that her college work was completed. And she would learn how to pleat even if it wasn't to her liking.

One month and 500 pleated caskets later, Sara took a mental inventory. All the fiberglass caskets they had molded in the shop were sold. What had Steve done with the money? She phoned the Mears' to check if Steve had paid them anything on their loan, as he had promised.

"Not a cent," Howard reported.

The next two nights as she faithfully showed up at the warehouse, there were no workers but Steve and herself.

"What's wrong, Steve?" she asked. "Why haven't the men shown up?"

"They're striking for higher wages."

"I didn't see any pickets. There's no one around."

The next day it was obvious that they weren't asking for more money, but only for the back wages owed them. They would sue if they didn't get it immediately. Sara wondered why she didn't join them. She hadn't seen any money, either. Steve's idea of getting rich overnight was to be important from the start. Bills mounted and a lawsuit hung over their heads with her name on it. The workers assumed that she was a partner. After all, hadn't she faithfully shown up each evening to work as the wife of the boss?

The coffin business ended as suddenly as it had began. Forced to close down, Steve resumed his eerie behavior pattern. Sara's reprieve was over!

CHAPTER SEVENTEEN

Rocking on the Precipice

BANKRUPTCY! That awful word from Sara's past bounced off the kitchen wall. Unexpectedly Steve arrived and walked in the unlocked back door.

"What are you doing here?" she asked gruffly, startled to see him.

"I've just filed for bankruptcy in the casket business," he announced.

His venture was as dead as the people who had used his product.

The power company had just left after turning off the electricity. Sara was stunned to learn that the bill hadn't been paid.

The children were in another room, eagerly waiting to leave on Sara's promised Saturday-afternoon outing. Purposely she had hurried to get her work done so they could have the afternoon together. The lunch dishes were being removed from the dishwasher to do by hand.

Steve's words devastated her. She leaned against the counter for support.

"How much more of this is there, Steve? You've been in charge of the finances. I'm not part of this bankruptcy. I've done my share to clear your debts. You've picked up the bills and said you paid them. But you haven't. Because of that the electricity is off."

While she continued wiping the counters, she picked up the butcher knife to place it in its special holder. Without warning Steve grabbed it from her. The blade's tip touched her throat.

"This is it, Sara! Your last day on earth!"

The children came bouncing into the kitchen. Quickly Steve turned the blade to make it appear he had just taken it from Sara.

"Your mother is trying to kill me," he ranted.

Chad, now seven, wasn't sure if it were true or not. Stacy, too small to comprehend, seemed not to notice the danger.

Sara urged them to play in another room. If Steve was going to kill her in the kitchen, she didn't want them to see it. The moment they left he held the knife to her throat again. In a nerve-shattering voice Steve announced with hideous laughter, "I am Fear!" It was the voice of another creature living inside him. He was the slave of a supernatural power who had given him the right name.

Sara wondered if Steve was really down there somewhere, or was he absent from his body and others were using it? Had he lost control and demons commanded him? Had they entered through his mouth when he took those pills the first time? Now he was controlling Sara and "the thing" was controlling him.

Steve's piercing blue eyes were cold and icy again. He glared at her, then picked her up from where she had been standing by the sink and plunked her down on a kitchen stool. Firmly he grabbed her head between his hands. She knew what was coming—more head bangings. He beat her nearly senseless against the wooden door frame.

"Get into the car!" he commanded roughly.

Gripped by fear and pain, she obediently headed for her car. Steve yanked on her arm.

"No, no! Not your car! Mine!" he yelled, while continuing to twist her arm. "Slide through to the other side," he bellowed, then pushed her over to make room for himself.

Driving wildly and without seeming purpose, Steve headed through the hilly back roads, weaving past avocado groves. Then he made a sharp turn onto another road and the car careened dangerously.

"He doesn't know where we're going," she decided, "but we've got to get there fast." At last the road came out onto a foothill community.

The pain in her arm was excruciating, but she blocked it out. Giving her undivided attention to his driving, her eyes were riveted to the road. Finally they left the exclusive residential area where Steve turned onto Highway 139.

The black, blue, and swollen arm was throbbing along with her head. Thoughts of her children momentarily replaced her own concerns. She checked her watch.

"Two-thirty. They're probably all alone. How could Steve do this to them? I wonder if Chad will think to take Stacy to Sue or Fran. Will I ever see them again? Who will care for them if I don't. Certainly not Mother. My sisters? Do they care enough for me to raise my children? They're so far

away. Mom taught them to hate me. Anyway, they're married now and have their own families."

On and on Steve drove until they reached the ocean
frontage. Turning left, they passed gorgeous homes dotting
the hillside of the Palos Verdes area. On the rugged shoreline
road, Sara saw a sign indicating they were on Palos Verdes
Drive. On their family outings during better days, Steve never
brought them this way. But this was no sightseeing trip!

"Why are we here? What is he up to? Why doesn't he say
something? The silence is deafening. Even listening to his
other voices would be better than this silence."

Moving at breakneck speed along the spectacular strip of
coastline, Sara knew there would be no law enforcement to
slow them down. She saw the curve coming—just ahead.
Steve made no attempt to slow down for it. Suddenly, without warning, he veered off the pavement, braked sharply, and
began edging the car forward. Maneuvering ever so carefully,
he positioned the car so that it was draped in space over the
precarious precipice, then turned off the engine.

This was no trip to watch the sunset. With the front wheels
suspended in air, the car's balance was delicately divided between front and back. Steve leaned forward, then backward,
tilting the car like a teeter-totter. When he added his horrible
laugh, Sara was sure this entire episode was born in the pit of
hell, where this fiend had come from.

"How come I'm part of this? I'm afraid to turn my head to
look out the back window. It might tilt the car too far. With
that sharp curve in the road, no one will see us."

While Steve leaned forward, Sara concentrated on pushing
back as hard as she could. Her mouth was dry and her heart
felt like it was in her throat. The balancing act went on and
on. Each time the car tilted forward, she saw the huge boulders jutting out of the deep water far below. Waves broke
with great force, spewing water high over the rocks. She
closed her eyes and made a desperate plea.

"Oh God, let me die right here in this car. Why let me
live?"

At 3:25 they were still teetering, and Sara wondered how
much more of this the car and the edge of the cliff could take
before something gave way. She could hear the car creak
with each motion.

Steve added a new and terrifying element to the horrendous adventure. He grew tired of rocking to and fro like a
child. Suddenly he grabbed Sara's left ear and began scream-

ing directly into it, as a child who has lost self-control. His screams were ear-splintering. It was madness!

"Oh God, please deafen my left ear so I can't hear his screams."

Immediately his voice faded into the distance. It was a miracle. She opened her eyes and watched as his mouth made grotesque shapes. The sounds were barely audible to her. But he had not let go of her ear.

"If Steve plans to kill me here, why is he still in the car with me? I know he doesn't intend to die. If we ever manage to get off this cliff safely, will he try to kill me some other way?"

Suddenly Steve let go of her ear, then turned the key in the ignition to start the car!

"This is it!" Sara braced herself against the dash, closing her eyes. "We're going over!"

Steve pressed firmly on the gas pedal and the car lurched. But not forward! He had put the gear into reverse. When Sara opened her eyes, the wheels were spinning, making a tremendous cloud of dust. Marvel of marvels! They were clear of the cliff and back on solid ground.

Immense relief swept over her. That much was over. Prospects of his allowing her to live were brighter. He had still not spoken a word (only screams) since he had ordered her into the car nearly three hours ago. It reminded her of the 70 miles she had once gone without Gary speaking. But that had been an innocent game ending with a good laugh. There was nothing innocent about this. Her fists were clenched tightly, digging into flesh.

Thoughts returned to her children. They were better off at home all alone than in this car with a madman.

The gas gauge read "empty" and Steve pulled into a service station. The instant the car stopped Sara jumped out.

"Run, run, run," she thought. But her legs would not obey. Her heart thumped furiously. Scenes of a movie flashed through her mind where lipstick was used to write an urgent message for help on a mirror. She reached the restroom door.

"Locked! Now what? I'll speak to the attendant.

"My husband's crazy. He's been trying to kill me!" she blurted.

"She just got out of the hospital. They gave her a hallucinating medication. She doesn't know what's she's saying," Steve explained. "I'm taking her home now."

Quietly he spoke to Sara. "Come, dear, get back into the car."

"What can I do? The attendant believes him."

At home, Steve opened the kitchen door and shoved Sara inside so forcibly that it sent her sprawling across the floor to the kitchen table. When her head hit the edge of the table she slumped unconscious to the floor. Steve left her where she fell.

At 6:15 Sunday morning she awakened. At first she wondered what she was doing on the floor, then decided her body had taken over when she could take no more mentally and emotionally. "At least I'm alive." As she got up from the floor, she sensed intense pain from Steve's abuses. Her left ear was so sore she could hardly touch it. The back of her head felt like one mass bruise from the head-bangings on the door frame, and her right arm seemed broken.

"Some battle scars," she thought. "But how lopsided. I never even engaged in combat." Thoughts of herself quickly vanished as she wondered about the children. She found them huddled together in her bed. She tried to imagine the nightmare it must have been for them to be left alone for so many hours.

"Thank God, they're safe!"

She headed for the shower. But there was no hot water. She remembered that the electricity had been shut off and it was Sunday. There was no way to get it connected today.

"How will I cook? I wonder if I can substitute the barbecue for the stove. I could make a game of it with the children. I've never cooked eggs or made toast there. Some game. But it's better than the one I was in yesterday."

A little past eight the phone rang. At least it hadn't been shut off.

"Sara, this is Marilyn Mears." After greeting one another, Marilyn said, "Howard and I both know you aren't responsible for our loaning Steve $10,000, but we did it in good faith. Tell me honestly, Sara, where do we stand? Will we lose it all?"

"Marilyn, I wish you had checked with me before you got involved. Steve is so smooth and believable. I should know. I didn't plan to marry a crook, but that's what he is. I know I can't make it up to you, but I want you to know I've really tried. I put the interiors into 500 coffins believing it would help get your money back. I don't know what Steve has done with the money he got from selling them.

"My life's in jeopardy at this very moment, Marilyn. Yesterday Steve tried to do away with me. He may try again. I'd like to stand by you, but right now I just don't know how. I don't want you to be cheated. I'll still try to get it back for you. I really will."

Chad came in as Sara hung up the phone. His lips quivered and tears filled his eyes. Her heart went out to him.

"What's wrong, Dear?" she asked, taking him into her arms.

"Mama, please don't make me go to school with diapers. I didn't mean to wet the bed."

Sara could have both laughed and cried with relief. She had expected him to complain about being left alone. Instead he was telling her he had wet the bed again. Her bed!

"If you wet the bed once more, you'll have to wear diapers to school," Steve had warned after Chad began a bed-wetting cycle.

"It's all right, Dear," Sara consoled him. "No one is going to put you in diapers for school. Daddy won't be scolding you about it again. He's not going to come here anymore!" she announced.

There! She said it! And she knew she would never let him into the house again.

"It's really the last time," she determined. "He's not going to hurt us anymore."

CHAPTER EIGHTEEN

Off to Jail in a $600 Suit

JACK'S FAVORITE chatting place with Sara was in their side-by-side driveways, where they often parked their cars parallel.

Over the top of Sara's heaped basket of soiled clothing, Jack noticed her partially closed eye but acted as if he hadn't.

"Hi, Sara. What's wrong? Washing machine break down? Use ours."

"Thanks, Jack. The washing machine is okay. It's the electricity. It's been shut off. Can't use the stove. No shower and no coffee—a great way to start the day. Thanks for offering your machine, but I couldn't impose. I know what Sundays mean to you. A neighbor running in and out of the house is a nuisance.

"Sara Benson! I thought we were friends. I can understand your not wanting to use the washing machine, but not coming over for coffee? You know us better than that. I'll run a heavy-duty cord from our house across the driveways. Use our electricity on your machines. Let me know if anything goes wrong. Keep the cord until your electricity is restored."

"Jack, that's swell. But I still don't have hot water."

"I overheard your predicament, Sara," Sue said, arriving on the scene carrying a box. "Here's cold-water soap. It'll do the job."

"Thanks, Sue. I'll try the hookup Jack offered."

"Jack, why don't you ask Ted Bailey to help Sara? He could run a cord from his place. Then she can do the laundry on our cord and make coffee and use kitchen appliances on his. Sara, feel free to use our bathrooms for showers.

"I'm barbecuing chicken for lunch. Bring the kids and join us at two. Is Steve around today? It's hard to say this, Sara—he scares me."

"We'd love to come for lunch, Sue. Don't be concerned about Steve. I'm not letting him back in! Look at me! Red ear, swollen eye, black-and-blue arm—and those are only the bruises you see!"

"Sara, let me help you, Let's put an ice pack on your eye. I just knew Steve was responsible for this. I'm so sorry."

"You people are the dearest friends I have. I'm okay. I appreciate your concern. Thanks for all your help."

Ted Bailey, Sara's neighbor on the other side of the house, responded to Jack's idea. Soon the two of them finished stringing extension cords to Sara's house.

"We need to feel needed," Jack told her. "And Sara, you need us. You shouldn't have to face what you've been through alone. Sue and I know what it is to go through severe storms of life. But we've got a new manager now. He's made all the difference in our lives."

"I can't imagine you people having troubles. What do you mean about a new manager?"

"It wasn't very long ago, Sara, that Sue and I were on the verge of breaking up. Now our marriage is better than ever."

"How did you manage that, Jack?"

"We'll tell you about it at lunch if you're interested."

Hurrying to complete her chores now that she had electricity again, Sara could hardly wait for two o'clock to come.

Out on the Worths' patio, Sara asked, "What did you mean, Jack, when you said your lives are under new management? Do you have an agent handling your affairs?"

"Yes, I think that says it very well, Sara." He paused, searching for the right words. "Shortly before you moved into your new house, Sue and I had been at each other's throats. Our marriage was in the pits. We couldn't stand each other. We tried marriage counseling and everything that was suggested for us. Nothing worked. We were at wit's end. We were making each other's lives miserable, destroying one another. One evening friends called, asking if we would go with them to a Billy Graham Crusade at the Anaheim Stadium. 'Sure why not?' I told them. I was curious, and it was better than fighting with Sue.

"We were so antagonistic toward each other that we wouldn't even sit together in the car or at the meeting. The place was packed out. Everyone listened intently, including me. During Billy's message I felt my hard heart softening. By the end of his talk I made a decision to put Jesus Christ in control of my life. Would you believe I walked down the aisle? If anyone had told me I was going to do that I would have said, 'Impossible. It's not for me. I'm too sophisticated.'

"What I didn't know was that Sue had gone down another aisle to the front. Down there I gave Jesus my life—lock, stock, and misery. I asked Him for forgiveness. I gave Him all my hurts and asked for His healing. Then I gave Him my future, my marriage, and my family. For the first time in my life I felt clean and forgiven.

"You know, Sara, the amazing thing is that I became a better lover, a better husband, a better father, a better provider, and a better man at my job. We have a wonderful relationship in our home that we never had before. And we've got someone to help us with our problems.

"On the way home from Anaheim, sitting beside Sue, I fell in love with her right there—all over again. And I boldly announced to everyone in the car, 'I asked God to take over the management of my life tonight. I feel like a ten-ton load has been taken from me.' Sue squeezed my hand. Then I found out she had gone forward too."

"I could hardly believe my ears," Sue broke in. "I told him, 'Jack, I did the same thing.' Big miracles began happening. I fell in love like never before. Our marriage and home were healed. Relationships with other people improved. Jack's business began to prosper beyond imagination. We're not free of problems, but now, no matter how weighty or small, we give them all to God. He sees us through them with a peace we never knew before."

When it came to having someone else manage her life, Sara wasn't ready. "Someday . . . when I'm old and gray," she thought. With lots of good visiting, good feelings, and a nice meal, Sara returned home bolstered in spirits.

At home she plugged lamps into neighbors' borrowed electricity—humiliated, realizing they knew the electric bill hadn't been paid.

In bed, the mental gears were racing. "Tomorrow, during lunch, I'll pay the power company and hope they restore service before another night. What I need next is an attorney. My neighbor, Dick Gardner, is a lawyer. The Gardners were the first ones to invite Gary and me to dinner. I'll drop into his office on my way home from school. He didn't handle my divorce from Gary because he knew both of us. But this is different."

At Dick Gardner's law office, the receptionist asked Sara to wait.

Soon Dick appeared and asked, "To what do I owe this honor, Sara?"

"Dick, I'm planning to file for divorce from Steve," she began after he ushered her into his office. "Since he's used up all my finances, I need to make plans to cover the legal fee. Tell me, approximately how much money will I need to get a divorce, and what do I do first? I want custody of Stacy, too. Do all attorneys charge about the same, or should I go bargain-hunting? This may sound strange to you, but I don't know where to begin. Gary did all the paperwork the last time."

"It all depends on property settlement, Sara. With filing, the cost is fixed; but without a list of assets and liabilities, I couldn't give you a fair estimate. Why don't you make up a list? Then we'll know how to proceed."

"Dick, there's another matter. How can I keep Steve from invading my house again? He's dangerous."

"An injunction will need to be filed with the court, Sara. I've got an appointment now, but call me at home this evening around eight o'clock. In the meantime, draw up a list of financial assets and liabilities."

At home, waiting for the electrical servicemen to come, she began working on the list Dick wanted.

ASSETS	LIABILITIES
Two children	Steve, who blighted my reputation and wrecked my life
Insurance policy worth $10,000	
Mercedes 450 SL, 3 years old	Missing furniture and wardrobe stolen by Steve to get cash for himself
Retirement fund (not negotiable unless I quit or retire)	
Equity of $10,000 in house at 1441 Circle Hill Drive, La Habra	A lawsuit of $2,890 from Steve's former employees (unpaid wages)
House improvements:	Title to house is in my parents' names (promised to me after balance of $20,000 is paid)
$4,000 carpeting	
$2,500 draperies	
$5,000 swimming pool	
$17,000 a year teaching salary	Disowned by parents
Ability to hold a second job	Unpaid house bills and who knows what else Steve owes in my name
Self-confidence: slightly damaged	
A sturdy body	Two wrecked marriages and ten years of my life down the drain
Age: 30	

"There's nothing here a court would award the wounded party," she thought while looking over the list. "This is ridiculous! Pathetic, too! Imagine a woman at my age with nothing more to show in life than this." She folded the paper neatly. "It's an embarrassment! I'm not eager to show it to anyone."

The arrival of the power company interrupted her thoughts. After disconnecting the borrowed extension cords strung throughout the house, she returned them to the neighbors. At eight o'clock, after dinner and the children's baths, she phoned Dick.

"What's this about your being afraid for your life, Sara?" he began.

"It's Steve's insane behavior. On Saturday, he put a knife to my throat and threatened, 'This is it, Sara.' Then he forced me into his car. After a frightening drive, we ended up on the coastline somewhere in Palos Verdes. He found a cliff, drove to the very edge, and with the front wheels hanging over he rocked the car to and fro to get it to fall into the ocean. When it didn't, he brought me home; then in the kitchen he knocked me unconscious. I haven't seen him since.

"Dick, we're not safe anymore. What legal steps can be taken to keep him away from us? I can borrow on my car to pay you."

"Let's put first things first, Sara. You can't afford not to have an attorney. Let's not get hung up on fees at this point. If you decide not to use me after I've seen your assets and liabilities, there'll be no charge. First you need a court injunction to keep him away from your house."

"Will you go ahead with that, Dick?"

The legal paperwork was completed without a word from Steve. Six weeks later Steve arrived. This time he was not alone. Instead of a white Continental it was a late-model Rolls Royce. He drove it into the driveway as though he still lived there. Next to him sat a gorgeous blonde. He got out of the car and walked to where Sara was picking roses.

"Sara, I'm going to be married," he abruptly began. "I know that's a relief to you. You won't have to put up with me any longer. Barbara is a little embarrassed to meet you, so she stayed in the car until you clear the way."

"Until I clear the way? What do you mean, Steve? And what's this about your getting married? We aren't divorced yet." Sara's mind reeled.

"His personality has reversed again. One moment he's a

liar and the next he makes me out to be one. Why are his intentions always evil? He plots what he can do next to hurt and destroy. But the demon who possesses him doesn't seem to be in charge today. Can demons be gentlemen?" Sara wondered.

"Barbara doesn't know we're still married," he went on boldly. "We've announced our wedding plans, and gifts have started to arrive. If you sign this paper we can legally be married and I'll be out of your life forever!"

"What a conversation," she thought. "Steve's super confidence usually causes him to come up with instant, smooth answers. But this is just too much. I should be glad Steve is getting out of my life. I'd like to hit back just once! Cram a garden hose down his throat, water running full blast. That would be a good ending."

Revenge! It's both bitter and sweet. At first she almost told him "I'll not sign anything for you." Then she remembered that Steve was out of jail on bail. A light flashed.

"You don't often catch Steve off-guard," Sara thought. "But this may be it."

"Wait a minute, Steve," she began. "I have something in the house for you. I'll just take along your paper to read and see if I should sign it. You can wait with Barbara.

"Now's the time to tell the sheriff's office about the last attempt on my life. When they check on his probation, they'll put him away for a good long time."

Sara went to the bedroom and dialed the well-known number, asking them to come quickly while she stalled him. A plan rapidly formed to keep Steve busy till the deputies could arrive.

"I'll meet that blonde now," she decided. "The only way to catch a liar is to be one. I'll have to tell one now."

"Steve, a letter came for you, but I can't find it now," she told him. "Why don't you introduce me to Barbara, and then I'll sign your papers."

While they were talking the deputies arrived with handcuffs. Sara sighed! They had already had a warrant out for his arrest on another matter. This was far better than the garden hose!

There was Steve in a $600 suit, a gray Rolls Royce, a beautiful almost-bride, and handcuffs. Sara was glad she hadn't killed him. This was legal revenge, and she didn't have to go to jail for murder.

CHAPTER NINETEEN

Go Live on the Street

NEVER HAD Sara felt so relieved! The divorce was final. Steve was gone! Washed out of her life! No more deputies. No more unpaid bills. No more strange events or terrifying scenes. She was free. Free! It was a glorious feeling.

"One thing spoils it—that name, "Benson." I've got to get rid of that name!"

Picking up the day's mail beneath the door slot, she noticed an envelope from a bank she had never heard of. She was about to throw it in the wastebasket when she noticed that it bore a first-class stamp.

> Please report to the general manager, Mr. Roger Hill, as soon as possible regarding your $2,500 loan. This account is now overdue. Failure to respond will result in a court action.

"There's got to be a mistake. This can't be for me. Why should I report to a bank I never heard of about a loan I don't know about?"

At the bank Mr. Hill was abrupt.

"Are you married to Steven Benson?" he asked.

"Not anymore." She was relieved she could say it.

"He has a loan drawn on this bank with your name on it. Since he has not paid, and the summons for him appears undeliverable, you are liable."

"Will you go over that again, Mr. Hill? You say *my name* is on the loan? I've never been to this bank before and I never signed for a loan. May I see the loan application, please?"

When the form was presented to her, it was her turn to be abrupt.

"That's not my signature, Mr. Hill. It's a forgery. A bad one at that. I've always had very poor handwriting. For once I'm glad. It's my name, but not my signature. Bring in your experts to check."

They asked her to sign her name, agreeing that it appeared

to be a forgery. But as Steve's divorced wife, she was responsible.

It was time to use Dick Gardner as her attorney again.

"Dick, why should I have to pay Steve's bill when I'm not married to him anymore? My name on that loan wasn't even a good forgery."

"Sara, there's an antiquated California community property law that is in a long, drawn-out process of being revoked, but it's still in force. Divorce doesn't absolve you from responsibility for Steve's bills."

Instead of fighting it in court, Sara let the bank attach her salary to collect it. The next paycheck dumbfounded her. It was for 34 cents. The rest applied on Steve's loan.

Deputies arrived, serving more papers showing that Steve was in debt everywhere. Why hadn't she kicked him out when she first suspected he was a con artist? she wondered. Now she learned that he had used 31 charge cards, all in his name, but with different account numbers.

"No wonder he wore $100 shoes and $600 suits. He bought them with credit cards that he applied for from banks far and wide. And now I'm paying for it all. The old law says I'm responsible."

At the living room bay window, she watched the sheriff's car pull away.

"I thought we were through with this kind of thing. I'm still living in a glass house. How many more unpaid bills will show up? At the rate of arrival it might take the rest of my life to clear them up. The neighbors probably think this visit is because I've done something wrong."

Camile arrived without any greeting, delivering an ultimatum.

"The last police car has come to this house. There will be no more ruining the neighborhood with the goings-on you are up to. I want you and that lunatic husband of yours out of this house by the end of the week. Do you understand me? Out! Your husband doesn't have a steady job, and you owe a month's rent. Neither of you are any good. No good!"

The last sentence was as old as a worn-out record, but the others cut Sara to the core. With fire in Camile's eyes she continued the barrage of unpleasant words.

"I don't care about you or where you go!"

It wasn't enough for Camile to order her out. She didn't even care what became of her after she was out. Sara staggered under the weight of this new blow.

"Mom, you are behind times in knowing what's happening. Steve doesn't live here anymore. I've only missed one payment with you, and it's just two weeks late. I don't have any money right now. I don't have any place to go. Can't you wait until I can arrange to pay it?"

"Go live on the street! You're no better than a street woman anyway. That's where you belong."

Camile's hands were fixed on her hips. She hadn't batted an eye.

"I have two children to think about, Mom. You may not care about me, but think about them! They're your grandchildren. Give me a little time."

I've got $10,000 equity in this house. Some months I've paid ahead. So I'm not really behind in payments. Besides the $10,000, I've paid $4,000 for carpeting and $2,500 for draperies. Then there's the $5,000 swimming pool added to the value of the property since I've lived here."

"That has nothing to do with it. I want you out of here no later than the end of this week. I don't want to hear about you or your problems. You've made your own life; now suffer the consequences."

"You can't do this to me, Mom. It's not right. The law says you have to give me 30 days. And I'll expect my equity when I move out."

"If we sell this house, we will return your equity to you."

Since there was no contract in writing, Sara didn't have any way to fight back. Being family, they had concluded that they didn't need a legal agreement. "We're people of our word," they had always claimed.

Sara's back bowed! She was angry with her mother, angry with the world, angry with Steve, angry about debts she had nothing to do with, and most of all, angry with herself. Without relief, Sara knew she was bound to crack somewhere.

One night Sara went to bed with pains in both arms. After swallowing several aspirin she finally dozed, but awakened later with additional pains in her chest.

"Wonder if I'll make it till morning?" was her first thought. "Should I drive to the emergency center? Should I call for a doctor? Is this a heart attack?"

Hoping it would ease, she waited till morning. When it didn't, she went to the doctor.

"It's both dull and sharp," she told him during the examination. "It nags at me. Sometimes it's momentarily quiet, but the next thing it flares up so intensely I think I'm going to die."

"The electrocardiogram indicates you have a heart condition," the doctor told her. "It's my guess you've been living with severe stress. Unless you adopt a new life-style you're in for a prolonged bed rest."

"New life-style? That's already my problem. Mother is forcing me to adopt one and I'm resisting."

In the car on the way home she reached a decision. That's what she would do . . . just what the doctor said—a new life-style. But it would not be as a street prostitute, as Mother suggested. Her aims were higher. She could draw better bait than an ordinary woman on the street. There were other ways . . . with better streets.

At home when tears came, she got into the swimming pool.

"Hey, Sara, mind if I join you?" Ted Bailey called from the gate.

"Great, Ted. Come on over."

"Sara, for a long time I've pictured you making a change in your work. I've got just the job for you." He hesitated, waiting for Sara to respond. When she didn't, he went on.

"You've got everything it takes to be a top-notch model. Every day our advertising agency passes up dozens of women applicants from modeling schools and agencies because we're looking for someone of your type and figure. The job pays better than teaching and offers far more opportunities. Why don't you give it a try? Come to my office after school tomorrow. I'll introduce you to my partners. It'll help you decide."

"Whoa, Ted. I like what I'm doing. It gives me time to be with my children. They need me. Modeling is demanding. I'm not sure I'd like it. If it didn't work out, I'd have no place to turn. I don't think so. Teaching is worth more to me than the money it brings."

Later, while preparing dinner, she thought it over.

"What's wrong with me? I'm behind in house payments and no other solution is in sight. I've thought about living on the street, but not Mom's way. Maybe Ted's got the answer. I'll give him a phone call."

"I've been thinking, Ted. I believe I'd like to come to your office after all. Is tomorrow at five okay? You know what the freeway is like after school."

Ted's agency was in Century City, a prestigious business suburb of Los Angeles. Sara was introduced to executives who were used to selling ideas and making split-second decisions. Ted had her change to street clothes, then bathing suit, and finally sportswear to model for them.

"Why don't you consider joining us here?" asked Harley Curtis, one of the partners.

"I've watched Sara in her yard with a ribbon tied around her hair and she's ravishing." added Ted. "You've a natural talent for this, Sara. And you wear perfume like no one else I've ever met."

"Why haven't we seen your face before?" one of the executives asked. "Where have you been working?"

"In a classroom. I'm a public schoolteacher."

"No kidding! I can't believe it. How'd you like to change that?"

The cameraman's lights focused on her as they talked.

"Tinted or dyed?" the makeup artist was examining her hair.

"Neither. I've never had color on it."

High pressure executives in Ted's elaborate suite of offices made it sound so promising and easy. It certainly wasn't what her mother had in mind when she had told her to go live on the street.

"Is this the break I've been waiting for?" she wondered on her way home. "What about my heart? I know I've ignored the pain signals. Will this be too much for my body? The doctor's orders were clear. Yes, I'll do it; I'll obey his orders. I'll call Ted when he gets home."

"Ted?" She tried to sound casual. "I have a few questions. First, are evening or weekend jobs possible? I still have five weeks of school."

"Sure. You can work out a schedule with the crew. Are you saying you'll go to work for us?" He sounded as eager as she now felt.

"I have more questions, Ted. When would I begin? What about rates? Would it be a contract, or is it free-lance work?"

"We'll draw up a contract, and if you approve you can go to work right away. We have you in mind for a major cosmetics firm's TV commercials. I'd like to use the pictures made today and contact them. Will you agree?"

"Ted, if I can teach and just work part-time for you, I'll say yes."

"I know you won't be sorry, Sara. We'll treat you right."

Sara's anxieties were not so quickly erased. She wanted the sense of security that Ted was depicting, but needed more evidence—like signatures on the dotted lines. But she wasn't out of the woods yet.

CHAPTER TWENTY

In the Gutter with Gutter People

"THIRTY DAYS, Mom said. It isn't much." Sara cupped her chin, deep in thought. "I'll not lose this house! Not without a struggle! By cutting the budget to the bone, I think I can make it. Mom will give in when she has the money in her hand.

"Why can't I clean the pool myself? I've watched the maintenance man use our equipment. What's so difficult about it?

"The swimming-pool heater will need to be turned off. And I can discontinue water-softener service. It's a luxury I can't afford now, even if it uses less soap.

"Where did the rule come from that women aren't supposed to cut grass or wash windows on the outside of the house? Why should it only be man's work? I don't have to put on a false front. I know how to push a lawn mower, edge, trim shrubs, and cultivate. Being self-sufficient has some advantages."

Looking out the window, she noticed that the grass needed cutting. She jotted down the phone numbers of each service and began dialing. When she finished canceling the last one, she went outdoors.

It isn't overwork that caused my heart to go bad on me. It's the stress I've been living under. It won't hurt to do a little yard work.

"A moving van costs too much, and I don't even have the first and last month's rent to secure an apartment."

She got the lawn mower out of the garage, but before she was finished she realized how tired she had become. "Get the job done no matter how you feel," was inbred into her. The patio furniture seemed to be beckoning.

At least Steve hadn't included it when he sold the other furniture, crystal, and gifts from her marriage to Gary.

As she put the mower away, an excruciating pain hit her in the tailbone. When she tried straightening, she couldn't. Her body refused to respond. Ted Bailey called to her from over the block wall.

"I've got good news. We've lined things up for you to be at the agency at seven o'clock tomorrow evening. Here's your contract, Sara, ready for your signature. We've outlined a special around you for a cosmetic company. It's really a good deal."

"I'll feed the children and then study it, Ted. If it's okay, I'll sign it and send it back with Chad."

The pain was intense in her back now, but Ted didn't notice her stooping.

"How can this be happening to me now, just when I've got the answer to keeping this house? Unless my back improves, I'll be unable to make it to work tomorrow."

All night Sara tossed, turned, moaned, and groaned as she felt the new job slipping away from her.

I'll have to be better by seven or call a substitute teacher. I need a chiropractor, but my finances are down. There's barely enough fuel in the car to get me to work and drive to Ted's agency. Staying home means Stacy and Chad will be with me too.

"Which is worse—staying home with the kids when I'm in misery, or going to work in agony?" She forced herself to dress.

By noon she knew she could not remain in the classroom any longer and wrote the principal a note asking to be excused. Then she sent for Chad. When Brad arrived she left to pick up Stacy at the child center.

At home Sara took two aspirins, groaned, and sat down at the kitchen table to join the children with their sack lunches. Suddenly Chad decided to sit on her lap. He was already too big to hold. She squelched the desire to tell him to get off. When Stacy saw Chad, she wanted her share of loving, too. Crawling onto her lap, she asked, "Love me too, Mommie!"

It was a touching moment, with all of them needing special loving, but Sara was screaming inside, "Oh, my aching back!" With more troubles than she could bear alone, she began unloading them onto the children.

"If I can't go to work tonight I won't get any money. I suppose I'll have to sell everything that's left in the house. I'm sure glad Steve didn't take the two of you when he was taking everything else.

"Chad, you can help me think of things I can sell. We can make a list together. Please get a tablet and pencil from the desk for me."

Chad brought the writing materials, then disappeared.

When he didn't return, she checked his bedroom. There she saw him banging his head against the wall while crying.

"What's wrong, Dear?" she asked tenderly, trying to comfort him.

Between smothered sobs he answered, "N-nothing."

But his tears did not stop. Had he learned to do this kind of thing by watching Steve knock Sara's head against a wall? What was wrong with the boy? And what was wrong with her back?

It was hard for Sara to admit defeat. She saw herself in the mirror, and the bent-over-back was pitiful. How ridiculous to think of showing up at the Evans, Bailey and Curtis Advertising Agency listing like a sailboat in a storm! It would be a waste of everybody's time.

"I don't want to give in to this, but it's not just me anymore," she argued with herself.

At last she picked up the phone to call Ted at work. It was nearly 4:30, and was getting late to cancel the appointment.

"Ted, will you believe this? Last night I threw my back out of place. I'm unable to stand straight. I'm in agony and my face shows it. Could you rearrange the schedule for next week? I know it's already late. I'd come if I could."

"I'm really sorry about your back, Sara. We'll work out another time. I'll check back with you at home. Things were all set up for you to begin—the contract's been signed with the cosmetic firm using you. We'll just have to postpone it."

In the kitchen Sara took a quick inventory.

½ quart milk	½ loaf bread	1 can tuna
2 eggs	3 raw carrots	lettuce
		cereal

1 box macaroni and cheese
a little peanut butter in the bottom of a jar
about enough cheese for 2 sandwiches

There was no money for groceries. With the paychecks drained by Steve's unpaid bank loan, her finances were zero. The prospect of lasting till Monday, when she could use the car as collateral for a loan at the bank, was dim. And it was too embarrassing to ask friends for help.

Another mortgage payment was due, and she still hadn't paid the last one. The phone, water, and light bills were due again. Credit at the child-care center was sagging badly. She scolded herself for not going to the bank earlier about a loan.

The car should easily bring $1,000, and that would help meet current expenses.

On Monday, still dragging, Sara made herself go back to work. It was Chad's crying that did it. He had cried spasmodically all weekend.

"Chad, I'm not going to punish you. I don't know what's bothering you. I wish you'd tell me. I don't know how to help unless I know what's wrong. I love you and don't want you unhappy or hurting. Please tell me what's wrong."

No answer.

"Chad, do you hurt somewhere?"

"No."

"Why are you crying?"

"I don't know."

"Is it because you're wetting the bed again?"

"No. I don't mean to."

"I know that, Dear. Mother loves you no matter what goes wrong. I want to help. I wish you'd tell me what's bothering you. Won't you do that, Dear?"

No answer.

"Why do you hit your head against the wall and bed?"

"I don't know."

They were getting nowhere. She decided to go back to work. The house was a depressing place. Away from it things didn't seem as bad.

Three weeks later, Chad's crying spells hadn't cleared up and Sara's back had improved little. She had to tell Ted to postpone his plans again.

Fran hadn't heard from Sara for a long time and felt impressed to check up on things. Inside Sara's house, Fran was shocked at what she saw.

"Sara! Where's your furniture?"

"Steve sold most of it, Fran. My crystal and sterling, too. He took it when I wasn't home. Stole it would be a better word."

"How awful! It was beautiful. I loved your dining set. Ethan Allen, wasn't it? I'm sorry about this, Sara. You deserve the best, not this."

"Thanks, Fran. But that's not the worst. My back went out about three weeks ago. At the same time Chad began a crying spell. It hasn't stopped yet. To make it worse, he's hitting his head against the wall. Between his crying, head-banging, and my back, I'm going under. He's too old to be doing this kind of thing . . . and bed-wetting, too."

"Sara, you know about the family guidance center here in La Habra. They have trained counselors in these kinds of problems. Let's get an appointment for you right away. I'll call them."

At the center the counselor listened sympathetically.

"Mrs. Benson, when did you first notice this? Try to think back."

"Chad and I were both so glad the bed-wetting problem was clearing up after his stepfather moved out. But then it returned, along with this constant crying and hitting his head against the wall. The crying began the day I came home from work with a bad backache. Chad wanted to sit on my lap, and he's heavy. Then both children wanted to sit on it. I had a pity party with them, feeling sorry for myself because I was going to have to move. 'Grandma says I should live on the street, but that's no place for you,' I told them. I asked if they would help look for an apartment.

"I told them I was glad their father hadn't taken them while he was taking everything else to sell. Then I asked Chad to help me make a list of things I could sell because we needed the money. Instead, he went to his room." Sara paused. *"You don't suppose he thought I'd sell him?"*

"Let me talk to him alone, Mrs. Benson."

In no time the problem was verified.

"Mommie is going to have to sell me. She needs the money real bad."

"A more tranquil atmosphere must be restored, Mrs. Benson," the counselor told her. "Undoing damage and healing deep hurts requires extreme patience with lots of loving."

A peaceful atmosphere! Sara couldn't remember when they had last known peace. Repairing damaged emotions was going to take lots more than loving.

Money borrowed on the car was almost used up, and Sara sold the bikes in the garage to help meet another house payment. With check in hand, she headed across the street.

"Hi Pop," she greeted him as he answered the door. "I know I'm late with this money, but I brought it as soon as I could."

"You'll have to talk to your mother. She's in charge of business matters." Marc had never been able to call Sara by her given name, nor could he stand up to Camile. It had always been like this for him, except when he wanted to move. Neither of them invited Sara inside. This invisible sign had been posted for her when Gary left. It read, "KEEP OUT, SARA."

Camile took the check, then studied it without speaking. Sara counted on Camile's weakness never to turn down money.

"This will not go toward your mortgage. That has ended. This is your overdue rent. We're waiting for you to move out. You cannot stay. Your 30 days are more than up! When school is out for the summer you will be out or we will be forced to take legal action."

"Mom, don't try to cheat me out of the money I've invested in the house. It belongs to me and I expect you to return it."

"If we sell the house, you will get it back."

Apartment-hunting with a still-aching back wasn't easy. On the second floor, where rents were less, Sara found a small one, with no air-conditioning and poor ventilation. The tenement neighborhood, with quarreling neighbors whose problems often brought police, was no place for her and the children. A grocery store, five blocks up the street, was in an even-worse section. On the way there she spotted men propped against buildings who wined without dining.

"Mom thought her neighborhood had become run down because of my problems. She ought to see this cheap, crummy one. Wonder if she'd come here if I got sick? No chance," she decided.

When it came near moving time, Sara sat down with the children.

"What shall we do with Penny? I know this will be difficult for you. We can't take him with us. They don't allow dogs."

"Why do we have to move?" Chad's lips quivered. "I don't want to leave my friends. Penny likes it here and I don't want to give him up."

"I hate Grandma!" Stacy added, with tears falling. "She's mean!"

"Moving is something we have to face. You're both smart. You want Penny to have a good home. Think about it. You'll come up with a good answer for Penny. I know how you feel. I don't want to give him up either. I love him, too."

That evening Chad carried Penny into the kitchen. Stacy spoke for them both.

"Mommie, we know what to do with Penny. Jill and Don love Penny, too. They don't have a dog. We want them to keep Penny for us. They will let us visit him. He'd still sorta be ours. And if we want him back they'd give him up. And his doghouse can be loaded onto a wagon and moved to their backyard."

"Good thinking, kids!" Sara complimented them. "But you'll have to ask the Worths if they approve of the idea as much as you do."

Sara advertised a garage sale to dispose of everything she couldn't keep. She needed every penny she could raise. People took advantage of her distress. Up till now she hadn't realized that most friendships have a price. She watched everything go, including things bought by so-called friends who acted as though they had done her a big favor by buying things at rummage-sale prices. They looked at her circumstances and she thought they judged her accordingly.

"I'm still basically the same person, but now I'm down to one sofa, two chairs, and three beds, with not enough room for them. The refrigerator is too big for where I'm moving and there's no place for the washer and dryer. The car's no longer mine and doesn't fit the neighborhood where I'm going. Some assets!"

At the last minute Sara's real friends appeared. Ted Bailey got a truck from a rental lot. Bradley Owens, her principal, carried out the heavy things. Jack drove the rental truck and moved Sara's belongings to the apartment.

At lunchtime they were still packing and loading. All the wives showed up with a potluck meal. Sue suggested that they all go to her patio to eat.

"I never knew you cared so much," she told them. "As soon as I get on my feet again I want to put on a special dinner—to express what I can't say."

The Worths stayed until the last piece was put into place and only one carton remained packed. Sue made beds and hung clothes in closets. In the kitchen she arranged the cupboards according to Sara's plan. When everything was done, Sue set a large basket of fresh fruit on the counter of the tiny kitchen.

"There," she said, "doesn't that make things look homey?"

"Sue, you don't know how much you mean to me!"

Jack lugged in three bags of groceries, announcing his arrival imitating a horn.

"Ta ta! A house-warming present, Sara." He knew she was too proud to accept it any other way.

Alone at last, and with the children in bed, Sara faced the

little she had salvaged from life. In the shower she let tears fall unashamedly. She was entitled to a few brief moments of weakness. Where she was living now and how she felt seemed to go together. It was the kind of thing she had read about in cheap magazines.

"For just a little while I thought I wanted to live on the street. Maybe I really do. But this isn't the street! I feel like I'm in the gutter with gutter people. I don't like it! If I have to make a living on the street, it will be in a good neighborhood, not this one!"

The allotted time for self-pity had passed.

"Better things have got to be ahead. I'm a hard worker, honest and still decent! I have two precious children. We haven't anyone but each other, but that's no reason to stay in the gutter."

CHAPTER TWENTY-ONE

Receiving Signals

THE GRIM DEADLINE that Camile set to "be out of the house when the school year ends" had barely been met. Mercilessly Camile had bamboozled Sara into moving out against her better judgment and the attorney's advice.

The old rule, "Don't talk back," made Sara the loser. Camile had knocked her down, and after she was down, just for old time's sake, she gave her another kick. No more! This was the beginning of a reversal of difficulties, and Sara was ready and eager for a new start!

The backache plaguing her for several weeks had improved, and the little discomfort remaining could be ignored. When the doctor announced that she had heart trouble, he didn't know that it had been brought on from a broken heart. But now even this seemed mended.

With packing, selling household goods, and moving, the last day of school had come and gone without its usual fanfare. Giving her students loving well-wishes and a final good-bye was as important to her as the enthusiastic reception she gave them on the first day. It was this sincere kind of caring that made her both popular and successful as a teacher. But now these students were no longer hers, and next year would bring a new group. Or would it?

If success was to be hers with a modeling career, it could mean an end to teaching. Her entire future was at stake. For the first time in weeks, she felt excited and equal to whatever lay ahead.

Last night's tears acted as a catharsis, washing her wounded pride and damaged ego. The shabby surroundings fit yesterday's problems, not today's. The low point had passed. She wasn't going down the drain.

In the unfamiliar apartment she found a tablet. *Call Ted Bailey for an appointment*, she wrote at the top. This potential career had been interrupted by her wrenched back and her mother's order to move. Remembering Ted's words, "Now that you're settled, Sara, you might give me a call about that job," encouraged her. With great confidence, she added the forceful word "SUCCESS" to her pad, underlining it in red.

"Success doesn't keep company with failure," she thought, "I'm tired of failures and I want to be where successful people are found."

The telephone serviceman was due to connect the phone, but she couldn't wait. Somewhere in the neighborhood she had seen a pay phone. But where? It made her squeamish to think of wandering around in this neighborhood to find one. The manager offered her phone, but Sara wanted privacy and found one in the next block.

"This is Sara Benson," she told Ted's secretary. "I'd like an appointment with him at his earliest convenience."

"Please wait while I check with Mr. Bailey."

While waiting for an answer, she added a note to her pad, "Get rid of the name Benson. Change back to Carlisle."

"Mr. Bailey will see you at two and he's delighted you're coming."

Sara's mind raced as fast as her pulse. The agency seemed anxious to have her! "More like eager than anxious," she decided. "Good sign!"

The new outfit she had purchased recently was one extravagance she had allowed because she was desperately in need of clothes. It was the best she had since Steve stole and sold her elegant wardrobe.

"If I knew where he sold them, I'd try buying them back," she thought, standing before the mirror imagining herself walking into Ted's office with a straight back. The pained expression from her face was gone. "I'll use all the grace and charm I can muster."

At the Evan, Bailey and Curtis Agency she was ushered into a lavishly furnished dressing room. There, Craig, the makeup artist, and Doug, the head cameraman, went on a flaw-finding examination. Craig tweezed a few hairs from her hairline and restyled her hair. She had thought she was coming for an appointment to see Ted about going to work. Instead, she was being put to work!

In the mirror, she could see Craig studying her nose. For a painful moment she remembered her father's terrible name to her, and the surgeries.

"What about my nose? What's wrong with it?"

"It's nothing that will show," Craig told her. "I thought I detected a trace of a scar. You have a marvelous nose, Sara."

For five hours, Sara sat under hot, bright lights while they focused on her features, making the most of every facet of her face. She posed in positions she didn't know her body could get into.

At 10:30 she left the studio to pick up her already-sleeping children at Fran's house. Life had quickly taken an upswing, but she knew how short the span of a modeling career can be, and she had started late. Hal Evans told her, "You'll be promoting an entire line of well-known cosmetics. It's everything from lotions to lipsticks, Sara, with at least two to three years of work ahead. If you hadn't shown up just when you did, we'd have been done for with that company. They had approved our layout using you."

The salary would be more in one year than in five years of teaching. Too bad Steve's debts would eat up so much of it!

"Ted mentioned evening and European sessions. What am I getting into? This is no eight-to-five job. And what of my children? Mother neglected me for a career; I don't want to do the same."

The contract Sara signed had a cleverly inserted clause—"travel as required for the job." She hadn't realized it would mean leaving in two weeks for a European assignment.

Fran and her family were going on a summer vacation, and Sara would need to make other arrangements for the children.

After a few days Sara confidently approached Hal Evans about her schedule. Since he had shown unusual interest in her career, she was sure he would be understanding about her problem. After all, wasn't he the one who half-promised to draw up a schedule to her convenience?

"Sara, don't tell me your family troubles," he told her bluntly. "I have enough problems on this job without adding your kids. You'll just have to work it out yourself."

His callousness hurt and surprised her. Each day the solution appeared more elusive. This glamorous new career would virtually come to a grinding halt if she couldn't work out these peculiar working hours with a dependable baby-sitter. She had tracked down every possibility for full child care for the time she would be away. It always ended the same—unworkable. An idea crossed her mind, but seemed almost too remote to consider.

With Sara's schedule becoming so tight, she had lost touch with the Worths, who had moved her and provided electricity and food, standing by her when she had needed them most. And what had she done for them? Nothing.

"I'll take the Worths to their favorite restaurant in Whittier. Eating together is the best way to sustain friendships. I'll drop by to invite them out."

That morning she forced herself to turn onto Circle Hill Drive to see Sue. She felt a knot in her stomach before she got there. The house she had lived in for five years was hard to face, whether empty or occupied. And her parents! They hadn't yet repaid her money.

As she pulled up in front of the Worths, she spotted her parents at work in their yard. They saw her, too, but pretended they hadn't.

"That's okay," she decided. "I'm not going to let it get me. I refuse to act as they do."

"Good morning!" she called out cheerfully, as though everything were right between them. Her father lifted his hand feebly while Camile kept on working.

"Pop would speak to me, but he doesn't dare. Mom would make him pay dearly for it."

The house she had so recently called home was equally hard to face. She tried not to notice the strange car where hers once stood. Someone else was enjoying her house! It hurt. But when Sue opened her front door, Sara felt as though she were the most important person in the world.

"Sara! You're the joy of my day! There's no one I'd rather see!"

"Sue, I wanted to have coffee with you this morning, but I'm short on time. I stopped by to invite you out to dinner Friday evening. You know how cramped my place is. Would you and your family be my special guests at Federico's on Friday at seven? After dinner could we come back here to talk? I have a problem I'd like to discuss with you and Jack."

"That's great, Sara. Our kids miss your kids and I miss our special relationship. It'll be good to be together again."

Penny came racing into the living room and jumped onto Sara's lap.

"Oh, Penny. We've missed you so much. It was like leaving one of the family behind to leave you. Stacy and Chad will love seeing you again."

On Friday, at Federico's, when the waitress brought their dinners, Jack bowed his head to pray. It was as though it were a natural thing to do. Aloud! Sara couldn't believe it! In public? She was sure that everyone in the place was watching and listening. Was she embarrassed! She had heard him do this before, in his house, and thought it nice. But here? Suddenly her attention turned to what he was saying.

"Lord, we know You've got some special reason for us to be together with Sara, Chad, and Stacy. We ask you for an opportunity to be of help to her. You know we're willing to be used."

"Willing to be used?" How uncanny that Jack should put it that way. "To be of help?" How could he know what she had in mind? Sara was perplexed.

After dinner they returned to the Worths' house. Sara waited until the children were at play before bringing up what was on her mind.

"You know I've been working at Ted's agency. I'm grateful for the job because it's helping pay off debts Steve left me. But with odd working hours, I can't take care of the children properly. Fran's a great help, but she's leaving on vacation and I've got to come up with another answer.

"The agency is sending me to Europe in two weeks for a cosmetics-company layout. I've tried everything—contacted everyone I know who might take Chad and Stacy. I just can't bring myself to lodge them out. It would be like boarding them in a kennel!

"You know what my children have been through. Where we're living now isn't good for them."

Sue and Jack's faces showed that they understood what Sara meant. She went on.

"I've been thinking, 'If my kids could be in a home like the Worths', I'd accept the two-week European assignment without hesitation. I know it's asking an awful lot of you. You've got your own family and don't need a bigger one. With Jill and Don each having their own bedrooms, and being the same ages as Stacy and Chad, I wondered would you consider their staying here until school begins?

"The two of you are outstanding examples of living harmoniously . . . something I wish my marriages had. You have such an overflow of love. It's what I've always longed for."

Sara reached into her handbag for a tissue to blot unexpected tears and give herself time to regain her composure.

Jack sent Sue a signal. They couldn't have known what lay ahead when they had prayed at dinner, but they had lots of love to share.

"We believe it's the right thing for us to do, Sara. And we'll do it!"

CHAPTER TWENTY-TWO

Delicate Negotiations

RELUCTANTLY SARA said good-bye to Chad and Stacy, who had come to the airport with the Worths. Aboard the chartered plane were the camera crew, makeup artist, producer, and others in charge of special equipment. Filming was due to begin in London tomorrow afternoon. Five days later they would proceed to Athens, then to Switzerland, and then back home.

Hal, who sat beside her, appeared relaxed, but Sara felt uptight. Mother's words, "My Sara isn't qualified," rang in her ears.

"You know, Hal, in college friends urged me to become a model. When I brought it up at home, my parents were horrified. 'It's immoral,' they said. Without training, I'm wondering what I'm doing here."

"Put your fears aside, Sara. You've got what it takes! Stop worrying. I've produced movies, and I know talent when I see it. Your natural flair for this business is better than training at school. Ted's discovery of you was one of the best things that's happened to us. This project was ours if we could come up with the right woman, and you were it!"

"My heart is in teaching, Hal. I'm a born teacher and that's hard to give up."

Here it was the middle of July, and she still hadn't told her principal she might not be back to work in September. Leaving the door open to return was wiser than nailing it shut—just in case.

"If only these debts were paid off. I could make a down payment on a home of my own. That's what's holding me to this job," she admitted to herself. "I don't have any business being away from the children. I wouldn't be in this predicament if my parents had repaid my investment."

In London she quickly forgot these concerns. Completely at the beck and call of the agency, she felt monopolized, with no time for fun, like seeing Buckingham Palace or riding a double-decker bus.

The cosmetic firm's London office arranged a cocktail

party for fashion experts and people in related fields. To Sara it seemed like a coming-out party. Surrounded by successful people, it was spoiled by one flaw—a chaperone! The agency had appointed one to keep Sara in the limelight and tell her what to do.

"Limit your conversations to five minutes or less," she instructed Sara. "Your job is to mix with the crowd. Don't leave unless I'm with you. It's for your own good," she said firmly. "The demands on your vitality need to be protected so you'll be your best before the cameras. That's why I'm with you."

Those at the party seemed counterparts of the Madison Avenue crowd, except for one distinguished-looking fellow who stood out above all the others. It wasn't only the cut of the English made-to-measure suit. And Sara certainly recognized one when she saw it.

"Wonder why he's here? He could be a model, but I doubt it." Out of the corner of her eye, she knew he was noticing her, too.

Hal introduced Rex Page to Sara. The usual stuffiness and arrogance of this profession were missing in his manner. All evening she had heard the usual phrases of the trade spoken with a British accent: "You'll go a long way in this business" or "It's good to have a fresh, beautiful face with a new kind of glamour." They made it sound so cold and trite.

"Hal told me you're new in this business, Sara," he began. "I've been wondering—what did you do before this?"

"I'm a teacher, Mr. Page—a fifth grade teacher, and I love it!"

"Say, I like that! But there weren't any teachers like you around when I went to school, or I would have turned out differently. I imagine every boy you ever had in class suffered a case of puppy love over you. They'll probably never get over it, either!" His brown eyes sparkled.

He reminded Sara of a student she had just had. Gates would get out of line, then look at her with talkative eyes. Before she could discipline him, she melted beneath his impish look.

"What are you doing in London, Mr. Page? I notice the absence of a British accent."

"It's Rex. I'm a golf enthusiast on vacation. But at home I'm a broker. Hal invited me here tonight because he knew I was in town. We're golfing buddies. I really don't belong in this crowd."

"Are you in stocks, real estate, or commodities, Rex?"

"I'm not in any of those fascinating things, Sara. I buy futures, but not on the commodities market. I'm an independent produce buyer and shipper in Latin America. I go where they grow pineapples, celery, bananas, coffee—any produce that's marketable at home—and I buy the field before it's grown."

"That's very interesting, Rex. You must be away from home a lot."

"Yes, I don't get to spend much time there."

"Oh, that's too bad. It must be hard for your family. But having someone waiting and needing you makes life worthwhile, doesn't it?" Sara knew she might be treading on personal grounds and didn't want to appear overly interested.

"You're right, Sara. But no one's waiting. My wife couldn't take my being away from home so much. She divorced me to marry someone else who stays home."

"I'm sorry, Rex. I'm afraid I've embarrassed you."

"Not at all, Sara. It's nice to have someone care enough to ask."

"You say you're a golfing buddy of Hal's. Where do you golf?"

She was relieved to get the conversation to less personal matters.

"Do you know where La Habra is, Sara? I have a house at the Foothill Country Club. A golf course is my frontyard, lemon and avocado groves border my backyard. I can begin a round of golf by sliding open a patio door."

"Rex!" she said, grabbing his arm firmly. "You've just described my former neighborhood! Can you believe my house was less than five blocks away, on Circle Hill Drive?" She released her hand, embarrassed by her action.

"You can't mean it! That's my street, too. Imagine being neighbors there and meeting here! That's really exciting."

The chaperone, standing within hearing range, was eyeing Sara and tapping her watch. But Rex was now asking if she were married. Carefully she weighed her words.

"I've gone through two divorces and have a child from each marriage—a daughter, whose third birthday is next week, and a son, ready for second grade. It's my first time away from them."

"I'm sorry. I know you'll make it up to her when you get home. Sara, I came here without dinner. I'm starved. How about you? Can we slip away? Do you have to stay?"

"I'd love to leave, Rex, but the agency has me locked up tight. And my chaperone has been within earshot ever since I got here. She's sticking to me as if I were in the Miss America Pageant."

"When can I see you again? Hal told me you're leaving Monday."

"Yes, I hoped they'd allow time for socializing and sightseeing, but they haven't. We're going to Athens next."

"I'm sorry, Sara. But don't be surprised to see me at the airport."

It was a nice way to end a conversation, Sara thought—like saying "I'll be seeing you" when you know very well you won't. Rex hadn't even asked the departure time for Athens.

Dutifully Sara mixed with guests while Rex found his way to Hal.

"Tell me, Hal could I buy a seat on your charter to Athens?"

"I don't see why not, Rex. Just be sure to be aboard our bus at the Hilton Hotel by five on Monday evening. Great to have you along. Maybe we can squeeze in a golf game there."

With a new lilt in his steps, Rex returned to his hotel. As he ate a late dinner he plotted his way into Sara's schedule.

"I'll work on the chaperone. I'll invite her to join us for dinner."

He congratulated himself on his delicate negotiations to see Sara again.

CHAPTER TWENTY-THREE

Let the Dust Settle

EACH TIME SARA passed the small shop next to the hotel lobby, she paused in front of the window. The dress was just her color—a luscious shade of green. The few minutes she had allowed to make the purchase were barely enough before the five-o'clock deadline. It was her last chance.

"If it's a size eight," she told the clerk, "I'd like to try it."

Pleased that it fit perfectly, she wore it. The airport bus was already waiting at the side entrance. She greeted the driver, then took a seat near the front. Looking out the window, she noticed dignified-looking men heading home from work carrying attaché cases and swinging umbrellas, and wearing pin-striped suits.

"Aren't there any working-class men in this part of London?" she asked the driver. "They all appear to be executives."

"Ma'am, these are the average working-class men of the city," he responded, amused by her observation. "This morning their attaché cases probably contained their lunches."

There was only one distinguished-looking person whom Sara wanted to see again, and she doubted that he would appear at the airport, as he had said. A double-decker bus rumbled by. This very morning the agency had rented one for her to pose on its steps. When she wanted to go to the top, she noticed that it had been roped off. She still felt cheated that she hadn't been given the opportunity to see London from the upper deck. Yet she had many good feelings about the completed assignment.

She was still looking out the window when Rex nonchalantly boarded the bus. Sara didn't see him.

"Hi, Sara. You don't mind if I sit here with you, do you? Say, that dress is a knockout on you—color and all."

"Rex! I didn't expect to see you again." She knew her delight was far too evident. "I chose this seat hoping for a good look at London on the way to the airport. I hope you had a good tour of the city."

"Yes, but have you ever tried driving on the left? That

took the fun out of it for me. Someday I want to come back. But you haven't asked what I'm doing on this bus, Sara."

"I *am* wondering, Rex. What are you doing on it?"

"I came to ask if you'd go sightseeing with me in Athens."

"Athens? Are you going, Rex? Of course I'd like to see it if they'll let me."

"Remember, Sara, I told you I'd see you at the airport today. Hal arranged for me to join your flight."

Sara was still trying to hide her feelings. Inside the airport terminal she stopped at the souvenir counter.

"Would you help me pick out gifts for my children, Rex? And the Worths, too. They're the family taking care of my children while I'm away."

"What about these, Sara? You wanted to see Buckingham Palace."

Rex held a pair of little palace-guard dolls, complete with fur hats.

"Their clothing and shoes are authentic reproductions," he added.

When he noticed a toy double-decker bus, he laughed.

"I want to give this to you in memory of the ride you didn't get. You said Stacy's birthday is due. Maybe she'd like it."

"Rex, it's thoughful of you to buy the bus. Imagine being in London and missing the changing of the guard, Houses of Parliament, and Big Ben!"

Warm feelings flowed between them as they boarded the flight for Athens. Sara relaxed as Rex pursued their friendship.

"Your chaperone interrupted us the other evening. I put a mental bookmark where we left off. You had told me of your two children and two marriages. I'm sure you've been deeply hurt. Want to tell me about it?"

Up till now no one ever cared enough to ask. Only her attorney knew, and he had been paid to listen. Here was someone who wanted to listen without pay. Bits of the story burst from her like a broken dam.

"My husband's last name meant nothing but trouble," she began. "He brought me misery, bills, bills, and more bills. Because of him, my pay has been attached and I was forced out of my house. I became liable for debts I knew nothing about. He forged my name on loans. With court costs and attorney's fees, I'm in over my head—all because I have his name."

All of the sudden she realized what she had done—probably killed a romance before it had a chance to get off the ground by telling so much. Too late now. She might as well go on.

"Everytime I'm asked 'Are you Mrs. Benson?' I cringe," she continued. "I don't want to be Mrs. Benson. I die when I hear that name. It usually means another court action or bill. I want it wiped out of my life! My next appearance in court will be to get back my maiden name—Carlisle."

"I feel for you, Sara. I'm sorry you got hurt. Maybe sharing helps a little. I'm a good listener. I think it's great that you're making a new life for yourself."

"If Rex had any interest in me before this, he has no doubt changed his mind," Sara thought with chagrin. "He knows I'm *not* bargain-basement material. The price tag attached to me is too big! I even pulled it out for him to examine. Debts, two children, lawsuits, bad name, and hostilities. No it's no bargain he's looking at!"

But Sara had struck a responsive chord in Rex, and he seemed more interested than ever. To him she was like a lonely, hurt, abandoned child needing love. Already he had a strong urge to say, "There, there, It's going to be all right. I'll help you. Wait and see."

In Athens they behaved like two children playing hooky from school. The chaperone was delighted to be included in some sightseeing. Rex manipulated her and the schedule to include intimate times. Behind oversized menus, he even sneaked in hand-holding right under the chaperone's nose.

Rex tagged along to Switzerland as if he were part of the advertising company. In spite of the chaperone hovering over them, they romanced. Before leaving Switzerland, he phoned his home office requesting that a company car meet them at the Los Angeles Airport. He was trying to do all the right things to pave the way for a closer relationship. Sara's guards were weakening. When he said, "I want to see you and your children safely home," she wondered if the children and Rex would respond well to each other. "Love me, love my kids" was as important to her as her own feelings about him.

Trying to sidetrack Rex by having him drop her off at the Worths, she told him they would take her home. It embarrassed her to have him see her cheap apartment and run-down neighborhood. But Rex was persuasive.

"I insist, Sara. I'm not one to do a half a job."

Before they arrived at the Worths, Sara told Rex they were

the kind of people who would care for her children as if they were their own. "You'll like them. They're my dearest friends."

Stacy and Chad screamed delightedly as they saw her arrive. Warmly they hugged one another. Rex stood taking it all in.

"Mommie, don't go away again," Chad pleaded. I like it here, but I want to go home."

Sara's heart wrenched. They couldn't know how difficult it had been to leave them. Finally she realized she hadn't introduced Rex.

"We met in London and discovered we were neighbors," she explained to the Worths. "Rex has a house at the Foothill Country Club. He offered to bring me home from the airport. He's become a dear friend."

Rex was remembering when he returned from buying trips, and Peg, his ex-wife, would call out, "So you're finally back?" Yet she had claimed she couldn't stand to have him leave. He had been drawn to Sara when she said, "Having someone waiting and needing you is what makes life worthwhile." Yes, this is who he wanted to have waiting and needing him.

After a stop at the grocery store, they unloaded their luggage and Rex said good-bye. Dead tired from the long trip, she went to bed wondering what Rex thought of her apartment. The phone rang.

"Sara, I had to call you. You've become very important to me. being with you the last two weeks has been the highlight of my life. I loved meeting your children tonight. They're great kids. You've done a terrific job with them. It makes me realize what I've missed. And your friends, the Worths—they're my kind of people, Sara! When you told them I had become a dear friend, I was pleased. But you know, it's more than friendship for me. You don't mind, do you?"

She responded cautiously. "No, I don't, Rex."

Two weeks later, Sara reminded him that school was due to begin in a week.

"I have another plan for you, Sara. I want to marry you now!"

"Rex, you have no idea what you'd be getting into. I'm paying off Steve's horrendous bills and still have a long way to go."

"I'll help you pay them, Sara. I want to. Don't worry. Business has been good. Why don't we sit down right now at your desk? Tell me the amount and I'll write the checks. You address the envelopes."

Sara's mind shifted automatically into the same old gear that she had used when Steve pressured her into marrying him. At first she thought it was too good to be true—security, thriving business, gorgeous home! A lovely big car for himself and a smaller one for her. Wonderful father for the children! Gentle, loving, thoughtful, and generous. What else is there? But were there no flaws in him? Or were all the flaws in her?

"I have plenty of love to give the right man. Is he the right one? I must make sure. Has he no hidden past? Hal Evans thinks he's great. They've been golfing buddies for several years. That speaks well of him. It hardly seems to warrant further investigation. I believe he would even pass Mom's scrutiny." At last she turned to speak to him.

"Rex, I'm deeply moved and grateful. But it's just too soon. I need to know if I really love you, or whether this is just a way out of my problems. Neither of us can afford to make another mistake. The dust hasn't had a chance to settle from my last marriage."

"Sara; I had counted on you saying yes before the next buying trip. I've waited because I didn't want to leave without you. If I don't go now, business will suffer. It'll be three weeks before I get back. Say yes now! We'll make it a combination honeymoon-business trip."

"I have to finish up the contract with Hal's agency, Rex. And school is about to start. If I marry you, how would you feel about my teaching? You're gone so much. I would need something to keep my mind busy."

"If that's what you want, that's what I want. But you wouldn't need to work. I'm able to support us all. You know what caused me to be interested in you from the first? It was your words 'feeling needed.' I want you to feel that you need me more than anything else. I need you!"

"Give me more time, Rex. Let's wait till you come back."

Part Three

CHAPTER TWENTY-FOUR

The Shoebox Account

BACK FROM HIS LATIN AMERICAN business trip, Rex spotted Sara on the other side of the airport customs inspection area. A fenced partition, intended to discourage smuggling between passengers and waiting friends, was all that separated them. They sent little signals to each other while Rex waited his turn in line.

After clearing customs, Rex made his way to Sara, dropped his bags, and swept her into his arms. Long and tenderly they kissed. All the questions she had wrestled with in his absence suddenly faded.

"The best part of coming home is finding someone waiting," he laughingly reminded her, "and getting hugged and kissed by someone you care about."

In the parking lot Sara handed Rex her keys, asking him to drive the 45-minute trip to his house. After only a few minutes on the freeway, he abruptly took an exit. Sara wondered where he was going, but said nothing. She knew what was coming. Before he left, she had promised to consider his proposal, and now he wanted her answer.

After finding a quiet street, he pulled to the curb and turned off the ignition. Under a big shade tree he took both her hands in his.

"I want to marry you, Sara. I want to find you waiting for me when I come home. I'll move heaven and earth to make and keep you happy."

"I don't know how to play games, Rex. I want to say yes. I really believe I love you, but I'm afraid—afraid because I've been burned before and don't want to be burned again. I couldn't take it. And I'm not just thinking of myself.

"You've had a bitter experience too, Rex. I want this to last. I want to give you my love—unreservedly. I want to be supportive of you and want you to be supportive of me. I don't want fantasies. No false pretenses."

"We both want the same thing, Sara. Like you, I've been burned and hurt deeply. I've learned a lot about what makes a marriage fail. Believe me, I don't want to go through that again!

"On the trip, I decided we should move into another house. I don't want either of us pointing our fingers at the past and tripping over ghosts. Old memories have a way of interfering.

"Sara, before I left, a large lot was for sale a little ways up the hill from mine, in the country-club complex. It had enough room for a swimming pool and a play area for the children. If it's still available, I'd like to buy it and have a home built there to suit you . . . my wedding gift to you. The deed would be in your name. We would live in my house until the new one is ready. Marry me now, Sara! If you'll say yes, we'll see if it's still for sale. Let's pick up Stacy and Chad to look at it."

"Rex, I'm overwhelmed! We ought to wait. We need to know each other better."

"Okay, Sara. Today is October 4th. Let's set the wedding for October 14th. Is that long enough?"

"Oh, Rex! I really need to pay off all Steve's debts. Let me clear that up first. Then I'll think about being married."

"Sara, I told you I'd pay them. We'll do it tonight. Then that obstacle will no longer stand between us. And let's never bring it up again—either of us."

"I don't know, Rex. This is really a big debt. I expected to use my TV residual money to pay it off, but it hasn't come in yet."

"Sara, is it more than $10,000? I can handle that right now. You mean more to me than money."

"I believe you mean it. It's true, it is an obstacle between us, but it's my obstacle, not yours. I should pay it. But if you pay it, I would treat it as a loan and pay you back as soon as I can."

"Sara, you don't know how happy you've made me. I take that as a yes answer." He pulled her to him. When they came up for air, he said, "Let's go on a Latin American honeymoon, Sara. I know how you feel about leaving your children, so we'll take them with us. You are all my family now. My next trip to Colombia is scheduled for the middle of October. Can you arrange to take a leave of absence from school? And have you finished your modeling assignment yet?"

"I believe I can get a leave. The agency asked me to do a follow-up commercial for the cosmetics line. I haven't committed myself. I had planned to work until Steve's debts were paid off. Rex, you have my mind in a whirl. Things are moving too fast for me."

"Sara, let's pick up the kids now."

When they arrived at the lot, Rex sketched his idea of a house plan and then paced it off, showing Chad and Stacy where he thought their rooms would be. It was obvious that he had won all their hearts.

"Let's go to my house so I can phone an architect right away. I'll ask him to confer with us on the site. But first I need to call the realtor to purchase the ¾-acre plot."

Two weeks later the children were back at the Worths. Rex and Sara left on their business-honeymoon trip to Latin America. Rex had eagerly offered to take the children, but Sara decided they should go alone.

At each airport on their trip, Rex rented a car. It was evident that he had often been there before. The plantations he inspected were often a long way from the city. Rex was buying everything from coffee to pineapples, just as he had told Sara when they first met. She didn't object to his conducting business during their honeymoon and usually remained in the car while he examined planted fields. Sometimes she heard him discuss deals in Spanish with owners or workmen. Her French was no help to her now.

As they drove from place to place, Rex shared his feelings with her.

"I want you with me, Sara. We belong together. I don't ever want to leave you."

Sara felt the same. Being together was satisfying whether they talked or remained silent. She was content to drive for miles without a conversation, and the honeymoon was all she had hoped for.

In each major city they visited, Rex asked Sara to open a bank account in her name, listing him power of attorney. When his reasons seemed vague to her, she pressed him about the legality of it.

"You know how much traveling I'm required to do, Sara. If anything happens to me, it will be easier if your name is on the account to make a withdrawal. I must have cash in advance to buy these crops."

"I don't understand, Rex. Why do you use cash in your deals? Why don't you use company checks instead?"

"I am the company, Sara. When checks are drawn on a foreign bank, there's a delay in their being forwarded back to the home bank. The rate of exchange fluctuates. These farmers don't understand this. Our company isn't equipped to transact in foreign currencies."

When the honeymoon ended. Sara found that the movers had transferred her belongings from the apartment to Rex's garage. Compared to his lovely furnishings, the things in the garage looked ready for a rummage sale.

"Sara, I want you to buy new things for you and the children. And I think it's time for you to begin planning to furnish the new house. There's over $20,000 in this shoebox. I want you to use it as you like. From time to time I'll give you more. Open an account in a local bank in your name, and give me power of attorney."

"Why so much, Rex? And why is it in cash?" she questioned.

"Sara, remember that I must have cash available for foreign transactions. Those people I do business with are afraid of checks bouncing. It's all legitimate. I own the company. I'm not cheating anybody. It's my money in the box, not the company's. Don't worry about it.

"I want you to use this for yourself and get things for the house. Keep a record of house expenditures."

Soon there were accounts in more banks than Sara could keep track of. Rex announced the need for another trip to Switzerland for financial purposes. It was getting too complicated for her. When he insisted that she go along, she jumped at the chance. Switzerland was beautiful and she wanted to see it again. But even more, she would be learning about his business dealings, and that intrigued her.

"We'll all go," he suddenly decided. "The kids will love it. You're my family now, and I don't like being away from any of you."

"How kind and considerate he is. How fortunate I am," Sara thought.

In Switzerland, Rex rented a car and they all went sightseeing and attended some sporting events. In Geneva, Rex asked Sara to accompany him to the bank. She was more than willing.

"I want you in on the discussion with the bank officer," he told her.

The officer recognized Rex immediately.

"Gangsters and con artists use Swiss banks," Sara thought while they talked together. "But reliable businessmen? I can't see how this all fits together. I've heard about 'laundered money' in foreign banking, but this? Mountains of cash are displayed every time I turn around. I've mentioned how risky I think it is for Rex to carry such large sums."

The bank officer interrupted her thoughts when he brought papers for her to sign. When she hesitated, he explained.

"It's just a formality, Mrs. Page . . . a protection for your husband and security for you in the event of his death."

"Why a foreign bank, Rex?" she asked later.

"Sara, you're an intelligent woman, but you've become overly concerned. Swiss currencies are recognized everywhere. They don't fluctuate. I can easily obtain cash with a check drawn on a Swiss bank. I've tried to be completely open with you. Don't you trust me?"

"How do you manage to keep it all straight, Rex? Don't you get mixed up on what's yours and what belongs to the company? And what about the Internal Revenue? I'm probably just apprehensive because Steve was a wheeler-dealer. You've been completely open about everything, and I'm grateful, Rex."

He made no effort to keep Sara in the dark. His attaché case was full of foreign checkbooks and bank statements. It would take an accountant to keep track of it all.

"How come Rex never writes down anything?" Finally she decided to ask him.

"Mathematics is my dessert, Sara. I have a photographic mind when it comes to numbers. Why don't you check me out? Write down the next deals I make. Don't let me see your notes. Wait two or three weeks, then ask me to recall them. To me it's like memorizing a script.

"Imagine having to write down all these transactions. I'd be doing bookkeeping, not making sales. In Los Angeles I sit down with Paul, my accountant, and bring him up-to-date. It's just that simple."

Okay! She could buy that! She would check him out as he suggested, but she was satisfied that it made good sense. He didn't have to write things down. Why hadn't she observed that about him before? She had fretted for nothing. She was married to a genius!

When they returned from Switzerland, Sara was delighted to see the new house already under construction.

"That's why I insisted that you go with me on this trip, Sara. I wanted to surprise you. I had hoped they would have even more finished."

More and more Sara was giving her time to Rex, the house, and her family, and less time was left for things at school. But she felt good about it. With all the love and affection she was getting at home, she was an even better teacher. Her students weren't neglected. And this new house and the love Rex was sharing with her was the dream she had wanted her childhood friend, Melissa, to see. How she wished they had kept in touch!

When Rex suggested that an interior decorator be called in to help with the new house, Sara hesitated.

"Sara, there are color coordinating, drapes, carpets, kitchen counters, and cabinets to select. You'll want to choose your own bathroom fixtures and lighting. You're too busy to do it all. You need help."

The interior decorator and Sara chose the carpeting, light fixtures, linens, and draperies. Rex ordered the driveway concrete to be poured. New furniture was selected along with appliances, and when everything was set in place, they moved in. Rex came home with a new car to occupy the third space in the massive triple garage.

"Since everything else is new, I felt that your old Mercedes didn't belong. Here are the keys to your new one."

Too many good things were happening all at once, and Sara shed tears of joy.

When summer vacation arrived, Rex asked Sara to plan another Swiss trip with him by way of Central America.

"I have a few matters to take care of in Panama. We'll go there first and take in the Canal. It will be interesting experience for the children. And Sara, you'll need to locate those checking accounts from our last trip there."

Rex's spending caused Sara to wonder how it was possible for a produce business to be so profitable. Was there such a huge markup on fruit, vegetables, and coffee?

"Let's take in England, too," Rex suggested. "We'll do up London to celebrate our having met there, and we'll see the things you missed. Don't worry about taking a lot of clothes along. I sold the other house at a good profit. We'll all buy new clothes over there."

CHAPTER TWENTY-FIVE

The Swiss Money Manipulator

THE RUMBLING in the long private driveway made Sara uneasy. The children had gone to bed and she was working at her desk. Vibrations sent shock waves through the very foundation of the house. She abandoned her project in alarm and hurried to turn on the floodlights.

This residential area of the country club closed at eight, when the patrolman left his post for the night. An electronically operated switch opened the iron gates at the guard station. After he left, access was possible only with a special perforated card, changed each month.

"It can't be Rex. He's only been gone six days. He's supposed to be in Mexico for ten days. I wonder if I should call the police."

Whatever was coming up the driveway lacked power and was laboring to make it up the long incline. How had it managed to gain entrance at this hour of the night, she puzzled? Straining for a glimpse of it, she saw a truck rounding the final curve of the slope, barely moving. Its springs sagged badly from an overload. It wouldn't have surprised her to see it break down right on the spot. When Rex stepped from the cab, Sara was stunned.

"Rex! I didn't expect you! What are you doing with a truck? And what are you hauling? It made the whole house shake."

Realizing how she must have sounded, she held out her arms to him. He responded warmly with loving kisses.

"I'm so glad you're home ahead of schedule," she told him as they walked arm-in-arm toward the house. "But you surprised me by arriving like this. "What's in the truck?" she asked again.

"I bought all the aggregate stepping-stones this rented truck would hold, Sara. They cost 17 cents a piece. I'm sure I can sell them for at least a dollar. That's $1,245 after expenses and a good profit. We'll have to store them in the garage until I can sell them. I'll get them unloaded tomorrow. The cars will have to be parked in the driveway."

"Aggregate stepping-stones? The kind landscape gardeners use? Is there a market for this, Rex?"

Three weeks later the stepping-stones were still inside the garage, and the three cars were outside, weathering. Is this why he had insisted on a triple garage? It irritated Sara, and she finally spoke up.

"I've invited a few friends to dinner tomorrow evening. What about those stepping-stones in the garage? The driveway is a bottleneck with our three cars, and with guests coming there isn't room."

"The stones will be gone in a day or two, Sara. The profit was far better than I expected, so I'm going back for another load."

"Will you have to stack them in the garage, too? It looks to me like we're getting ready for a rummage sale. Couldn't you at least keep the garage doors closed? That's our front entrance."

"Okay, I'll take care of it. It does spoil the looks of things."

Two days later the first delivery of stepping-stones had been removed. But within a week they were to be replaced by another load.

"Won't the management be upset with your conducting business here? The rules state 'no business may be conducted on residential premises.' "

"You shouldn't be upset, Sara. I'm not conducting business here, just storage. I can't rent space and make a profit. It's only temporary."

When the next delivery arrived, Chad wanted to help unload. He started to pick up one.

"Chad, I don't want you underfoot! Stay out of the way and don't touch them. Do you understand?" Rex snapped.

Chad's feelings were hurt and Sara was puzzled by Rex's outburst.

"He only wanted to impress you by helping, Rex. You could have explained that they were too heavy and he would get hurt."

"I'm sorry, Sara. I'll make it up to him. I guess I'm just tired."

A few days later Sara was brought home from school ill. When she didn't trust herself to drive, Brad brought her home in his car.

"Don't worry about your children or your car, Sara. I'll see that they get home. Be sure you're over the flu before you come back. Some teachers have returned too soon and had a setback."

Too ill to notice Rex's car in the parking area beside the house, Sara went right to her bathroom, took two aspirins, and hurried to bed.

Off in the distance she heard a faint, steady tapping, but was too sick to care. Later, when her temperature dropped, she got up to open a window. The tapping sounds became more distinct.

"It can't be the gardener clipping shrubbery. He's here on Fridays. Even though I'm weak, I've got to find out what's going on."

Rex and a helper were seated at a workbench on the patio. She was surprised to see Rex at home. Several piles of steppingstones were neatly stacked beside each man. Picking one up, Rex studied it carefully by rubbing his hands over the entire aggregate surface. Then he put it aside without doing anything more to it. He took another, examining it the same way. The workman was doing the same thing to his stack. These inspections continued as they searched for something special.

"Why such a thorough investigation?" Sara wondered as she looked out the den windows onto the patio. When Rex found what he was looking for, he stopped and picked up his chisel.

Carefully, like a jeweler working on a priceless diamond, an imbedded stone was removed from the slab's surface and placed on the workbench. From the indentation left by the stone's removal, Rex carefully lifted out a small plastic bag filled with white material. He placed the bag in a small box beside him, then glued the stone back where it had been. Some surfaces appeared to have a raised stone while others were smooth. They continued, unaware of Sara's observations. She returned to bed, now sick at heart as well as body.

Was Rex engaged in smuggling? When did this start? Had he done this before they married? Is this where the money came from to pay off Steve's debts and build this house? Steve was a crook. But Rex . . . ?

Did Rex have other methods of getting illegal drugs? Was the produce business a cover-up? And what about his frequent trips to Switzerland? Did he have her name on those foreign bank accounts so he wouldn't get caught? Is that where he stashes his drug money? Was Sara implicated?

Her mind reeled with unanswered questions.

"Is that where the shoebox account came from? Is this why Rex uses cash instead of checks in his dealings? I thought I married a bright businessman. How could I have been so sucked in?" she groaned. "Wow! This is too much for me! What do I do about what I know?"

About four o'clock the tapping ceased. Sara heard sweeping and knew that the stepping-stones were being neatly stacked back in the garage. When all the evidence had been removed, they got into Rex's car and drove off.

"Their timing coincides with when I normally come home from school. Thank God he didn't come into the bedroom! He doesn't know I came home sick. but what happens when he finds out? Will I be safe or will he . . . ? Just like the last marriage. How could I do this a second time?"

At 4:30 a teacher from her school who lived nearby brought Chad and Stacy home.

"Your car isn't far behind, Sara. I'll just wait here so I can take Mr. Nelson home. He's driving your car. Maybe you can call the gate so he won't have trouble getting in. The guard didn't want to let me in until he recognized Stacy and Chad. You're sure fortified here, Sara. It's like getting into Fort Knox. Lovely place you have."

"Thanks for helping me out, Rita. I'll call the gate now."

"Let's not say anything to Daddy Rex about my not feeling well," she told the children. They agreed and she started dinner, ignoring her illness as well as she could. If they caught what she had, that was just too bad. After dinner she quickly cleaned up and excused herself.

"Rex, I'm going to soak in the hot tub and go to bed. I feel a little achy all over," she finally admitted to him.

"I'm sorry, Sara. If you had told me earlier, I would have done the cooking. If you're not better tomorrow, I'll take over in the kitchen. I'll get the kids to bed."

In bed, Sara was still trying to come up with a solution.

"I'll say nothing and keep my eyes open," she finally decided. "Maybe I can get some actual evidence. When Rex mentions his next trip, I could ask to go along. Maybe if I had done that when he wanted me to, this wouldn't have happened. I've done almost the same thing to Rex that Mom did to Pop. But I really love Rex. And I'm sure he loves me. It's evident in everything he's done till now. I've been the rags-to-riches route before, and I'd settle for rags rather than dishonesty.

"I've only got the flu, but Rex has money-fever and he won't be recovering from that in a day or two. Is there no end to finding dishonest men, or aren't there any honest ones anymore? Will he end up in prison? Giving him up wouldn't be easy."

Each morning at 5:30, Sara walked down the long drive-way to get the *Los Angeles Times*. On the way back she would unroll the paper, check the headlines, then open the paper to hold old rose petals she picked up on the way. Near-ing the house, she would look up at their bedroom window, where Rex would usually wave to her. She would wave back. It was routine.

Two days later, feeling better, she went to get the paper. Stopping to pick up petals from one bush, then another, she came upon a small plastic bag near the doorway of the ga-rage. During the night a load of stepping-stones had arrived with a new driver. Rex had met him at the gate and they had unloaded late into the night. The plastic bag must have fallen to the ground in the dark when they broke a stepping-stone. Scooping up the bag as if it were a rose petal, she shook the paper into the trash can along with the plastic bag. She would retrieve it later.

Horror filled her mind. Was Rex watching her through the window, as he usually did? Had he seen her pick up this evi-dence? She went about her chores as usual, but inside she was a mess. A nervous wreck!

"Should I remove the plastic bag from the garbage can, or wait until evening, hoping it will still be there?"

Often Sara noticed pieces of cement from stones in the trash, and knew they had broken some stones. Surely that was why Rex had been so upset when Chad offered to help unload the truck. He was afraid one would break and reveal the incriminating contents. If she left the plastic bag in the garbage can, Rex might notice it and retrieve it himself. Then she wouldn't have the evidence.

Purposely she took out the kitchen garbage as she left for school. With one swoop she grabbed the plastic bag from in-side the trash can and pushed it into her purse. There! She had pulled it off! Her trembling hands could hardly get the key into the ignition.

"Now that I have evidence, what will I do with it? I can't

leave it at school, and I can't keep it in my car! I certainly can't leave it in my handbag! It might incriminate me. I know! I'll take it to the bank during lunch and put it into my safe-deposit box. It's in my name alone. Yes, that's at least a temporary answer."

CHAPTER TWENTY-SIX

Good-byes by Bits and Pieces

WITH THE EVIDENCE safely locked away at the bank, Sara should have been relieved, but she wasn't. Back at home, seated across the dinner table from Rex, she studied his unusually handsome face. The twinkle in his eyes was still there, but did not speak as loudly to her as in days past. It cut her to the core to have him spoil all they had together.

"If Rex had seen what this did to Steve's body, would he handle drugs? she asked herself. "What I do about that plastic bag will affect us all. I know the evidence must be turned over to the law. It's an international offense and the FBI will be involved. This is something I have to do all alone."

The die was cast. It might cost Rex everything. It could cost everything that mattered to her. The risks were great. That was life! She had always lived in the high risk area.

"Tomorrow I'll make the call to the FBI from a pay phone where no one can overhear. They'll instruct me what to do. It will have to be secret. One step at a time. No point in shattering lives until necessary. Whatever it costs, the next shipment must not arrive. If they need more evidence, I'll ask to go along on his next trip."

Carefully she gathered up the foreign bank deposit books. She felt and acted like a spy. She was a crusader out to stop a racket from getting any more victims.

During lunch the next day she wrote a brief note to the Worths.

> Dear Friends:
> Since I've been doing a lot of traveling outside of the country lately, I believe someone ought to have this. I trust you. Please keep the small envelope I've enclosed and open it in case I'm dead or missing.
> Love,
> Sara Page

The smaller envelope, marked *OPEN IN THE EVENT OF MY DEATH OR FAILURE TO RETURN*, contained a statement about Rex's illegal operations and some foreign-banking information. Putting the smaller envelope inside the larger one, she sealed it, then placed it in the mail for the Worths.

Promptly at three she locked her classroom door and hurried to the car. She would pick up the children after making the call to the FBI. There was a phone booth a few blocks away, on Whittier Boulevard. As she turned the corner onto Whittier Boulevard, an explosion rocked the car. Like a cold hand, fear clutched Sara. She lost control, and the car veered from the street and jumped the curb, snapping off a small palm tree. As the car leaped the curb, Sara hit her head against the roof frame.

Shaking like a leaf, she got out of the car. Dazed, she walked to the front and tried opening the hood, but couldn't. As traffic swerved to avoid the accident, a car pulled to the side and a man jumped out.

"What happened?" he asked.

"Something blew up!"

"Are you hurt?"

"I'm not sure. I hit my head on the ceiling of the car as it jumped the curb. I'm not bleeding and nothing seems broken," she said, trembling.

"You're white as a sheet. Maybe you'd better sit down."

"No, no. I'm not hurt. Just terribly scared. Someone's trying to kill me. There was a violent explosion under the hood."

He finally forced the hood open and began inspecting. A police car pulled up.

"Is anyone hurt?" he asked the crowd that had now gathered.

"Oh, officer. I'm glad you're here. Something blew up. My life's in danger. This was meant to kill me."

When the officer saw how shaken she was, he insisted that she sit in his car while he joined the man in his search.

"Ma'am, your car won't run," the officer reported after they closed the hood. "I'll call for a tow truck."

"I see that you're in good hands," the man said to Sara, waving good-bye.

"Tell me," the officer said to Sara again, "What's this about your life being in danger?"

"I don't know where to begin. I've been waiting all day to get to a pay phone to call the FBI. I have evidence for them.

I just left the school where I teach," she said, pointing toward the school up the street.

"I was turning onto Whittier Boulevard when this happened. Whew! I'm almost too shaken by this to think straight. I don't believe this was an accident. Someone wants me out of the way. I know too much."

"That's a pretty serious charge, lady. We'll investigate it."

The tow truck arrived. Sara asked to have her car taken to the Mercedes garage nearby.

"You can ride in my car," the officer volunteered. "I'll write my report after your car is checked out."

"This is a put-up job, all right, lady," a mechanic told her at the garage. "Look at this thing! Two more inches and it would have ignited the fuel line. You're lucky it didn't blow up the whole car."

A piece of the timing device used to set off the explosive was handed over to the policeman, who took it as evidence. Then he escorted Sara to the police station, where she told her story again, asking for an FBI agent to listen.

A call to the child-care center let them know that she would be late. When the FBI agent arrived, she told the story. Since the bank was now closed, they agreed to meet there the following noon, when she would turn over the evidence. The agent was finally convinced that Rex would not harm her, and he agreed to let her go home. The FBI needed time to build their case. Sara could help by acting as though she knew nothing and that the accident was a mere mechanical problem.

Two hours later Sara bravely returned home minus her car.

"I was going to run errands after school when my car broke down," she said casually, then hesitated. "I'm glad it's nothing serious. A policeman was kind and picked up the children and brought us all home. That's why I'm late. The children had to wait nearly two hours for me. They're hungry and tired, Rex. So am I. Could we eat out tonight?"

"I put out steaks, but I like your idea better," Rex answered.

Being alive was cause for celebration, Sara decided.

"Strange, he's not surprised to see me alive and well. He doesn't act as though I'm not supposed to be here. I'm sure he had to be in on it. I don't get it. Do you suppose he doesn't know?"

"Everybody in the car in ten minutes," Rex announced. "We'll take a vote to find out where we're going to eat."

Fortified by the knowledge that the FBI had promised her that the house would be under surveillance, Sara returned after dinner feeling like a crusader. She was pleased with her performance. Rex hadn't questioned her story. At breakfast, he surprised her by announcing he was making a quick trip to Switzerland.

"Could you arrange to go along, Sara? I hate going without you."

At first Sara was tempted, then backed off.

"No point in sacrificing my life in a foreign land," she decided. "He may do away with me on the trip. If I have to die, I want to do it in my own country, not off somewhere where no one would know."

During Rex's absence the noise of a prowler awakened her one night. Armed with a butcher knife, she slid the glass door open and hid behind a bush, waiting for the intruder to pass. She wondered what had come over her to stimulate this reaction. The large blade was pointed in the direction she expected him to come, and she was ready to cut him to pieces. She waited and waited as her heart beat louder and louder. Suddenly it came to her.

"This is no prowler! It's one of Rex's henchmen hired to knock me off. Of course! Rex failed in his attempt with the car explosion. Now he's trying to get rid of me another way."

Her mind raced back to the morning she had picked up the plastic bag.

"No doubt he saw me do it and realized I'm now his archenemy."

When the prowler failed to show up at the rear of the house, Sara gave up and went indoors. She closed both doors to the windowless dressing room so the prowler would not detect light. She found the special "day-or-night" number the FBI agent had given her. Using the identification as she had been told, she was soon connected.

"This is Sara Page. Somebody's trying to gain entry to my house."

"Yes, I know. I've been watching him, Mrs. Page. He's gone now. Just stay inside with your lights out."

"What do you mean, 'you're watching him?' "

"I'm in an old beat-up car on the vacant lot just up the block from you, watching through strong binoculars. Don't worry, Mrs. Page. I'll be here the rest of the night and then someone else will take over."

Even knowing about the agent, Sara was restless all night.

Nearly a month passed with nothing significant happening. Rex returned from his Swiss trip and seemed no different from usual. However, no more stepping-stones arrived. Sara thought the FBI had crossed the matter off their list when she did not hear from them.

One day Rex didn't show up at home by 6:30, as he had said. The hours dragged by, and finally Sara called the special number for the FBI. Her heart sank as she was told that Rex was being interrogated at their offices. A truck full of pineapples was unloading at his place of business on the docks when they placed him under arrest. The pineapples had been used to smuggle the illegal drugs across the border.

For three years Rex had been bringing cocaine and marijuana across borders of Latin American countries. Plastic bags filled with costly powders were carefully concealed inside coffee bags, bananas, pineapples, and stepping-stones. By removing some of the contents of the produce, the drugs remained unnoticed. An occasional spoiled pineapple or banana hadn't aroused suspicion. To speed things up, he had decided to use the stepping-stones. He had devised this method when he became impatient.

At the FBI headquarters in Los Angeles, Sara sat with Rex, now a broken man. During the questioning she reached for his hand.

"Tell me, Rex, why did you get involved in this? I only wanted you, your loving care, and to have us belong to one another. I wanted that more than anything. And you've freely given it. It wasn't *things* that I wanted."

"Sara, it seemed so easy and lucrative. I couldn't resist. That's my only excuse. I knew it was wrong before I got involved. I wanted to give you the security you lacked in your previous marriages," he groaned as he slumped in the chair.

"I've gotten by without being caught till now . . . I trapped myself. Your name on those accounts made me feel safe, and that involved you too. I'm sorry, Sara. Forgive me."

Sara squeezed his hand, too choked to speak. Finally she did.

"Rex, did you know I had found out what you were doing?"

"I wondered, but wasn't sure. The syndicate that bought the stuff worried about you. I tried reasoning with them, but it was you or me. The attempt on your life, with the timing device on your car, was done without my knowledge, Sara. They wanted you out of the way. You could ruin me and that would ruin them. They knew you taught school so they tampered with your car in the school lot. I had no way of knowing how or when they would try again, so I chose to make a hasty trip to Switzerland to make a big deposit. I wanted you to go along, feeling that you'd be safer with me. I didn't want anything to happen to you. When you chose not to go, I thought, 'Okay! I won't be around to get blamed.' I'm no hero.

"Sara, I wanted only the best for you. I never planned for you to get hurt. I've loved you more than anyone in my life. I know this finishes us for good. I'll file for divorce!"

In shock, Sara rose to leave.

"Please move out of the house before anything else happens," he called to her.

Imprisoned, Rex's business and manipulative deals ended. Sara turned over all foreign bankbooks and records to the FBI for evidence, and signed a release on all claims and rights to that money.

"I'm numb all over. It seems like what's just happened was to someone else, and I was only watching.

Slowly, feeling returned. "I don't ever want to go home. I hate that place now. We've got to sleep there, but I don't want to stay a minute longer than necessary."

"Let's go out to eat" became a frequent solution to escape having to face the house without Rex. It was a game to see how long she could avoid coming to grips with the pain associated with his leaving.

"When's Daddy Rex coming home?" Chad asked frequently. "I don't like it when he's gone."

"Let's go to a movie," she told the children, or, "we'll go to the library after school. Then we'll have a nice dinner at a restaurant."

"I've got to find a substitute to fill the enormous gap Rex left, and not a man, either," she decided.

One night she went to bed early. Sleep would not come.

"A wife ought not to rat on her husband. He would have been caught eventually anyway. It's the law of averages. I should have let nature take its course. But I turned him in! Why am I both right and wrong? It's too much for me. Caged again!

"How come I could face these things while they happened?

But now that it's over I'm wracked with guilt. I can't stand being guilty. There's nothing worse! It's a punishment I can't take. And why should I be punished for doing what's right?

"I've paid and paid in the past and it never got me anywhere. There's got to be a way out. Where is it? Why can't someone help me?"

CHAPTER TWENTY-SEVEN

The Hundred-Dollar Lady

"I'M PHONING BECAUSE I want to stop by this evening. Would it be okay, Sara?" It was Ted Bailey.

Facing friends with still another failure was hard.

"Sara, I'd like to help," he told her when he arrived. "You've been through a lot. Come back to work for us. It'll help you over this rough spot. We'll make it well worthwhile."

Ted had caught her while she was weak, like warm wax. That was okay. She needed to feel needed even if their reasons weren't the same. An excuse to get rid of this house is what she had been looking for. And here it was! Why not sign it over to the government and move into a nice apartment? It had been built with contaminated money. And the shoebox account? There was still some money in it. What should be done with it? Earnings from the agency would allow her to get back on her feet again, even if it seemed to take forever before it came in.

When the moving van backed up to the front door, the children didn't want to leave, and cried, "Why do we have to move?" Remembering the time Marc had brought up the subject of bankruptcy and what it did to her, Sara decided not to tell them they couldn't afford the house any longer.

After a few days in their new apartment, Sara came home from school before heading for the agency, and awaited the arrival of the baby-sitter. Chad was nearly 11 now, but she wouldn't leave the children alone.

Sara spotted a letter from an attorney as she sorted the mail. Memories of similar envelopes with lawsuits because of Steve's unpaid bills caused her heart to skip a few beats. She ripped it open, wondering what news it held. Trembling, she pulled out the folded letter.

"Divorce papers? From Rex?" She wilted.

"I didn't believe him when he said this is what he would do. What a blow! He doesn't want me anymore? This can't be! Maybe he only wants to set me free. Or maybe he stopped loving me. So what! I'm not going to let it put me out of commission, like Bruce Lane's letter did. Anyway, nothing matters anymore," she tried to tell herself.

When the baby-sitter arrived, Sara headed for her car, parked in the basement garage. Dean Kelly lived on the same floor as Sara. She had first met him in the basement garage when he parked his car next to hers. While he admired her Mercedes, she admired his good looks. As she stepped from the elevator now, he met her. She didn't mind taking a second look at this tall, muscular, blue-eyed blond.

"Sara! Am I glad to see you! Every day I park next to your car hoping to bump into you again. I wanted to invite you to go with me to a party in a friend's apartment here. It's this Saturday night at eight. You will go with me, won't you? It's one of those all-night affairs, but we can leave anytime."

Sara had always stayed away from that sort of thing. She knew what it would lead to, and hadn't wanted it. But now it was different. Dean wanted her and Rex didn't! That was reason enough.

At the party it was another story. Sara wondered why she had come. It was not good friends enjoying each other's company! She preferred meaningful conversations and hoped to make new friends. She really knew better. That's not what they wanted!

"They've come for another reason—to encourage and arouse base desires. To me it's just lewd and illicit sex," Sara thought. "I don't like flaunting it in front of others as though it's meaningless. It shouldn't be treated this way. It's a private thing."

When the keys were dropped into a container, Sara stiffened.

"Well, I'm not dropping mine in! I want out! No switcheroo of partners for a night for me!"

Dean sensed that Sara was uncomfortable, and suggested that they leave.

"Let's get out of here, Sara. Your apartment or mine?"

They went to Sara's apartment and she paid the baby-sitter. It was 11 o'clock. Dean darkened the room a little and pulled her to him.

"Why am I receptive to Dean's overtures now when I've always rejected this before? Even the slightest suggestion turned me off earlier. What's really so different tonight? Is it losing Rex that's done it? I wish I understood myself. Am I this hungry for sex?"

With Dean's advances, she allowed her emotions to take

over. When he suggested that they go to bed, her reasoning was thrown to the wind. Yielding without a struggle, she made no effort to suppress the desires that by now were raging within her like a forest fire out of control.

In bed with the lights out, she didn't picture Dean next to her. She really had no feelings for him. Instead, she pictured Rex there beside her and responded as though it were he. That thought restored a sense of morality to it. Dean's body aroused a force like a tidal wave within her as his hands cradled her in a special way, and the touch of his warm skin on hers quickened her response.

Blotting out who he was allowed her imagination to roam at will. All she could think of was that the raging fire within her must be quelled. The power of his body and strong muscles brought a response that washed over her like a flood as they molded together. She surrendered to him fully, and their bodies joined in blissful moments of passion.

With the fire gradually dying within her, her conscience reared its head. To subdue it she reminded herself, "I'm making believe it's Rex beside me," and that brought the peace needed to fall asleep.

In the morning, the shock of being with a stranger had worn off. Reasoning returned, and with it the thought, "So what! He cares for my body! He even thinks its worth a hundred-dollar bill. How dumb!

"Mom told me to go live on the street. Well, here I am and this is *my* street. I've lost nearly everything I ever cared about, except my children. Now who's around to care? My pride is wiped out!"

After Dean left, she went to the shower. It took far longer this morning. She remained under the water to wash away the ugly thoughts that surfaced.

When a client at the agency invited Sara to dinner, she accepted. It didn't even matter that Brian had on a wedding ring. Over dessert, he propositioned her.

"Sleep with me tonight, Sara. I want to be with you. I don't expect something for nothing. There's a hundred-dollar bill in it for you."

"How quickly I've changed. He wants me . . . Rex doesn't. I can pick the time, the place, and the men . . . not from bars . . . not off the street. I wonder what Mother would say now. Father said, 'You're a whore!' Mother urged me to 'live on the street.' Well, now I've done both. There are lots of opportunities."

Brian was a good lover. She gave herself to him freely, but felt degraded after it was over. It was as if she had gotten dirty deep inside, and no amount of washing could make it clean. Ten showers wouldn't help.

A few days later, when a representative of the cosmetics company made a similar pass at her, she went to bed with him. The next night it was the same. And the next. At first she accepted money. Then she decided that money was unimportant.

"Each time it's been a hundred dollars. I don't want to be known as 'the hundred-dollar lady.' I won't charge. I'd rather not be paid. I'm not in it for the business. Anyway, I wonder how you report this on your income tax."

"I like what the men say—'Sara, you're a tiger in bed. Sleeping with you is really something. In bed you're another person. Wow! You really have it!' Well, at least I'm good at something.

"I'm not a good business manager. Probably never was. I certainly can't manage myself, and I'm not managing my body anymore. As long as the fellow is clean, good-looking, and of at least average intelligence or better, and wants me, that's all that matters. It's just to fill a void in my life."

Bo, an advertising executive, nice to be around and extremely successful, invited Sara to dinner several times. When she accepted his invitation to see his house in Bel Air, she knew very well what it meant.

"Isn't this neat? Look at me!" she thought as they drove up in his expensive Jaguar. "This guy thinks I'm something! He even takes me to his gorgeous home in an exclusive neighborhood. This is the right street all right."

Bo turned down the lights and put on soft music. There wasn't anything new about it. Was it the forbidden fruit in the Garden of Eden? she wondered.

"None of these men would marry me. They just want to look at and use my lovely body. It's so empty afterward. Before this I only gave myself within the marriage commitment. I never felt degraded then. Now it monopolizes me. I thought my conscience would be salved by refusing the money, but money or no money, it's the same.

"Bo wants me to live with him. He thinks I'm good enough as a steady bed partner, but not to be his wife. When he says, 'You're mine, Sara. You belong to me now,' I want to ask, 'For how long? What risks will you take for me? Will I belong to you when things go wrong? Will you belong to me when the bottom drops out from under one of us? Where will you be then?' "

"What happens if one of us gets sick? Who's around to care? You don't care about my kids. 'Here's money for a baby-sitter,' you say. 'Let's cut out.' Or, 'Put them in a boarding school. I'll pay the bill. What's money?' Money? It's not a substitute for being loved.

"It's coming home and belonging to someone that counts. It's being wanted and needed day after day. It's sharing hurts and pain and going through deep problems together. Bo doesn't want that. He just wants to use me."

"I hate what I've become." She hesitated. "I hate what I see and how I feel. It's like I've become two people—a schizoid. The turmoil brewing in me has got to be stopped! Suicide would be a blessing—a sweet release."

That night she went to bed with Bo, and after the good feelings had passed, the bad ones emerged and engulfed her. Lying there with him, she started to cry softly and couldn't stop. She didn't want Bo to know, but her body would not cooperate. Tiny convulsions gave it away. This went on hour after hour until faint signs of daylight appeared. Bo thought she was out of her mind, but her conscience was killing her!

"Why should it bother you, Sara?" Bo asked. "Mine doesn't bother me. Forget it! It's the natural instincts in us. We're made this way!"

"Bo doesn't have these guilty feelings. He thinks I should be able to turn them off—like a switch—and then they'll be gone. I wish I could."

A few days later Sara's body began sending signals that all was not well. It started with a cough that wouldn't stop. In the faculty lounge, the teachers asked about it.

"Sara, you're too thin. You've been losing weight. Something's wrong. Aren't you well? Better take it easy, Sara," they warned.

Ted gave her notice that if she lost any more weight it could result in a temporary layoff. She was working at the agency only part-time, but the coughing spells interfered with everything. Finally she had to stay home. After a few days in bed, things weren't any better. She lay there thinking, "My bank account is dwindling and I can't afford this expensive apartment any longer. I'm not up to moving. If I can't work again soon, it's back to the slums for me!" she moaned.

"Now that I need the money, no one wants to sleep with

me because I'm sick. It's just as well. My kids have seen far too much. I'm not a fit mother!"

Sara had always taken great pride in her appearance. Now, when she was able to make it to school, she felt as though they were saying, "What's happened to Sara? She looks terrible."

"Face it," she told herself. "You've cracked and people can see the real you coming through the cracks."

Finally she made herself hunt for another place to live, and phoned the doctor. He arranged for tests and X rays. When they were completed, he reported his findings to her.

"You should have come when you began coughing. Mrs. Page, you have pulmonary tuberculosis. You will have to have complete bed rest."

"Tuberculosis? It can't be! Are you sure? I thought that disease was extinct. Isn't it infectious?"

"Let's take it one at a time, Mrs. Page. Until a few years ago it was considered incurable, but not today. Fortunately your case hasn't progressed too far. With eight to ten months of bed rest, proper care, and nutrition, you should make a good recovery. You have a relatively healthy body. But you must stop working immediately! Don't expose your students to this another day. Your children should also be examined. Check back with me within a week."

"Doctor, if I don't work, there won't be any income for me or my children."

"You know what must be done, Mrs. Page. I'm sure you'll find a way."

Thoughts of suicide were now becoming an obsession.

"What's there to live for? Somewhere on 'that street' I chose to live on, I picked up this disease. It's the natural consequence for living like I have . . . the penalty I have to pay. Besides, I broke the law of God.

"There's no way out this time. And nowhere else to run!"

CHAPTER TWENTY-EIGHT

High Risk

"WHY ISN'T DADDY REX living with us anymore?" Chad asked Sara. "Why doesn't he ever come home to us? I want him."

It ripped Sara's heart to be reminded. She wanted him too.

"Me too," Stacy added. "I love Daddy Rex and want him to be my daddy."

To make a distinction between "Daddy Steve" and "Daddy Rex," Chad had come up with these identities for them.

"I don't like those men who come here," Stacy went on. "They're not nice to us."

"Yeah! I don't like them either," Chad reinforced Stacy's feelings. I hope they never come back."

That did it! Their remarks were like fingers pointing out the guilts already plaguing Sara. Well, "the men" weren't coming back, but it was because she was coughing too much.

"Let's go back to our house at the country club," Chad pleaded. "I like it there 'cause Daddy Rex lived with us and he was good to us."

He thought moving back would restore the good times.

"We can't, Chad. I'm sick. We can't stay, and we won't be going back."

"Mommie, you didn't used to cough before Daddy went away. I wish you'd stop. I don't want you to be sick. And I don't want to move, either."

In a run-down neighborhood, Sara found a little house. The owner insisted on the first and last months' rent.

"I'll be gone long before the two months are up," she felt like telling him. Shopping for a place to live exhausted her. The next-door neighbor greeted her.

"Hi. I'm Norman. Could I be of help?"

"Yes, I'd appreciate that, Norman. I'm Sara. Are you sure you really want to? My car has a removable roof. In the trunk is a hoist and winch. Could you install it from a beam in the garage?"

Norman opened the trunk to examine the equipment.

"Sure, Sara. No problem. I'll have it done in no time. I'm a mechanic and know about these things."

The fancy Mercedes 450 SL coupe that Rex had given her didn't fit into the scene. The $30,000 it cost would have made a substantial down payment on a nice home, but she wasn't up to that kind of thinking now. The car stood in the driveway lined by an overgrown hedge. Wild grasses and weeds peeked through the cracked pavement. The house needed lots of renovation.

"We really match," she said aloud, as if the house could hear. "Both of us need repairs." Talking to the house made about as much sense as choosing to live in it. "Nobody cared enough about you to fix you up, and it's the same with me. This place looks like a garbage dump, and that's the way I feel I look."

As a student Sara had always been number one in her classes. In teaching she had become the epitome of accomplishment. And finally, as a model, she had been given the best assignments. "You're at the top, Sara," they told her. Well, she was at the bottom now.

The first Saturday in the house she woke up early—coughing. Before she got out of bed, she knew what she would do. A baby-sitter was needed before she could do it. Finally she got hold of one, and when she arrived Sara left in her car.

"My rib cage feels like it's been torn loose from the rest of me. Along with coughing, it's a slow death that I can't take any longer."

As Sara began driving—first aimlessly, then furiously—a plan was forming. She had always been a fast driver, especially in these low sports cars. It was the same way that Steve had driven that day they hung over the cliff. Then something clicked!

"That's it! That's where I'll do it! It's the perfect place to have an accident that won't look like a suicide. I wonder if I can find it? I never thought I'd want to see it again.

"A trial run—that's what I'll do—to study the situation."

The road seemed all curves. She wanted to go fast but couldn't—between curves and coughing, it was impossible.

"This looks like it. I'll find a safe place to park."

Sara sat awhile to think things over. Then she got out. Cautiously she leaned over the cliff to investigate. Far below, waves crashed against a few large boulders.

"This has to be the place," she decided. Hastily she stepped back from the edge as another coughing spell began. A few pebbles dislodged with her hasty movement and tumbled down the cliff.

"I've got to be careful. I'm weak and wobbly. I don't want to die today. I've still got things to do. Besides, it would look like suicide with the car parked over there, and that's not the way I want it! Tomorrow is the day. I'll go home and get things in order."

Memories of hanging and rocking to and fro on that precipice were too much. She hadn't come to remember but to decide if this were the right place to end it all.

Quickly she returned to the car and drove away. About a mile up the road she decided to go back, and she made a U-turn. Slowly she approached the bend, calculating where to speed up so it would look like she had missed the curve. Satisfied that the setting was right, she headed home.

Organization had always been one of Sara's strong points. She would need to work late into the night. There were bills to pay. Coughing interrupted, but she kept on anyway.

"Mustn't leave any loose ends. Make a list . . . check on insurance and teacher-retirement program for coverage. Check the will . . . make sure the children are full beneficiaries, not my parents. Leave the house neat."

With the last check written and the last stamp licked, she stacked the envelopes next to her purse. In the morning she would mail them on the way to her death.

"I've always heard that people with suicidal plans don't think things through. Their depression rules their actions. I guess I'm different. I want to die as much as anyone ever has. But I don't want to be sloppy about it. I've always been methodical, and I want people to be able to say, 'Sara was always the neat one.' It's important to me."

Most of the night she plotted and planned to be sure that each detail had been covered.

"I won't leave any notes for others to read. It's best not to leave something they would remember and talk about. I'm a fast driver. My friends know that. They'll say, 'She didn't make the curve.' And they'll think I was only out sightseeing. I'm known for doing that."

One thought really bothered Sara—the children. The insurance and teacher-retirement policies would be sufficient security for them. She couldn't find anything about suicide in the policies, but she had never been one to read the fine print. Anyway, they would have trouble proving it was suicide.

A decision she reached during the night surprised her. She would go to church first. It was a risk, but hadn't she always lived in the high-risk area? It had been years since she had been in church. Her mother had dragged her there against her will when she was little. Father stayed home, but Mother had to go. After all, Grandfather Lambert was a minister. Sara had finally rebelled and quit going.

The last time she had gone to church was when she married Gary. She would go this time because the sermon might help her make peace with God and keep her out of hell for killing herself. A slender thread of hope that she might even change her mind as a result of the sermon was buried somewhere in the recesses of her subconscious thinking.

"I'll go to that stately church I've passed so many times. It isn't on the way to the cliff. So what? Time doesn't mean anything now. I know a few people who attend there. It might be good to be seen by them. They would say that I didn't look like a potential suicide."

At last everything was done and she headed for the bedroom. As she came to the children's room, she paused, then went in. She sighed heavily.

"I wish I didn't have to do this to you." Tears dropped freely as she leaned over to kiss each of them good-bye. Sorrowfully she collapsed into a chair, watching them in the faint light from the hall. Another coughing spell began, and she hurriedly left the room.

CHAPTER TWENTY-NINE

Decision at Dead End

IT WAS ABNORMALLY EARLY to get up for a Sunday morning, but this was not the time to rest. She had all of eternity for that—after she dumped herself and her guilt into the ocean. There was no other solution. She had spent years looking for one, and it had eluded her.

At 5:30 she plugged in the coffeepot. In the bedroom she chose a pale gray suit and a long-sleeved, bright-red chiffon blouse. They matched the silver-gray metallic finish of the car with its red leather upholstery. A bit of red would show just beneath the jacket sleeves.

Back in the kitchen, Sara felt her heart grow colder. A strange, heavy sensation swept over her. She was going to hell! She would be living there! It was a terrible place—too horrible to think about. She tried to quiet these tormenting thoughts.

"What are you waiting for?" she asked herself roughly. "What are you trying to do? Are you making peace with yourself? Are you trying to make peace with God?"

Suddenly the coldness changed to fear. Trying to ignore it, she left her unfinished coffee to go to the garage. What a dump it was!

The hard top was suspended above the car. Yesterday she had used the winch to lift it off the car for the trial run.

"I wonder why it seemed important to have Norman put up the hoist and winch. I didn't plan to be around long enough to use it. Which car top shall I use to drive over the cliff? The hard top might prolong drowning. I don't want to drown and I don't want my hair messed up for church.

"Should I use the convertible top? The last time I put it up I noticed some small holes. It could leak water. I want the impact to kill me. The hard top will do that better than the soft one."

Besides its distinctive elegance, what had originally impressed Sara with this car were its safety features. The sales manual pointed out extremely high standards of the seams and welds. It was as though it were saying, "It won't leak water." Would using the hard top make it so watertight that she would suffocate inside?

"That's what the plaster of Paris face mask did to me before surgery on my nose. Well, I don't want to drown and I don't want to suffocate! I want to die from the impact! Dying is hard. I thought it would be easy."

Other features from the sales manual came to mind.

"It seems to me I read something like 'If you ever bump an unyielding surface, the steering column and wheel are designed to collapse from impact.' I know the interior is padded for safety."

The car seemed to be telling her, "It's not going to be your death trap." She pushed the button for the soft top to rise. It had dried and cracked from lack of care. It was in need of repairs, but this was not the time. It was too late.

At last the decision was made to use the hard top. She cranked to drop it into place. It was exerting, and she coughed again.

"I'll save the cough medicine for just before church."

She finished dressing, applied her favorite perfume, and left the house. It was eight o'clock. On the way she mailed the checks she had written the previous evening.

In front of the impressive church she spotted one last parking place. It seemed reserved for her. The sign in the church yard announced the service for 8:30. She had ten minutes. The sermon title on the sign caught her attention: *"ONE LAST CHANCE!"* With an agonizing moan, she leaned her head over the soft steering wheel.

"Oh, God, if You really do exist, I've got to find You today or I'm finished. *This is my last chance!* I've already gone down the drain. There's no more desire in me to search for answers. I've had a lifetime of guilt and it's got to go! Today is it!

"You know I'm on my way to do away with myself, God. I don't know what else to do with the guilt but take it with me to the bottom of the ocean. If there's an answer I've overlooked, it's up to You to show me what it is."

It was time to take the cough medicine. Without further hesitation, she walked inside. No usher showed her where to sit, so she chose the back. Glances told her "You're new here. You don't seem to know we each have a designated seat." Listening to the organ music brought back memories.

"When I was younger, Mother made me sing in the choir. I hated it. I remember sending notes to people in the choir to make them laugh. Mother would be furious with me. Then there was the Sunday the organist was absent. 'Sara, you play the organ today,' Mom ordered. I can hear it like it was yesterday. 'Mom, you know I can't,' I pleaded. 'Of course you can. We paid good money for you to learn to play the piano. Just sit down and play.' I refused, and at home she sent me to my bedroom, locking me in. Not knowing how to play made no difference to Mom. I should have done it because I was told to."

She coughed a few times, and people turned to look at her. "The cough medicine doesn't really help anymore. I could leave, but I might miss what I came for."

An hour later she walked out of the church as empty as when she had walked in. The sermon had been dull and the service mechanical. It hadn't met a single one of her desperate needs. What a disappointment!

Outside, she spoke to a few people she knew. Today they seemed as cold as the church service. Soon there was no one. She got behind the steering wheel, leaned over it again, and let the tears roll. Earlier she had decided that there would be no more tears, but now they would not stop.

"Oh, God! You weren't there! Do You really exist? I didn't find You and I was looking! Are You so hard to find? Don't You know how desperate I am? I can't cope any longer. I've already told You that if I don't find You today I'm finished. This is it!

"I think what hurts almost more than anything is that I thought someone in there would care. *They're supposed to care.* Well, I don't care anymore either!"

Uncontrolled sobs came. Convulsions of grief engulfed her, shaking the car. The last straw of hope was gone. There was nothing left to do but drive over the cliff. Finally Sara started the engine and drove out of town. With at least eight ways to get to the ocean, she had trouble finding the route she had used on Saturday. Starting at a different spot had confused her. It was Steve who had known the way. At last she found herself on a strange, crooked road. It didn't matter if she were lost or not. She had been lost yesterday too but had finally found the place. It was as though someone else was in charge.

"I don't know where I'm going, but I've got to get there fast. I've got to dump these terrible feelings. I can't stand this slow death by my conscience any longer. No more creeping death for me. Get it over now!"

More curves and many roads later, Sara made still another wrong turn and found herself in a beautiful residential area. The beach had to be nearby. She remembered a small forested area she had passed on the first try.

"I must get off this road and find the right one. This is ridiculous. I know I'm heading in the right direction . . . not deliberately trying to escape! Keep looking," she told herself. "Take it easy. No need to panic."

On the next turn, Sara noticed that it was a dead-end street. She pulled into a driveway and turned off the engine to get hold of herself.

"What am I doing here? It's as though someone else is in control of this car. It's not going where I want it to! I'm trying to find the shoreline and everything has gone wrong." Her mind cleared. "How can something so simple become so difficult? I'm driving to the cliff that overlooks the ocean. When I find it, the rest is easy. Speed up on the curve, plunge over the cliff . . . that's it! But a dead-end street? It's where my life is—at a dead-end!"

A sign above the garage door read AUTOMOBILE TOPS, SEAT COVERS—NEW AND REPAIRS.

"I need a new top, but not now. This is my 'drive-over-the-cliff day!' Besides, it's Sunday and closed."

The auto shop was on the first floor, with an apartment on the second. She tried to concentrate on the matter at hand, but her mind began to wander. She thought of her children.

"I know they're up now. I didn't leave them any breakfast. Oh! I overlooked one thing—a baby-sitter. It may ruin the perfect suicide. What a rotten mother I've been—not fit for the job anymore! Too weak to take care of them now. And I've probably passed my illness to them.

"Oh, God! Please see that my kids get good care. Anyone is a better mother than I am!"

Tears were wetting her blouse now.

"Oh, God! Look at me! I feel like a drowning person going down for the third time. Here I am on a dead-end street. I'm the loneliest person on earth. Isn't there anyone to care about me and how I feel? Can't you see I'm abandoned?" she sobbed. "I've fallen apart. I know my greatest enemy is myself, but I can't handle my life anymore. I want to die! Right here! End it all."

Sobbing brought on another coughing spell.

"I have no right to live. Look at me—*I can't even find the cliff to drive over!* I want to dump me and my guilt in the ocean . . . I want to get it over with . . . NOW."

Sensing someone near, Sara opened her eyes and there she was—looking at her as though she knew her. It wasn't the stare of a stranger. She had the kindest face Sara had ever seen. There was something different about her. Her smile was warm and loving.

She tapped on the window, then opened the door and slid into the front seat alongside Sara as though she had been expected. Sara wasn't the least bit shocked or surprised. It was as if the car had brought her here to meet this woman.

"You're in trouble, aren't you, Dear?" she asked ever so gently.

Sara nodded in assent, unable to speak over her sobs.

"You think there's no way out for you. And you want out, don't you?"

Wondering how she could know so much about her, Sara nodded again.

"There *is* a way out for you, Dear. I'm here to tell you what it is. I was in my living room upstairs," she said, pointing to the second floor. "I was reading the newspaper with my back to the window when I was compelled to get up and look out.

"At first I didn't notice you, for you were directly beneath my window. Even when I looked down I only noticed your car. I was about to sit down again, but something made me take another look. Then I saw your hands on the steering wheel. That's the only part of you I could see, but in that instant I knew I had to come down at once! It seemed most urgent."

Remnants of Sara's sobbing lingered. Ragged shudders and coughs shook her body. When she quieted down again, the woman went on.

"My name is Marie Hall," she continued when she was sure Sara could hear her again after coughing. "I believe in God and I believe He prompted me to look out the window. He directed me here. I've come to be your friend. May I tell you why?"

Sara nodded. Marie's obvious concern baffled her. But she listened intently, waiting eagerly for Marie to go on.

"It's because God cares about you so much! He sent me to tell you *He* cares! And *I* care, too. Very much!" Marie hesitated, then asked "What's your name?"

"I-I'm S-Sara. Sara P-Page," she stammered, trying to control her breathing. "Do you mean it—that you care? I don't remember anyone ever telling me they really cared about me—just me. It was always the things I had to offer, or my looks, but not me."

Marie reached for a tissue in the box between them and handed it to Sara. She waited patiently until Sara was able to continue.

"I can't imagine you caring about me. You don't even know me. If you knew the rotten things I've done, you wouldn't even be sitting here next to me," Sara said bitterly.

"Oh, Sara! I not only care, I love you." Marie put her arm around Sara. It reminded Sara of the time Mrs. Goldman gave her a motherly hug. It made her feel safe, and oh, how she wanted to feel safe now.

"I'll tell you exactly why," Marie went on. "It's because I've experienced God's love for me so intensely—so fully that I love you even though we've only met! God knows you are in deep trouble and sent me to help. He wants me to tell you the way to escape."

"Escape!" Sara gasped. "How did you know I'm trying to escape?" Sara was startled by Marie's knowledge.

"I didn't know, but God did," Marie replied.

"I hate myself because of what I've become. I can't go on."

"Sara, do you hate your life because your guilt is so intense, so unalterably real?"

Sara reflected. So many people had tried to persuade her that her guilt was not real—only based on rules or standards that she and others had set for themselves. But oh, how real it was today!

"It's so real that I can't live with it even one more hour. I've got to get rid of it, Marie. My own conscience has pronounced the sentence."

"The reason your guilt seens so real is because in God's eyes it *is* real. The reason you can't live with it is a reflection of the fact that God cannot live with it. Not only is your guilt real, Sara, but hell is real, too. Everything in you testifies that that's where you belong. I have wonderful news! There's a way out for you."

Sara shook her head. "If there is, I haven't found it. I can't imagine what it would be. It's too late for me."

"I know you feel a great deal of pain over your wrongdoings. You're suffering from self-accusations. Does punishing yourself mean you're sorry?"

"Oh, yes. Yes!" Sara answered.

"But you know punishing yourself doesn't clear your conscience, don't you?"

"Do I ever!" she nodded again.

"God has another answer. He calls it repentance. It means being sorry in such a way that you turn your back on doing wrong; that you stop deliberately doing these things anymore. Is this the way you feel, Sara? That you don't ever want to do them again?"

"Oh, yes, more than anything!" Sara moaned. "But it's got to be paid for somehow. I can't just act like it never happened. I've tried that."

"That's right, you can't. And the payment is death, but not yours, Sara. You've been thinking of giving up your life for your guilt, haven't you? But Jesus has already given *His* life for *your* guilt. The debt's been paid. In full! It's canceled. You've been trying and trying to pay and you found you never could, haven't you?"

"Yes!" Sara sighed heavily. "I have! And it was never enough."

She was bewildered more than ever by Marie knowing so much about her, but she wanted to hear more.

"You never, never could pay, Sara. God knew you couldn't pay. That's why He sent His Son, Jesus, to pay it all for you. He loves you so very much.

" 'Sara Page,' Jesus says to you, 'I hung on a cross for you. I've taken your guilt and pain. I gave my life for it. I paid the debt in full that you couldn't pay. There's nothing left to pay. I took it all on the cross and died for it.

" 'Your guilt and sins are buried in the deepest sea.[1] They are gone. Washed away. You are forgiven![2] Pardoned![3] You can stand before Me free. All you need to do is believe in Me. Just believe I paid the price for your guilt."

"Receive that payment, Sara," Marie urged. "You don't have to pay with your life, because Jesus paid with *His* life. He was guiltless. Death is the payment, but if you died for your guilt, it would be nothing because that still wouldn't clear your record and you wouldn't be forgiven.

"God declared that His Son's death was sufficient payment. When the payment was completed, God raised Jesus Christ

[1]Micah 7:19.
[2]Luke 24:47.
[3]Micah 7:18.

from the dead. He is alive![4] And because He lives you can live. Along with forgiveness, He also gives you eternal life.[5] Won't you receive it, Sara?"

"I want to believe I can be forgiven." Sara hesitated. "I don't know if I can. Sometimes I believe there is a God. Then there are other times when I'm not sure. At times like this it seems like a fantasy. If there is a God, I'm not sure I can accept having His Son pay for anybody's guilt. Especially mine! I'm too rotten."

"I understand, Sara. But just for a minute, let's suppose that *maybe* you're wrong. What if there really is a God? And what if He really has a Son named Jesus Christ? You know that Jesus Christ really lived. History confirms this fact. You know that Jesus died, don't you?" Sara nodded.

"Well, I'm absolutely convinced He died for me! You may not believe it," Marie went on, "but I was as guilty as you. And I know He died for you, too. The best part is that I know He's alive. In fact, I talked to Him just before you came."

Sara grew quiet as she drank in every word. Marie looked at her compassionately. Sara gripped her hand, waiting expectantly for her to go on.

"Let me tell you what I asked Him to do just before you came. 'Lord,' I said to Him, 'who is the most needy person whose life you would have cross mine today? Let me share You with that person. You've done so much for me. I want You to let me share You with them so they can know You, too.'

"Sara, He heard your cry of distress today. That's why you're on my street. How else would you have come here? And how else would I have come to you? It's only for this reason—God wants to rescue you! He cares!

"He wants you to receive His forgiveness. He had you pass this way so I could tell you. Yes, it's absolutely true, Sara. God loves you very dearly. You are very precious in His sight. He knows you. He loves you, and Sara, He has a plan for your life and wants to put it into operation. He's been waiting for you to want Him. He wants to rescue you right now!"

Never in her life had Sara heard such wonderful words.

[4]Matthew 28:6
[5]John 3:15,16.

"Could this be the way out? I did ask God to send someone who cares," Sara remembered. "And He has."

"Sara, will you believe and receive? He wants nothing from you. There's nothing you can do but receive Him and His forgiveness. He's a gentleman and will not force you. He listened to you when you cried out today. While you were searching, He knew where you were all the time. Now you've found Him. *He's* what you've been looking for. He's the answer to your lifelong search. You're forgiven, Sara. But you have to receive Jesus Christ and His forgiveness. Won't you do that *now*?"

"I will!" Her own excitement surprised her. Then thoughtfully she continued, "Yes! I will! *I know now that this is what I've been looking for.* I don't understand it all, but I receive Jesus Christ and His forgiveness. Oh, Marie! It feels so good to say that!"

Tears of relief began to come as this truth sank in more and more. Then it began to explode inside her.

"I believe! *I do believe!*" Sara reaffirmed forcefully

Something broke as waves of relief flooded her. She began to feel warm and soft instead of cold and hard, light and free instead of heavy and bound.

"The tons of guilt are lifted! They're gone, Marie! I feel clean! For the first time in my life I feel clean!"

Marie said, "Sara, why don't you just say, 'Thank you, Jesus.' "

Without hesitation, Sara responded.

"Thank You, Jesus. Thank You for forgiving me. Thank You for making it possible. Oh, thank You for lifting the ten-ton load from me."

"There's something I think you ought to see, Sara. It's in the house. Will you come with me?" Marie urged.

Inside, Marie opened a book on the coffee table and handed it to Sara.

"These words sound like they may have been written especially for you. I think you'll agree. Would you like to read them aloud?"

"What happiness for those whose guilt has been forgiven!" Sara read excitedly. "What joys when sins are covered over! What relief for those who have confessed their sins and God has cleared their record!

"There was a time when I wouldn't admit what a sinner I was. But my dishonesty made me miserable and filled my days with frustration. All day and all night your hand was heavy on me. My strength evaporated like water on a sunny day until I finally admitted all my sins to you and stopped trying to hide them. I said to myself, 'I will confess them to the Lord.' And you forgave me! All my guilt is gone."[6]

"Oh, Marie! This expresses exactly what I feel. What is this?" she asked, then examined the cover. "It's the Bible. How wonderful! I didn't know it was like this. I must get a copy for myself."

"I'll give it to you. I'm sure you'll want to read it."

"Sara, I want to thank God for what He's done for you today. And I'm going to ask Him to heal you of your terrible cough. Marie got up, walked behind Sara, put both hands on her shoulders, and began to pray.

"Lord, You led Sara to my driveway today and directed me to her. Thank You for coming into Sara's life. Thank You for Your forgiveness and for what Jesus did to make this possible. You've made Sara clean and lifted the terrible weight of guilt from her. Help her to follow the wonderful plan You have for her life now that she has received You. Thank You for Your promise that You will never leave her nor forsake her.[7]

"Sara needs Your special touch of healing, Lord. I ask You in the name of Jesus to heal her and stop her cough right now. I thank you for it."

Sara turned as Marie opened her eyes. Then Marie spoke.

"I believe you're healed, Sara."

Sara answered, "You know, I've never heard anything like this in my whole life! I'm astonished by it all! But you know, Marie, I believe it too!"

Sara had carried her tissue box upstairs with her. Now reaching for one, she wiped her eyes, blew her nose, and took a deep breath.

"Marie!" Sara breathed deeply again as though testing. "The tightness in my chest is gone! GONE!" Her voice trembled with excitement. After still another deep breath, she continued.

"It doesn't hurt. My mind can't take it all in! I know I'm forgiven. I believe I'm healed! I'm a new person! I expected to die today. Instead, I'm going to live. I was going to drive over the cliff, but I can go home now!"

[6]Psalms 32:1-5
[7]Hebrews 13:5.

CHAPTER THIRTY

Dismantling the Cage

IT WAS AFTER THREE when Sara backed out of the driveway and waved good-bye to Marie. At the corner she turned left, carefully following Marie's instructions to get her out of the neighborhood.

First the street led through a forested area, then along a jagged cliff with expensive homes perched here and there. Far below, a thin line wove along the edge of the irregular coast like a mule trail.

"That's it! Four hours ago I desperately tried to find that road!"

At the first wide spot, she pulled over and stopped for a moment.

"I was so close! How could I have missed it? But Thank God, I did!"

She tried to comprehend the unusual series of events that had transpired. It was more than her mind could grasp. At last she checked Marie's instructions again and continued on her way. Winding down the hillside, the street she was on fed into a main road. She slowed to check its name. "Palos Verdes Drive." From here she could find her way home. Her eyes dropped to the speedometer and she chuckled.

"Fifteen miles per hour! What a difference from the way I drove this morning! Now it's like I'm in slow motion. My whole world is different. I'm different! I've never known anything like this—it's so wonderful. This morning I had given up on life, and life had given up on me. I expected to die! Instead, I've begun a new life."

A quick check in the rearview mirror showed no one on the road.

"Good. I'm not in anyone's way. There's no pressure from traffic. I can drive slowly and sort out what's happened. It's so big I can hardly take it in. I was in such a frenzy and now I'm at peace with myself.

"The only times I ever thought about God before were when I had my back up against a wall. Then I cried out for His help, wondering if He was real. Now I know He is! I met

174

Him. I don't have any doubts about it. The marvel of it is that after all I've done, He wasn't out to get me!

"What He's done for me through Jesus is better than a psychologist's couch or a governor's pardon. The guilt is gone! I don't have to run anymore. No more running from myself!

"Driving into that dead-end street and right up to Marie's house was no accident. I thought You had abandoned me, God, but You were planning my rescue. You were in charge and I didn't even know it.

"Even though I was lost, I wouldn't have turned onto an unmarked street and stopped my car in a strange driveway. And then to sit there like that! It wasn't like me at all. But it had to be that exact spot. Of all the people You could have chosen, God, Marie was the very one I could respond to. And to think I accused You of not caring. Oh, how much You cared! Thank You!"

A feeling of liquid love was flowing through her.

"This new warmth of God's love is reviving my cold heart—renewing me and making me a new person. I used to think people who talked about being 'born again' were peculiar. But it's the best way to describe what's happened to me.

"In one fraction of time everything has changed. Even the coughing stopped. Imagine that! Oh, thank You, God! Last night I had so many reasons to die. The list was so long. And now I have so much to live for. Those guilts aren't suffocating me anymore. They're gone. And I didn't have to die with them. Oh, God, I've never felt so loved!"

Sara reveled in this thought until suddenly she thought of the children.

"How selfish I've been! I've got to get home! They need me."

She pressed the gas pedal more firmly.

"I hope they're all right. They don't know it yet, but they're getting a new mother."

Sara's thoughts raced on as she quickened her pace in traffic.

"Last night my mental 'hate-list' monopolized me. I expected to die for it! At the top was Bruce, but now I can forgive him at last. He's never known about the bitterness I've carried in my heart toward him. Now it's gone! Completely gone. What a relief! I don't feel sick at heart when I think of him. Something inside me has been healed besides my lungs. My attitude has changed."

Somehow Sara linked Bruce with Grandfather because of what happened.

"Grandfather is dead, but what I've felt for him all these years wasn't. Now as I think about him it doesn't upset me. Poor Grandfather. He was old and needed love and affection and I never saw him get any. I didn't give him any either. I wish I had."

"And Gary . . . I've been sorry, but never told him. I need his forgiveness for hurting him so deeply. I hope it's not too late. I can't make it up to him, but I must write him right away. The sooner the better."

Her mind moved on down the mental list.

"Mother! All my life I've wrestled with feelings about her. When I was little, I tried to show her I loved her, but she rejected it. Then my love grew cold. Now it's revived. I believe I can love her even knowing that she isn't likely to return it. That's incredible! I never thought I could feel this way again. I want to run to her and just blurt out, 'Mom, I really love you! You don't have to say anything. This probably takes you by surprise, but it's true.' " Sara choked and her vision blurred. Momentarily she slowed down.

"I can forgive her for not loving me. I can even forgive her for not paying back my money. I can forgive her for turning the rest of the family against me. It's not so important anymore. That's a miracle!

"Poor Mother. She's lived with these terrible feelings all her life. She must be so miserable. That's why she makes everyone else miserable.

"And then there's Father! He's included. I must tell him he matters to me. I don't know if he'll respond. I do love him— really love him! Isn't that something! Imagine wanting to tell my parents these things. I've never told them. Never! They wouldn't let me. Even when I felt it. It could never be said. It was bottled up inside me . . . repressed. Now I want to say it. Out loud. It doesn't matter whether they respond or not. I believe I can love now without being afraid of not being loved in return."

Sara checked the rearview mirror again. A little traffic was building up behind her. Speeding up a little, she realized that people mattered more than ever now. How she treated them was important to her.

"That service station! That's where Steve bought gas after that terrorizing experience of teeter-tottering on the cliff. I tried to get away from him, but the restroom was locked.

"Steve Benson! I don't know. He's harder to forgive. He's done more to create havoc in my life than any of the others. Now suddenly I can think about him and it doesn't tear up my insides. What he did is the kind of things that shouldn't be forgiven. But I'm not angry anymore.

"He's under such bondage to that dreadful presence that controls him. It's worse than a ball and chain. His life must be a living hell."

Sara wanted to tell him, "I forgive you, Steve. I wish you could experience what I have today."

Rex was next on the list. What about Rex? He had already filed divorce proceedings. Their life together was over.

"I want to see him anyway, even though he's in a federal prison and it's far away. It will cost an airline ticket and time away from my job and children, but it's worth it.

"Maybe the prison officials would let the children see Rex. They really love him. He was good to them and I think he really loved them too. Taking them to see him might prove to Rex that I really care what's happened. It hurts me that he's isolated from all that matters to him. I'm sorry I didn't let him know how much it mattered to me what became of him. I'm sorry he lost everything and that we're separated.

"I wish it hadn't been I that turned him in. Why couldn't it have been someone else? But I had to report him. He was committing a crime and it was killing people. If only he had shown a little remorse. But he didn't. He would have continued if he hadn't been caught. He only seems to be sorry about that.

"I don't know if there's any future for us. I just want him to know that I've been given a new life and that he can have the same.

"Here I am, going back over that list, but I don't feel any turmoil. My responses are completely reversed. The anger, frustrations, and guilt don't overwhelm me anymore. The sharp edge is gone. There's a healing going on in me that affects everything.

She was nearly home now. There was one more item at the bottom of the list of those things she had expected to die for.

"I don't know if I can do it. It's the last link with my old, ugly past and the worst of the whole lot. *Me!* I went through the whole list feeling a new sense of love and compassion for each one on it. But knowing what I know about myself, how can I love *me*?

" 'Love your neighbor as yourself' I heard in the sermon

this morning. I don't know. I know God doesn't condemn me for my past, but can I quit condemning myself?"

This thought engrossed her as she turned onto her street. She sighed heavily.

"I'll deal with that later. I can't do it yet. It's too hard."

She caught sight of her dilapidated house, and a twinge of guilt stabbed her—that old feeling. She knew it well.

"I've abandoned my kids all day."

As she accused herself, something came to mind that Marie told her.

"Your past, present, and future deeds were paid for on the cross by Jesus. He took them *all*. Take care of your present guilts by asking for forgiveness. Keep short accounts with God. Don't let them wait. He forgives as soon as you confess it to Him. Don't run away from Him when you do wrong. Run to Him. Then you'll have peace again."

In the past, feeling guilty was natural. She sent up a quick prayer.

"I'm sorry I've exposed my kids to so much, things they should never have seen or known. And today I left them without making any preparation for their care. All I could think of was doing away with myself. Help me to make it up to them. Help me to share with them so they'll understand what's happened today. I want them to believe, too."

It was nearly 4:30 when Sara pulled into her driveway. At eight this morning she had left home, expecting never to return. But now all this was far in the past. The children were sitting on the porch steps when they saw her car drive up. They raced to the curb to meet her.

"Oh Mama! You're back!" Stacy shrieked excitedly. Her cheeks were wet with tears. "We thought we'd never see you again."

We've been so worried. Are we glad you're home!" Chad added. It sounded the way Gary would say it, Sara thought. He could get excited without making a fuss over it.

"We thought maybe you died and they had taken you away. You've been coughing so much. We thought all kinds of things might have happened. Do you know what time it is? You've never been gone like this before."

"First, let me hug you both. I love you so much. I'm terribly sorry I left you alone all day. Forgive me. I'm sorry you've been worried. I had something to clear up. Tell me about yourselves. Are you okay? Have you eaten?"

After their brief account, Sara made a hasty decision.

"Let's eat out! All your favorites—hamburgers, French fries, onion rings, milk shakes—the whole bit. We've got something to celebrate."

"Oh, goody!" Stacy responded, while Chad added a simple, "Swell. I'm hungry."

"Come to think of it, so am I," Sara responded. "I haven't eaten all day. It didn't matter until now."

"Mom, you look different! You look—happy. What's happened to you?" Chad asked. "Hey! You're not coughing! You don't even look sick anymore. You even act different."

"You're right, Chad. I am different. Oh, am I different! And am I happy! The cough is gone! Completely gone! A friend prayed for me. She asked God to heal me of the T.B. the doctor said I had. And God did! He answered her prayer. It's wonderful not to cough anymore. It's a miracle. Today I discovered God, and that He loves me. I never knew that before."

"Mom, was it Aunt Sue who prayed for you?" Chad asked.

"No, it was a new friend I made today. Her name is Marie Hall. And what a friend she turned out to be!"

"I thought it might be the Worths," Chad continued. "They pray. I heard them pray for you every day while you were in Europe. They talk to God just like I'm talking to you. They know Him real good."

"I'm glad you mentioned the Worths. Kids, what do you think of this? After we eat out, let's go see them. I want to tell them what happened."

"Hey, that's great!" Chad cheered. "We'll get to see Penny too."

At the restaurant Sara saw a phone.

"Let me call my principal and then we'll eat. I want to let him know I can come back to work."

With the call completed, Sara returned to the table smiling.

"Can you imagine it? I'm going back to work tomorrow. We've got more cause to celebrate than ever now."

As they got out of the car at the Worths, Penny began barking excitedly. The children hurried off for their own reunion while Jack and Sue had theirs with Sara.

"You look excited," Jack said, ushering her into the house. "You're actually beaming. I don't know when I've seen you look like this, Sara. And you've been sick? It certainly doesn't show. Tell us what's happened."

"I'm bursting to tell you. I want you and Sue to know before anyone else does. Remember the day you told me about making God the manager of your life? Can you believe I did that today? Me! Sara Page! I bet you never thought that would happen. When you tried to tell me what it meant to you, I couldn't comprehend it. But today Jesus Christ became real to me! Instantly He's become the most important Person in my life. It just happened this afternoon."

"Oh, Sara! The moment I saw you, I hoped it was something like this. You couldn't give us any better news," Jack declared.

"Tell us how it happened, Sara," Sue urged. "Give us all the details."

Without hesitation, Sara related the unusual episodes preventing her from carrying out her plan to commit suicide. Then she told about meeting Marie. It was easy to tell these friends who had experienced some of God's miracles in their own lives.

As she finished, Jack responded. "God knew He would have to do something unique to get your attention, Sara. He certainly chose a dramatic way to do it. We're so glad it worked."

"If you had succeeded in your plan, Sara, I would have felt responsible. You see, I've been putting off calling you. Each day I told myself, 'I've got to call Sara' I'm ashamed I didn't do it. But Sara, I got so excited just now when you were telling us that you asked God where He was," Sue continued. "It reminded me of what God says: 'You will find me when you seek for me, if you look for me in earnest.'[8]

"We saw you being disowned by your parents and know how that must have hurt. But did you know you're part of our family now?"

"I know what you mean, Sue. That's the way I felt about Marie—like we were related. That's the way I feel about both of you—so close." With a tremble in her voice, Sara shyly added, "And Jack, I've never had a brother before.

"This reminds me, I want to see my parents. It won't be easy, but I've got to. I feel so differently about them now."

"Sara, I believe your mother has left on a trip to your sisters," Sue reported. "I saw your father loading luggage into the car. I think he must have taken your mother to the airport. But he's at home."

[8]Jeremiah 29:13.

Part Four

CHAPTER THIRTY-ONE

Picking up the Pieces

"I WONDER IF POP will let me in," Sara pondered as she slowly walked across the street. Suddenly her pace changed.

"Mom isn't home. That's in my favor. Maybe we can actually talk. How do I begin? What will I say?"

With a lump in her throat, Sara rang the doorbell. She thought back to other days, when she hadn't been an outcast. Before she had time to pursue this thought further, the door opened. At first Marc seemed as cold and indifferent as Camile.

"Your mother isn't here," he announced stiffly. It never occurred to him that Sara might be coming just to see him. Without Camile to dictate a negative response, he was confused about what to say.

"That's okay, Pop. I came to see you. May I come in?"

Awkwardly he stood aside for her to enter, then pointed to a chair.

"You can sit down. Your mother is visiting your sisters," he said, sitting down in his recliner opposite her.

"I came for a special reason, Pop. It's to say something I've never said before. I came to tell you I love you very much. You don't have to do anything for me. There are no conditions. You really matter to me."

Marc was trying hard to retain his composure. A tiny spark of acknowledgement showed as moisture collected in his eyes. In this family, any displays of love and affection were restrained. Sara continued, undeterred by Marc's weak response.

"You're the only dad I have. But today I got a new Father."

Marc sat a little straighter. He was all ears wondering what Sara meant by a "new father."

"Over the years a terrible barrier has grown between us, Pop. It brought bitterness and anger to my heart that I didn't want to admit to myself. Today that wall was broken when I made God my heavenly Father. I never knew Him before. I found out today how much He loves me. This is why I'm here Pop—to tell you how much you mean to me. There have been times I wanted to tell you, but couldn't."

Marc's eyes were flooding now. Sara's words reached his heart. Tears clouded his vision, too. Quickly she rose from her chair to kneel beside him in his big chair. She reached for his hand.

"Oh, Pop! I love you! I'm sorry we never got along. So sorry. I've had resentment toward you for the way you treated me. I resented being shut out. I resented being the scapegoat of this family. But today those feelings left me . . . as if they were erased.

"I've been set free, Pop. God has forgiven me for all the rotten things in my life, and my guilt is gone. Because I'm forgiven, I'm free to love you! Even if you never let me in this house again, or if you never speak to me again, I'm glad I've told you. I hope you'll forgive me for the bad feelings I've carried in my heart."

Sara threw her arms around her father. She hugged him tenderly, then kissed him on the cheek. Marc's tears mingled with her own as he began to respond.

"I forgive you, Pop, for all the hurts you've given to me. I won't hold it against you anymore. I love you because you're my Pop. I want this to be a new day for us. Just accept my love. It's real."

Clumsily he returned her embrace, then kissed her. Words weren't necessary. Besides, Marc didn't have any.

Long ago Marc and Camile had stopped showing affection toward each other or anyone else. It was as though one day they made a pact never to show love in any form again. His response to Sara was a wonder.

"Pop, I need to go now. Could we get together again? Will you come over tomorrow evening? Have dinner with us. I'll come for you. We don't have to tell Mom. She's not here to object. It'll just be you, the children, and me. I'd like you to come."

"All right, Sara! I'll do it!" He said it as if it were a declaration of victory. "You'd better not come for me. Camile would find out. You know what would happen. Just tell me how to get there."

With the arrangements completed, Sara gave her father another hug and kiss, and left. What a good feeling! Communications with Father had been established. And he had even called her by her given name. It was another miracle in her life today. If it never went any further than this, the effort was well worthwhile.

Sara started back across the street, noticing the children at play.

"Maybe I can take another minute while I'm here to see Ted. I have some unfinished business with him. I'd like to apologize for my unbecoming conduct during the last weeks I worked there."

While she waited for an answer to the Baileys' doorbell, a sense of shame enveloped her. The door opened and Ted greeted her enthusiastically.

"Sara! Am I glad to see you! Come in. Heather is out with the kids now, but you and I can visit. You look wonderful. If I didn't know better, I'd say you haven't been sick. You're still underweight but look absolutely terrific. How are you feeling?"

"I'm lots better. The fact that I'm here and alive is because something tremendous happened today. As a result, I'm trying to straighten out my life. I owe you a big apology, Ted. That's why I've come."

To regain control of her quivering voice, Sara paused. She didn't want to get emotional. While she hesitated, Ted reassured her.

"I can't imagine why you owe me an apology. I can't think of a thing."

"I appreciate your attitude, Ted, but I feel I must make this confession to you. It's not easy. I'm ashamed, truly ashamed of how I blighted my reputation. I really messed up my life by involving myself with some of your clients. I'm sorry it reflected on your agency. That's why I'm here—to tell you how sorry I am."

Sara leaned forward to face Ted. With increased intensity she spoke.

"Ted, you may not understand this. I'm not sure I do myself. But I've changed so drastically that when I think of the way I lived, it's like it were someone else. There's a whole new life for me. I have to straighten out some things so I'm free to get on with it."

"You're right, Sara. I'm not sure I understand, but I like what I see. Forget what's happened. The important thing is that you're up and around again. I want to see you back at the agency after you gain weight. You're still invaluable to us."

"Thanks, Ted. I appreciate that. But that's not why I'm here. Unless I still owe you on my contract, I just want to teach."

"Well, if you ever change your mind, let me know, won't you? You've been a great asset to us. We still owe you residuals, so we'll be in touch. And Sara, I consider you a valuable friend!"

As she got up to leave, Ted put his arm around her shoulder.

"I can't get over it, Sara. You're still too thin, but otherwise I've never seen you look better. I wish you'd reconsider."

"I don't expect to, but it's nice of you to ask, Ted."

Back with Sue and Jack, she prepared to say good-bye. They walked out to the car with her. As they hugged one another good-bye Sara told them, "Today is the greatest day of my life."

"It's been a great day for us, too, Sara . . . the answer to our prayers," Sue told her.

CHAPTER THIRTY-TWO

Faded Scars

AFTER A PROLONGED ABSENCE, Sara was returning to school a radically different woman. Before she was forced to stop teaching, her condition was the subject of a daily news bulletin among the teachers.

"Have you noticed how bad Sara looks?" they would ask. "She's going downhill a little more each day."

"I hope she won't have to quit. But I don't see how she can keep going."

"I wonder what they'll think this morning," Sara pondered as she walked to the school office. "No one but the doctor and I know what the diagnosis was. I don't have to get a clearance, but I want to be able to prove I've been healed. I want the doctor to put into writing that nothing short of a miracle could have produced these results in so short a time."

In room D-3, Sara faced students who enthusiastically welcomed her back.

"It's a great day! We can do anything. There are no problems, only challenges," she proclaimed to her students.

"Want to paddle up the Amazon? Why not? Do you want to cross the Andes? Let's do it!" was the attitude she inspired and promoted.

"You know what I feel like today?" She answered her own question. "It's like a new student probably feels who's just enrolled and everyone else has already become acquainted. You know the feeling, don't you?"

A murmur of voices indicated that they understood the feeling. She went on.

"I'm glad to be back. I never thought I'd see you again. I have some exciting plans for us. I hope they won't be interrupted again."

At lunchtime she entered the teachers' lounge to get her sack lunch out of the faculty refrigerator.

"Hey, Sara! Glad you're back. We really missed you. This place is a morgue without you."

"That's right, Sara. Say, you're certainly looking better."

"Yeah, that's right. What happened?"

One teacher hardly finished before another eagerly confronted her.

"You're actually glowing! If a three-week rest can do that for you, maybe I ought to take a leave of absence. How'd you do it, Sara?"

"I'll bet it's a new man in your life. That's it, isn't it, Sara? Your eyes have that certain gleam that tells." This last remark brought a titter of amusement.

"Why, yes, you're right!" Sara responded with surprise. She hadn't expected them to make it so easy for her to tell. "There *is* a new man in my life, but I hadn't thought of it that way."

Here they were, putting the spotlight on her. Only this time it was more like a searchlight. It was natural for them to think she had another romance going. After all, hadn't she changed her name three times since being at Foothill School? Sometimes even *she* got mixed up as to which name to use. No wonder teachers and students sometimes called her Mrs. Cole or Mrs. Benson instead of Mrs. Page! They might not know about her domestic life, but with changing names so often, they knew when she had a different husband.

She put her sack lunch on the table, then sat down with them. They were waiting for her to continue. Her voice took on solemnity, and the room hushed.

"I've found someone whose love I can believe in," she began. "He loves me in a way no one else ever has." She hesitated only a moment. "His name is Jesus Christ. And He's forgiven me and made it possible for me to live with myself. And can you believe it? On top of everything else He's done, He's healed me of that terrible cough. Imagine it! He's the best thing that's ever happened to me."

"Oh, oh! You've done it now, Sara, haven't you? You've gone and got religious on us," one said.

"That's okay, Sara. Whatever it is, it becomes you. And I'm glad you're better. Welcome back with or without religion."

"It's all right if you want to call it religion," she replied. "I don't think about it that way. To me God's real and He's become everything to me."

Brad had finished his lunch, but lingered to hear Sara's explanation. He got up to leave, purposely passing Sara to put his hand on her shoulder.

"I agree, Sara. It becomes you. You look terrific. You sound great. That's what matters. I'm so glad you're back.

Sometime soon I hope you'll fill me in on the details. I'm really interested."

Leaving school that afternoon, Sara went over the events of the day.

"I made it! Imagine getting up from a near deathbed to work all day and still feel good. In fact, I feel great. Yesterday the cough left. I've still got energy to spare after a whole day of work. And I feel like cooking up a storm. I know it isn't my own strength that's seeing me through."

With the children in the car, she drove to the doctor's office to make an appointment. The receptionist recognized her and was surprised.

"Mrs. Page, I hope you aren't worse?"

"No, actually I'm well. I'm not coughing anymore. But I want the doctor to check to confirm it."

"Dr. Baxter will want to see you."

In the examining room, Dr. Baxter wasted no time in questioning Sara.

"What's this about being better?" he asked.

"No, not better, Doctor. I'm well!"

"Hmm. That's interesting," he said while checking her lungs with his stethoscope. "We'll need another X ray. Do you want to stay for tests or return tomorrow?"

"I'm having company for dinner, but since I'm here, Doctor, I'd like you to go ahead." Sara hadn't mentioned that she had gone back to work, and she decided that she would say nothing about it.

About a half-hour later Sara was called back to the doctor's office. Before him were the X rays. Another doctor pointed to one.

"There's no spot on this newest picture, not even a scar. It's as if the former X ray belonged to someone else. Something isn't right here. It couldn't clear up this quickly. There was a positive sputum test."

"If that's mine you're studying," Sara said as she watched, "I don't believe you'll find anything, Dr. Baxter."

"Sit down, Sara. This is Dr. Holt. I called him in for another opinion. I must tell you we find this hard to believe. You're right about our not finding traces of the disease. Your laboratory tests are negative. Because of the unusualness of the case, I want you to return again in 30 days. If you have recurrences of the cough, see me right away.

"I rarely say this," the doctor continued. "In your case it's as though the original diagnosis was incorrect. Yet—there it is!"

"Dr. Baxter, you're looking at a miracle of God. Isn't He called the Great Physician? Just believe what you see. I *was* sick. There's no doubt about that. But now I'm well! There's no doubt about that, either. Just for the records, Doctor, will you issue me a statement indicating your findings in both cases?"

"If in a month's time, after another checkup, no symptoms occur, I'll dictate something for you. Let's wait until then."

"It's hard to believe a miracle, isn't it, Doctor? If it hadn't happened to me, I wouldn't believe it either. I'll return as you asked, fully confident that you'll confirm it then."

At the market the children excitedly helped place items in the cart.

"How come Grandpa gets to have all his favorites?" Chad asked. "We never get to eat like this. What's so special about him?"

While Sara pondered an answer, Stacy quickly expressed her opinion.

"Yeah! He never came to see us before. How come he's coming now?"

Sara decided that she would answer their question with one of her own.

"You were glad we were getting these special things to eat. How come you don't want to have the person they're for eat them with us?"

"Mom, why is he so special?" Chad asked again.

"Because he's my father, Chad, and I love him. And he's your grandfather. That's what makes him special. He's lonely and needs our love."

In her heart she knew it was too much to expect Marc to be different just because she was.

"Does Grandpa get lighted candles with his special dinner?" Stacy asked.

"I'm glad you reminded me, Stacy. That's a good idea. Why don't you choose the ones you think will look best?"

Marc arrived on time. His reaction to the house was typical of him.

"So this is where you're living now. Whatever happened to that fancy house I heard you had?"

"I gave it up, Pop." One thing would call for another, and Sara didn't want to explain.

When Marc ran out of things to talk about, he was ready to go home.

"I don't think he likes us much," expressed Stacy after he left.

"It's up to us to make him feel we want him again," Sara responded.

There was one more task she had planned to do today—write Rex. But that would have to wait. It had been a long day.

CHAPTER THIRTY-THREE

Bridging the Past

ON HER WAY HOME FROM SCHOOL, Sara was engrossed in deep thought.

"I need to call the prison. I'd like to do it at home, but we don't have a phone. When I didn't plan to be around, I didn't need one. Now I want to know if they'll let me see Rex. And do they allow children? How often can he have visitors? And when?

"I've decided to have a phone installed," she told the children in the car. "We'll stop at the telephone company to order one. Please wait. It won't take long."

In the entry she noticed a pay phone. After checking to see if she had enough coins to complete a long-distance call, she dialed the operator to connect her. When the information she wanted from the prison was obtained, she ordered a phone. Then, anxious to begin the letter to Rex, she headed home.

In the kitchen she checked the food situation and was glad to find enough leftovers from their meal with Marc. This would give her the extra time needed for letter-writing. She changed to jeans and a T-shirt. When she noticed they fit too loosely, she knew she would have to go on a diet to gain at least ten pounds.

At the desk she sat staring at the blank paper. Then she leaned back and sighed. Finally she wrote the date and "Dear Rex." When nothing came, she tapped her fingers. The sheet of paper seemed to stare accusingly at her. She reached for an envelope, addressed it, then rechecked the identification number to make sure she had copied it correctly. It grieved her to think of Rex being a number instead of a name. Her mind went back to the unwritten letter.

"This is going to be harder than I thought. How do I begin? What do I tell Rex? That I finally don't condemn him anymore? Or that I'm sorry our home broke up? What I really want to say is that I care what happened to him." She rested her elbow on the desk and soberly cupped her chin. "But how do I say that?"

Four times she discarded her efforts and started over. "I

know what's wrong. I haven't asked God for help. 'Pray about everything.' Marie told me that's what the Bible says. 'Please God, guide me to say just the right things.'" This time the letter took shape.

Dear Rex:

Can you believe this is the fifth time I've begun this letter? I asked myself, "What shall I say to this man who swept me off my feet, brought me more love than I've ever known, and accepted my children as his own? What do I tell him after all we went through together?"

To sort out what really happened has taken so long. Watching our world crumble into dust devastated all of us. We seemed completely helpless to salvage what we had found together. We both sank to the bottom.

Rex, we had such a good marriage in the beginning. But the openness I thought we had with each other was an illusion. One day I discovered that it had never existed. It's this openness that I'm trying to establish.

I wanted so much to stand by you, but you didn't seem to want that. I hoped you would ask, "Will you be waiting?" But you never did. Our marriage didn't fail because you were convicted, Rex. It wasn't even because you were guilty. It fell apart because we didn't share what was in our minds and hearts. By your silence now, are you telling me you don't want me? Or do you think I no longer want you? I wish you would have asked me directly for a divorce. Then I would know if that's what you really want. I keep hoping, "Surely I'll hear from Rex." But there's nothing.

I'm not innocent either. When I realized you had lost the compass to regulate your moral judgments, I condemned you. I was so self-righteous. I didn't know that soon I would throw my own compass away.

A series of tragedies unfolded, mostly of my own making. I ended up deliberately doing wrong, and it dragged me deeper than I planned to go. The fears, hurts, and guilts that resulted ate at me like termites.

I can write now because I've been freed—from myself and from my ugly past! I'm no longer tormented by guilt and bitterness, either toward myself or others. I've found out that God loves me! I couldn't help myself, but Jesus Christ could. And He did! When I found out that He had paid my debt and offered me forgiveness, I received it. The moment I believed this, I was freed! That's why I can reach out to you now.

I didn't know how to stand by you when you were apprehended. Maybe it was because my world was falling apart too. You see, Rex, my world was you! I was totally committed to you and could only think about what you did and how it affected me. When I contacted the FBI and gave the evidence I found, I only wanted you stopped. Maybe if I had confronted you first, things would have turned out differently. But it's too late for that. Forgive me for my part in what happened.

Now that I can think clearly again, I realize I still care about you. The children miss you. They ask about you often. I miss you, too. They love you and I love you! I know you've already filed for divorce. I've accepted the fact that it's what you seem to want. But we've been your family, and we want to visit you.

There's no way to tell you what a visit to you will mean to me. The prison officials say you must sign a visitors' form before we're allowed to come. Would you do it, Rex? I phoned the prison today to ask about our visiting you. They say it would have to be a weekend. When I get the signed forms from you, we'll make arrangements to come. They told me there was a special visitors' place for picnics. Chad says we'll fix one so we can all eat together. We'd like that and hope you do, too.

Remember how you used to tell us "You're my family now?" We feel we still are. I'll check the mail anxiously till your answer comes. I'm sending a box of brownies made the way you like them. Hope the box reaches you in good condition.

I love you,

Sara

She sealed the letter wishing she knew a better way to say things.

"But I'm sure I've done the right thing in reaching out to him. If he doesn't respond, I won't go to pieces. I asked God for direction. He has a plan for my life, and however it turns out will be best for me and for the children.

"I need to write Gary, too. But I don't know what to say. I need time to think. Gary is a man of few words. It shouldn't be as hard. I'd like to write Steve, too, but I wouldn't know where to find him. The last time the lawyer tried to contact him, it was as though he had vanished. No one seems to know what became of him."

When Sara's phone was connected, her first call was to Marie Hall. How eager she was to talk with her again!

"Marie? This is Sara Page. I just got a phone installed. You're my first call. I want to tell you that what happened last Sunday is still so very real to me."

"Oh, Sara. I'm so glad you called. I've been waiting to hear from you. When you left Sunday, you had my phone number, but I had no way of contacting you. I've been so eager to know how you're doing."

"That's good to hear, Marie. Can we get together Sunday? Would you come to my place for brunch? I want you to meet my children."

"I'd like that very much, Sara. I was hoping to reach you before Sunday to tell you about a class I'm attending. It's primarily for singles over 30 who are no longer married. I wasn't sure if you are the right age, but I think it would be of interest to you."

"You're very kind, Marie. I'm eligible. Im 34 now. I'll soon be 35. My husband and I are separated."

Marie continued. "Let me tell you about the class, Sara. The teacher is a college professor. He's very interesting and really gets down to where we live. The subject is 'Who are you?'" The class is held in a bank. It's sponsored by my church, so the bank helped out by letting us use their meeting room. Now it's crowded out, too.

"Maybe you're wondering why I attend the class. At 47, I'm older than most of the others. I've been a widow for two years. Most of the members have gone through a divorce and have children. The class seems to be helpful no matter why you're alone. And what makes it more interesting is that there are about an equal number of men and women. Last Sunday, 74 attended. So you see it's becoming popular. I know it's a long drive for you, but would you be interested, Sara? Would you come, and then we can have brunch at your place afterward?"

"When does the class begin, Marie?"

"At ten. I'll be attending church at 8:30 and then walk to the bank parking lot. Could we meet there? Since it's crowded, I try to get a seat before it fills up. Does this plan sound all right to you, Sara?"

"It's fine, Marie. It might be just what I need. But I have a problem. I don't know what to do with my children."

"Bring them with you, Sara. We have children's activities at that same hour. I'll arrange to have a friend meet us at the parking lot, and she'll take your children with her. They'll be in good hands."

After detailed instructions on where the bank was located, Sara hung up, feeling really good about things. Her next call was to Marc. She hoped Camile hadn't returned yet so they could talk.

"Pop, I've been wondering how you are. I can call you now that I have a phone. Would you like the number so you can call me?"

"All right, Sara. Your mother is still away. After she comes home, it won't be easy to call you."

When she finished talking, Marc surprised her with an invitation.

"Come for a continental breakfast on Saturday, Sara. You know I can't cook, but I can fix one of those. Bring the kids. Is nine o'clock all right? They'll probably want to sleep late."

Sara was amazed. Here she had been thinking that nothing had been accomplished by his coming for dinner Monday evening. He had been so guarded in his responses.

"I can't believe it! He wants us to come or he wouldn't have asked."

On Saturday, Sara was delighted that Marc had gone to the trouble to set the dining room table for them. There was even a bouquet of fresh flowers.

"Everything's so nice, Pop. I'm so glad you asked us. Danish pastry, too, with cream-cheese filling! You went all-out. It's delicious."

"Even squeezed the orange juice. Picked them from the tree in the backyard this morning. Made hot chocolate for the kids, too," he said, obviously pleased with his preparations. "Hope it's all right."

"Yeah, thanks, Grandpa," Chad answered timidly. Until

their recent renewal they had almost been strangers to each other. But now the ice was melting between them. Sara hoped this was a new beginning.

"I don't think you're taking care of yourself like you should, Pop. Maybe you ought to eat all your evening meals with us till Mom gets back. Why don't you come at six each evening? I make dinners every night except Sunday. That's my day off."

"I'm not a cook, but I can heat TV dinners. Speaking of TV, Sara, I see you in commercials once in awhile. How did you get into that, anyway?"

"It's quite a story, Pop. The best part is that I'm not making them now."

They talked, laughed, and enjoyed each other. Marc seemed kinder to the children and even joked happily about Camile knowing.

"She always knows when I do something she doesn't like. I don't know how she does it, but she has a way of finding out."

They both laughed as though they were playing a good joke on her.

Sara left feeling high. It particularly pleased her that he was using her name after all these years of acting like she didn't have one.

On Sunday, Sara met Marie as scheduled. At the parking lot entrance Marie shook her head.

"The lot's full, Sara. But there are still places to park on the street. Before Sara had a chance to introduce her to the children, she said, "I'm Marie. I'm so glad I'm going to your house today. I want to get to know you both. Why don't you get out of the car here and go with my friend, Mrs. Walker? She'll take you to junior church, and we'll meet back here when you're finished. I'm sure you're going to enjoy it."

After the children hopped out of the car to leave with Mrs. Walker, Marie turned her attention back to Sara.

"While you park, Sara, I think I should go ahead to save us both a seat. I'll meet you inside. You won't have any trouble finding me."

An enthusiastic crowd eagerly waited for the teacher to begin. Sara was impressed to find the place filled. She drank in every word, and during the question-and-answer portion she was astonished at the perception these people had. No wonder the place was packed out. They not only shared a common bond, but they also had a keen sensitivity toward one another. They had experienced many of the same problems Sara had known. She leaned over to whisper to Marie.

"This is better than a therapy session. It's so stimulating and just what I needed."

At the end of the class they served coffee and doughnuts. Everyone was exceptionally friendly, and their conversations were more than small talk. The teacher, Dr. Edwards, introduced himself to Sara.

"I don't remember seeing you here, Mrs. Page. How did you learn about the class?"

"Please call me Sara, Dr. Edwards." Briefly she told of meeting Marie under extremely unusual circumstances. Dr. Edwards' face lit up.

"That's wonderful, Sara. In fact, it's a miracle. Would you give me permission to quote you in class—at an appropriate time, of course? Better yet, would you tell your story as a testimonial? I believe it's just the kind of thing our people need to hear to make us more sensitive to the needs of others. I think everyone would benefit from it. Perhaps you'd share it at our social. It's a week from Friday."

"Feel free to use it, Dr. Edwards. But I don't think I should tell my story just yet. This is only my first visit here. I want you to know how much this lesson means to me. It's exactly what I need. I'm so glad Marie persuaded me to come."

Outside, the children were watching for Marie and Sara. They eagerly ran to share their reactions, asking, "Can we do this again next Sunday? It was neat."

"I want to come back too," Sara replied, "even if it's 30 miles each way."

At home, while Sara fixed brunch, she could hear Marie and the children having a good time together. The children responded as warmly to Marie as she had. When Marie was ready to leave, she reminded Sara that she would expect to see her again next Sunday. "I'll give you a call, Sara."

When all was quiet in the house again, Sara reminisced on how different things had been a week ago.

"My outlook is so changed. God is so good to give me Marie as a friend. What a difference meeting her has made in my life! No more guilt. No more sickness. No more depression. I'm really a new person. And all because she introduced me to the One who gave me joy and peace!"

A few days later, Marc phoned Sara.

"I decided to talk to you while your mother is still away. When she returns, I won't be able to do this."

"Let's get together, Pop. Come over for dinner tonight."

While they were eating, Sara asked him to come again for supper next Sunday. "I don't cook big meals on Sundays. It won't be fancy, but we'll be together. I'm concerned about you, Pop. I don't think you look well."

It was the second time she had mentioned it to him, but he didn't seem to want to talk about it. Even though she sensed that something was wrong, she didn't press it further.

All week Sara looked forward to returning to the class. When Sunday finally arrived, she was more enthusiastic than ever. She had noticed how many others took notes, and she wished she had remembered to buy batteries for her little tape recorder. The class was so helpful that she wanted to be able to review what had been said. Not wishing to miss a single thought, she was kept busy writing in her notebook.

During refreshments she was impressed at how many in the class remembered her name. Several gathered around, encouraging her to attend their social on Friday evening.

"Sara, I'm Ray Riley. You can sign up to bring whatever you like. It's potluck. You shouldn't miss it. It's really worthwhile. This group helped me through the trauma of my wife walking out on me. I was going to pieces until I got into this class. We understand what it is to ache when the rug is pulled out from under us, and we're not embarrassed to share with one another. We find that it helps us to recover."

Now Sara knew she wanted to go on Friday more than ever. The matter of a baby-sitter on Fridays was often a problem. When Marc came for supper that evening, she mentioned it to him.

"When did you say you wanted to go, Sara?"

"On Friday, Pop."

"Your mother doesn't get back till Saturday. I'll be your baby-sitter! What do you think of that, kids?" he asked, sounding pleased that he had thought of it.

Sara nearly fell off her chair. For almost 12 years she had been a mother, and in all that time her parents had never offered to baby-sit, not even in drastic emergencies when they lived across the street from each other.

"I'm overwhelmed, Pop." Sara got up to kiss him. "I can't tell you what this means to me, that you'd do this for us."

On Friday evening she prepared a casserole to take to the potluck, making enough for Marc and the children's meal. When Marc arrived, he was unusually quiet.

"Anything wrong, Pop?"

"You remember your mother will be home tomorrow afternoon. I don't know when we can get together again."

It was as if he were saying, "We can't have any more good times together. Camile won't let us."

"Don't worry, Pop. We've had this much, and it's been great. We'll figure out something."

"I know you want to see your mother. I don't think you should try, Sara. She won't make up with you. Long ago she decided she would never let you back into the family again. You'll just get hurt if you try."

Sara knew it was true, but something within made her feel the risk would be worthwhile. The good feelings of having established a meaningful relationship with her father for the first time in their lives fortified her. She purposed not to give up on reaching out to Camile, and to seek God's help for it.

When she returned from the social, Marc commented on her cheerfulness.

"I'm really making wonderful friends, Pop. These people are different from any I've met before. It's what I've wanted and needed for a long time. I just didn't know where to find them till now. And I really enjoy the class. We all have a lot in common."

CHAPTER THIRTY-FOUR

A Bedside Good-bye

THE FIRST THING SATURDAY MORNING, Sara got down to the business of writing Gary. She had put it off long enough.

"Now I know what I must say to him. Rex disappointed me by not answering. I wonder if Gary will do the same. But this is no time to be discouraged."

The words seemed to fly from her pen.

> Dear Gary:
>
> I can imagine you're wondering why you're hearing from me. Nothing is wrong with Chad. He's fine. Soon he'll celebrate his twelfth birthday. Imagine that! You can really be proud of him. He looks more like you every day—so handsome! And he has your qualities of gentleness and kindness. He's never been a problem and is thoughtful and quiet.
>
> The reason I'm writing now is because something happened that's so tremendous I have to share it with you. It's revolutionized my life.
>
> A few weeks ago I was in the depths of despair with failures in health, marriage, and the ability to make right decisions. My values were terribly misplaced and my conscience was killing me. I wanted an eraser big enough to wipe out my ugly past, but I never could find one.
>
> Three weeks ago today, I prepared to dump my guilts—and me, with one grand sweep, over a cliff. Through circumstances too complex to tell here, I made a complete 180-degree turn. It happened when I realized that God really loved me . . . just as I was, and could forgive me! He was the only One who could. I received both His love and forgiveness that day. It's transformed my life, Gary.
>
> What happened from that made me aware that I needed to make amends to people I've hurt. I've never told you how sorry I am about the contempt-

ible way I treated you. I've relived my icy good-bye
to you a thousand times. It's been torture each
time! And to think I put you through this! Gary,
please forgive me for the anguish and grief I
brought you.

For years I've had a false pride that wouldn't let
me admit to you that I was sorry, even though I
was. I wish I could reverse my wrongs. All I can do
is to ask you to forgive me. I hope you can find it
in your heart to do it, Gary.

Sara

She had reached the end and pondered how to close the
letter.

"If I sign 'lovingly' Gary might take it wrong and think
I'm trying to get him back."

Suddenly it seemed very important to her to get Gary's letter in the mail right away.

"I'm going to the post office, kids. Want to come along?"

"Sure," they answered, and climbed into the car.

Since it was Saturday, the service window at the post office
was closed. But the rates were posted, so she dropped two
dollars' worth of coins into the machine for a special-delivery
stamp. As she placed the stamp on the envelope, she had a
good feeling.

On the way home she thought about the letter she had
mailed to Rex three weeks earlier. He wasn't one to postpone
answering. In fact, he prided himself on promptness. But it
appeared that he wasn't going to answer. Would Gary do the
same, she wondered again?

Something from last Sunday's class with Dr. Edwards came
to mind. Hadn't he pointed out how important it was to be
obedient in following through on good thoughts and im-
pulses? "Become sensitive to each one and decide what God
wants you to do with it." he had said. "Well, that's exactly
what I'm doing." Dr. Edwards had even shown from the
Bible how God uses actions that people aren't even aware of
to work out His plans.

"I'm the one in charge of acting on what I know is right
for me. What the other person does with it is not my responsibility. I'm only responsible for my actions. 'So, God, will
You take it from here, please?' It's strange—I felt so strongly that Gary's letter should be sent special delivery. I'm glad I
went downtown to mail it.

"Gary's sister, Althea, will probably be surprised when it arrives. We've kept in touch at Christmas, and Gary's child-support payments come through her. I don't know where he is. She'll see that it gets to him. She knows that Gary and I don't write to each other."

On Monday, Sara was still looking for a letter from Rex, so she quickly checked the mail at home. She had formed a pattern soon after her letter to Rex of sorting the mail each day. When she found nothing from him, the mail accumulated unopened on the desk.

On Wednesday evening she played the tape from Dr. Edward's class. It challenged her to attempt bigger and better things with her life. "I want my life to count for others," she determined. "I don't want to be self-centered anymore." When the tape shut off, she opened the mail. An envelope from the agency caught her attention.

"I'm not working for them anymore. I wonder what it's about.

"A check! For $40,000! I hadn't realized I'd be getting so much from that one series of commercials I made. Since I made more than the one series, there's still more due me. All those problems I had awhile ago made me unable to keep track of things.

"This money doesn't mean to me what it would have a month ago. I wonder why it didn't arrive when I really needed it. When I was at rock bottom, it would have seemed a lifesaver. But if I had had financial security then, I might not have found God's forgiveness.

"When I went to work for the agency, I wanted the money to buy a house. I believe that's what this should be used for. I'll begin looking. This will make a good down payment. I still like the neighborhood where the folks live. I'll contact a realtor about it."

It was nearly nine, and the children were getting ready for bed when the doorbell rang.

"Special delivery, ma'am."

"I didn't know you delivered this late. Thank you."

Immediately she recognized the handwriting.

"Gary! He answered! And so quickly. I'm almost afraid to open it. She fell into the nearest chair and ripped the envelope open. Out fell a folded check. Sara picked it up. It had Gary's own signature, not Althea's, as other checks from him for Chad's support.

"Two thousand dollars! What's this for! He's never sent so much at one time for Chad's support."

The letter was longer than any he had ever written to her before. But his handwriting was shaky. Her own hands trembled in excitement.

Dear Sara:

Althea brought me your letter. I'm in the hospital. Thanks for writing. Of course I forgive you. I've kept quiet all these years and sent everything through Althea because I couldn't face being turned down again. Sara, I felt I was the one who failed. So I need your forgiveness, too.

This makes it easier to ask if I can see Chad now. I mean here. You see, I'm sick. In and out of the hospital four times already. This time I probably won't get out. They give me three weeks at the most. It's the same hospital where you were when we met.

Althea and I have been talking about Chad coming. Could he come by himself? I don't think I dare hope you'd come too. I want to see Chad before I die. That's all that's left for me. Here's a check. If anything's left, count it toward Chad's birthday.

Strange, I found what you've found. About a year ago. I'm not afraid to die. I know where I'm going. I have the hope of heaven from God's promises. I'm so glad you found Him too, Sara.

Althea will meet Chad at the airport. She'll take care of him. She says if you come you can both stay with her. Please phone me here at the hospital. Let Chad come real soon. There isn't much time.

I've always loved you, Sara. There's never been anyone else. I never married again. How could I? I was still in love with you.

Love,
Gary

"He's too young! Only 36. What if I hadn't written?" Sara's face was wet with tears. She got up to get some tissues. As she passed Chad's room, he called out, "Good night, Mom." She would wait till morning to tell him.

"I wonder how he'll take it. How will I tell him? He doesn't remember his father. He was only three when Gary left.

"I think I should go with Chad, but I've just gone back to work. I hate asking to take a leave again when I've missed so much. It makes it look like I'm not dependable. But Brad is a very understanding person. I believe he'll approve of it when he knows the circumstances. It's Gary's dying request."

Recently Marie had prayed with Sara over the phone. After Sara had explained the problem to her, Marie had said, "Why don't we pray now?" "You mean over the phone?" Sara had asked, surprised. "Sara, it's no different from talking to Him anyplace else. He's always ready to listen."

It had seemed strange to Sara at the time, but now it was reassuring to know they could do it again. She dialed Marie's number and explained the situation. Marie didn't disappoint her. "Let's pray right now, Sara."

"Dear Lord, Sara has a big need and wants Your personal help. Will You give her the right words to tell Chad about his father? You know how important it is that they be kind and tender words. He'll always remember this. And she needs to know if she should go to Gary. Will You guide her to make the right decision by giving her a clear indication? Would You do this by the time she goes to work tomorrow so arrangements can be made? And Lord, Chad will need Your comfort. He's never faced this kind of sorrow before. Give him Your strength to face this."

The next morning Sara sat down on the edge of Chad's bed. Quietly she told him about his father. When he learned how much Gary wanted to see him, tears welled in his eyes.

"He won't live more than a few days, Chad. He wants to see you more than he wants anything else. I believe you should go. But how do you feel about it?"

"I want to go. But, Mom, will you go with me?"

This was the confirmation she needed. Now she could go ahead and ask Brad for permission. After they arranged to hire the same substitute she had had before, Sara called Sue.

"We'll love having Stacy again," Sue said without hesitating. Sara hadn't even asked. "She's like part of our family. We'll take you and Chad to the airport."

On the plane, Sara tried to prepare Chad for what was ahead.

"You've never asked why your father and I broke up. I'm sure you've wondered. I believe this is the time to tell you. It's not easy for me to say. Your dad was a wonderful husband and a loving father. He was so happy when you were born, Chad. By the time you were three years old, I was still trying to make your father over—into what I wanted him to be. It was so wrong of me.

"I urged him to move to California, but he was never able to get established. He didn't seem to fit into things here. His heart was still in Florida. I wanted a life he couldn't conform to. When an opportunity came along to say goodbye to him, I took it. I was selfish.

"I'm sorry it's robbed you of knowing your father. I can't tell you how sorry I've been that you missed his companionship. He loves you so much. When he left to go back to Florida, he could hardly put you down. He hugged and hugged you like it was breaking his heart to have to leave."

They were quiet for awhile, busy with their own thoughts. At last she continued.

"He'll probably be very thin, dear. He's so sick. And he'll be weak. His handwriting was shaky. You'll want to keep his letter. It's the only one he's written since he left us. It will be a good reminder to you of how much he loves you, and how he loved me. When we get home you might want to put it with your treasures. I want you to have it. You're the dearest person to his heart, and he never had a chance to show you. Now you're the one he wants to see more than anyone else.

"Your father may not know what to say when he sees you. Maybe we can make it easier for him. Shall we think about what we might say? Do you feel up to it?"

"Yes, I think so. What do I call him, Mom? I've always said 'my dad' when I talked about him. Do you think 'Dad' is okay?" When Sara nodded, he went on. "Would it be all right to tell him, 'I don't want you to die, Dad?' Oh, Mom, couldn't we take care of him, or do something?" His voice cracked.

"I wish we could, Chad, but I think it's too late."

Sara's own heart was breaking. She wished she knew how to comfort him. She had robbed both father and son of a rightful relationship because she wanted her own way. And she was sorry—oh, so sorry. But she had tortured herself with guilts long enough. Memories and regrets could not bring back the past. Instead, she was glad they had responded to Gary's S.O.S.

At the West Palm Beach Airport, Althea waved as Chad and Sara disembarked from the plane. It seemed there was no barrier between the two women even though Sara and Gary had been divorced a long time.

"Sara, I'm so glad you came. I really didn't think you would."

Turning to Chad, "And this must be Chad. You don't remember us, but I'm your Aunt Althea and this is your Uncle Greg. We are your family and want you to think of us that way. You're very special because you're the closest relative your father has. He's looked forward so much to seeing you. Why don't you and Uncle Greg pick up the luggage? We'll meet you at the car."

Walking with Sara, Althea brought Sara up-to-date.

"He's weakening fast, Sara. I was surprised at the amount of strength he summoned to write to you."

Arriving at the hospital entrance, Greg spoke.

"We'll park the car, then wait for you in the coffee shop. You won't want to stay too long. After dinner we'll all come back to see Gary. You can tell him we'll see him this evening. He's in room 707."

Walking down the hospital corridor toward Gary's room, Chad hesitated.

"Mom, I'm a little scared. Would it be all right if you go in first?"

Giving him a hug for extra reassurance and comfort, Sara answered, "Of course, Chad. Why don't you wait at the end of the hall? I noticed a sitting room there. I'll come for you."

In the room she found Gary with his eyes closed. She could partially see his face and was shocked at how gaunt he was. As she watched, he roused. Their eyes met. Sara's heart skipped a beat.

"Sara! You're here!" he said weakly. "I'm so glad you've come. I can't tell you what this means to me." He rested a moment. Sara came closer to take his hand.

"Let me look at you. Oh, Sara! Remember how I whistled the first time I saw you? I'd still whistle." He laughed weakly. "You're even more beautiful than I remember. Tell me about yourself. What are you doing now?"

Sara was having difficulty maintaining her composure. Finally she responded to what she was feeling inside, leaned over, hugged him, and kissed his cheek.

"Oh, Gary!" She tried holding back tears that were coming. "I'm so sorry for what I did to you." Her vision was clouded now.

"Don't do this to yourself, Sara. I don't want you feeling guilty anymore! It wasn't all your fault. I couldn't give you what you needed. There was nothing wrong with what you wanted. I just couldn't give it to you, no matter how much I tried."

"Yes, Gary. I was wrong to try to force you to be something you weren't. Forgive me."

"It's all forgiven, Sara. Let's remember the good times."

She realized how much strength he had used in those few minutes, and she wasn't here to focus on herself. She wanted to save his strength for the reunion with Chad.

"Chad's here. Would you like to see him now, Gary? He's in the hall. Are you up to it?"

"Oh, yes! I've been waiting for him to come."

Instead of sitting where she had suggested, Chad was standing outside the door. Sara signaled for him to come in. Without hesitation he walked to Gary's bed. The words seemed to explode from him.

"Oh, Dad! I want us to get to know each other. Mom's always told me what a great guy you are. I'm glad you wanted me to come."

Sara was surprised and proud. She needn't have worried that he would be at a loss for words.

"Chad! Son." Gary's voice broke with emotion. "Are you too big for a hug?"

Immediately Chad responded as though he had only waited to be asked. The hug Gary gave Chad belied his frail appearance. Neither of them would let go. Finally Chad sobbed.

"I don't want you to die, Dad. I want to take care of you."

They were both sobbing now. After a bit, Sara became concerned that this was too much for Gary. It was difficult for her to intrude. Gently she placed her hand on Chad's shoulder.

"I think your father needs to rest now." When she noticed that a nurse entered the room, she added. "We'll go for a little while, Gary, so you can be rested when we return. It's 4:30 now. We'll be back this evening. Is that all right?"

"Don't be gone long," he urged.

In the coffee shop, they found Greg and Althea.

"How did things go?" Althea asked. "With the excitement of your coming, I was afraid he might be worse."

"He was alert, and all of us seemed to make it. I know it took a lot from him. He was so happy. I'm really glad we came. We suggested that he rest and told him we'd all be back," Sara reported.

After dinner, Gary seemed anxious to speak with Sara.

"If there's any part of my life I could do over again, it

would be to let God into our lives. I believe we could have made it together then, Sara. Chad, I hope you don't wait. Put God first in your life. It's the best thing you can do."

These few words exhausted him. It was as though he had mustered false strength to say them. Now that his dream was realized, he was satisfied. He couldn't command this much effort again.

Gary was definitely weakening. Althea and Greg came in for a few minutes, but soon Althea signaled that it was time to leave. On Sunday, Gary lapsed into semiconsciousness. Rallying only briefly now and then, he went into a coma Monday afternoon. By Wednesday he was gone.

"You'll stay for the funeral, won't you, Sara?" Althea asked. "We'll ask to have it Friday and no later than Saturday. I know you need to get back home."

On Friday, at the funeral, Althea and Greg insisted that Sara sit with them and Chad in the family section.

"It's the way Gary would want it, and it's the way it should be. You meant more to him than any woman he ever knew. Just because you aren't married to him now doesn't mean you don't belong with us."

Sara was thankful for their thoughtfulness.

At the funeral, Chad and Sara's attention was captured by words the minister read.

"Even when walking through the dark valley of death I will not be afraid, for you are close beside me, guarding, guiding all the way. . . . Your goodness and unfailing kindness shall be with me all my life, and afterwards I will live with you forever in your home."[9]

When the minister finished, Chad nudged Sara and whispered "Dad told us he'd be living in heaven. Mom, he's there now! And He wasn't afraid to go because he said that it was God's home, and he was only moving from here to there."

[9]Psalm 23:4,5.

CHAPTER THIRTY-FIVE

The Glass Partition

"WHERE HAVE YOU BEEN, SARA? I've tried to reach you for a week, every time your mother was out for awhile. I even tried phoning you from a pay phone while the car was being serviced."

"I'm sorry I missed your calls, Pop. I took Chad to Florida. Gary wanted to see him before he died. It was very sudden. Yesterday morning we attended Gary's funeral, and we flew back last night."

"You don't mean it! Gary's dead? Sorry to hear it. He was a nice fellow. Too young to die. What was the matter with him?"

Sara was glad he was interested, and she filled him in on a few details.

"Your mother's at her regular Saturday hairdresser's appointment. Can't talk long. She'll be waiting."

Sunday morning at about eight o'clock the phone rang. They needed to be on their way by 9:15 if they were to be on time for Sara's class and the children's junior church.

"Hallelujah! Your mother's going to church to pray! Come on over for coffee. I want to talk!"

"Sure, Pop. Is it okay if I bring the kids? We'll be right over."

He sounded eager. He was more important to Sara than the class. She had missed last week's lesson by going to Florida, and she had really looked forward to this one. It was cutting it close. Maybe she could do both. Camile wouldn't stay away long, and it was about the same distance either way to where the class was held, in Palos Verdes.

On the coffee table Marc had placed a plate with doughnuts and two glasses of milk for the children. He ushered Sara to the kitchen. Camile never served meals at the kitchen table. It was a place to work and have coffee. Marc poured her a cup, then put out a plate of doughnuts for the two of them. Sara knew that after they left Marc would hurry to get rid of all the evidence that they had been there. How would he explain the missing milk and doughnuts to Camile? she wondered.

"Your mother will be back in about 45 minutes, so we don't have much time, Sara."

"Pop, you don't look well. Are you sure you're feeling all right?"

"Well, Sara,the reason I called you to come is that I'm going into the hospital Thursday for a checkup. They'll run tests and maybe I'll have surgery. It doesn't look good."

"I'm really sorry to hear it. May I visit you while you're there?"

"I don't know. If your mother knew, she wouldn't allow it. If you come, do it when she isn't around. I'll be at the Presbyterian Hospital."

"Would you phone to tell me if it's okay to come, Pop? You know I want to."

"I'll try," he promised. "If I'm not able, try the nurses' station."

As she left his house with the children for Palos Verdes, her thoughts were troubled. "I hope we won't be late. The class will pray for Pop if I ask them. They're caring people and believe in miracles."

Saturday evening at the hospital, Sara was told, "Sorry, no visitors."

"But I'm family."

The nurses seemed surprised. "Your mother said there was no family living here. She requested no visitors."

It was like Camile to shut everyone out. To prove she was his daughter, she got out her wallet to show the identification card inside.

"Please read the part where it shows who to notify in an emergency."

"In case of emergency, notify Marc Carlisle—father," the nurse read.

At last she was permitted to go in. Marc's back was toward the door. Sensing someone there, he growled, "Who's there?"

"Pop, I came as soon as I could. I had to prove who I was before they'd let me see you. Have the doctors found out what's wrong yet?"

"I'm not going to make it, Sara. They tell me I've got cancer and it's eaten me up."

"Oh, Pop, no! The doctors don't always know. It may not be that bad."

When he shook his head, she realized he hadn't exaggerated the seriousness of his condition. Her heart went out to him. Wanting to tell him a thousand things, all she could think to say were the words that had meant the most to her when she faced death.

"I'm so sorry. I want to comfort you. Let me tell you what got through to me. I felt so bad I tried to commit suicide. A friend told me, 'God loves you very much.' And for the first time I believed it! God wants you in heaven, Pop, and He says the way there is to believe in His Son, Jesus Christ. That's all it takes. Do it, Pop. If you do, I'll see you there. And I want that more than anything in the world."

Barely had she spoken these words when Camile walked in.

"What are you doing here? You aren't family. Get out!"

"Mom, I love him. I love you both. This is no time to exclude me."

"We don't need you. We don't want you. Get out!"

Little did Sara realize that this was to be her first and last visit to Marc's bedside. Ready to leave for school the following Thursday, the phone rang. The woman's voice had a faint hint of familiarity to it.

"This is a friend of your mother's. Sara, they operated on your father yesterday. He passed away last night."

Without allowing time for inquiries, she hung up. Sara was stunned. Thoughts of leaving for school were still on her mind when the impact hit her.

"My father—dead? I wonder who called?"

First she phoned the hospital to check this out.

"Marc Carlisle is no longer a patient," was all she was told.

Next she called her mother. No answer. She searched her mind.

"Who was that on the phone?" Finally she called Camile's minister. He already knew about it and gave her just enough information to allow her to follow through on her own. When she called the woman and identified herself, the woman hung up on her again.

Not realizing what had happened, Chad interrupted.

"Mom, we'll be late for school."

"Chad, your grandfather just died." Chad was as stunned as she was. He slumped into a kitchen chair and began to cry. Sara hadn't expected it to hit him so hard. He had seen Gary die, and now he had another sorrow. In spite of Marc's gruff exterior, the children had warmed up to him.

Sensing something amiss, Stacy came into the kitchen to inquire.

"What's wrong?"

After she was told, all three of them sat at the kitchen table and cried. Finally Sara remembered that Marc's sister lived in Los Angeles. She had sent Sara a Christmas card. After checking with the information operator, she made the call.

"Yes, Sara, your father is dead," her aunt told her.

"Do you know about the funeral or which mortuary is in charge?"

"Your mother told us not to contact you. But when I know more, I'll give you a call. Let me have your phone number, Sara."

Feeling completely excluded and heavyhearted, and crying inside, Sara forced herself to go to school. When her pupils were dismissed at three, she drove to her mother's house. The stranger who met her at the door would not allow her inside.

"Let me give you my phone number," Sara said. "I'll help in any way I can. Please tell my mother I'm available."

When a call came asking, "Are you Sara? We have an errand for you to do for your mother," she was eager to help. "Your sister, Stephanie, just arrived at the Los Angeles airport. Will you get her?"

Sara was willing to be a doormat again.

"I see you're living it up with a top-of-the-line foreign car," she greeted Sara at the airport. "And I hear your third husband's in prison. And you lost your house and are back on the street again! How rotten of you! Your despicable behavior caused Father's illness. No wonder he died! You and your escapades!"

Mother had poisoned Stephanie against her. What was there to say?

Driving in silence, Sara finally arrived at Camile's. While Stephanie and Camile greeted each other warmly, Sara slipped inside, unnoticed. They ignored Sara until it was time to eat. Not knowing what else to do, Sara went to the kitchen to prepare food for them. She set the dining table and called them to eat.

"You will stay in the kitchen!" Camile ordered.

"That's okay, Mom. I just want to help. I'm here to stand by if you need me. I'm sorry Pop's gone. I know you miss him. I loved him, too."

There! She said it. It was better this way than the way she had originally planned to tell her. This was a true test of

whether she really did love her mother. Well, she did! Even
with the painful rejection. It wasn't that Camile's words
hadn't wounded her. They cut as deeply now as when she
had been disowned.

"Mom's obligated to keep up the appearance of total rejection of me for Stephanie's sake. If she backs down for a
moment, she would look weak. She would rather add to her
misery by stabbing me to pieces. Even if it's painful, I'll do
as she asks."

No one spoke to Sara, and she desperately wanted to know
what was going on and be included. After all, Marc had been
her father! Out in the kitchen she could hear them talking
about her. They hadn't wanted her when Marc lived, and
they certainly didn't want her now. When they returned to
the kitchen for more food, they continued to ignore her. Finally she slipped out the back door and got into her car.

"A short time ago I would have thought I was a fool to expose myself to what they're doing to me. But when God
saved me from self-destruction, He did more than that. He
filled me with love. I determined not to live for myself, and I
chose to love. 'Oh, God, You know what being rejected and
turned down does to a person. But You just keep on loving
anyway. Help me to love like that, even when it's so hard."

All the way home, tears trickled down her cheeks.

The next day she went to the funeral home to take a last
look at Marc. Chad and Stacy asked to go too. Standing
beside his casket, Sara thought, "What I remember about you
are the good times we've had these past weeks. I'm so glad I
told you I loved you. That's a comfort now. It was such a
short time we had, but for a little while I had the father I always wanted."

Before the funeral, Sara went to see Camile again even
though Camile didn't want to see her. What she witnessed appalled her! Camile, sitting on the floor, was wailing and
crying out, "I killed him. I killed him!" There were no tears,
just rocking to and fro. Why was she wailing and crying
now? She hadn't done this the last time Sara saw her. Was
this a demonstration for friends and neighbors who were calling to express their sympathy?

"Grief is one thing. But this? Is this a wake? Maybe it's a
carry-over from the way Mom saw it done when she was
young."

Sara had never seen any member of the family behave this
way before, not even when Grandfather Lambert died. It was

difficult to keep from saying, "Get up! You don't need to make such a spectacle of yourself. We believe you're sorry he's gone."

Friends took Camile home the night before the funeral. A large sign was posted on Mother's front door.
CLOSED, TEMPORARILY RESIDING AT THE FOL-LOWING ADDRESS: 24061 Lambert Lane.

The morning of the funeral, Stephanie phoned Sara, asking her to pick up Sophia, who was arriving on a flight from Boston.

"Well, at least I'm good as an errand girl. I know they're using me, but I said I was available and I meant it."

Sara delivered Sophia to the address posted on the door. She rang the doorbell and a woman answered.

"We're Mrs. Carlisle's daughters. I'm Sara and this is Sophia. May we come in?"

"Your mother is expecting your sister, but she asked me not to let you in. I'm really sorry." Then she shut the door.

Sara stood there alone. Stubbornly she rang the bell again.

"I hear my mother crying. Please! May I come in?"

"I'm sorry. Your mother told me she doesn't want to see you."

When she continued to plead, the woman shrugged and opened the door. Camile was in a bedroom hitting her head against the wall. It brought distasteful reminders of Steve's abuses. Others in the room were crying and moaning with her. The sounds were weird, almost like a pagan ceremony.

"What a difference from Gary's family! They cried too, but talked about how wonderful it was that he knew he was going to heaven. And the funeral had words of hope. I've cried too, because Pop is gone. I control my grief, but they've accused me of not loving him. As far as blood is concerned, I'm part of this family. But that's all.

Later, as Sara thought about it, she wondered. "I could be wrong. Maybe there is therapy in getting emotions out in the open like that. Maybe it clears the way for healing to take place. We'll see."

At the funeral she told the usher she was one of the Carlisles. He escorted her to the special section curtained off for the family. In the mourners' room, behind a glass partition, Camile, Stephanie, Sophia, and Marc's sister were fighting about where Marc was to be buried.

"He's *my* husband! He *will* be buried here, not in your city," Camile commanded.

After each one expressed an opinion, Sara decided to take her turn.

"Why don't you let the body rest in peace? Give him a proper burial. What difference does it make which cemetery he's in? His soul has departed."

"You aren't family and have nothing to say. If you loved him like you say, you'd understand how important this is to me. And why are you here? This section is reserved for family," Camile hissed.

Stacy, Chad, and Sara were already seated. Only the curtained glass partition separated family from friends of the deceased.

"He's my father, and Stacy's and Chad's grandfather. I'm staying! Sara replied.

Marc's body remained in cold storage for two months while the power struggle continued between Camile and Marc's sister.

After the funeral, Sara's sisters helped Camile sort and dispose of Marc's belongings. The doorbell rang. Sara went to answer. Stephanie was at the door with a large grocery bag.

"Mom says this is all you deserve. It's from Pop's belongings. She says you can have it."

Stephanie tossed the paper bag inside and retreated hastily. Sara opened the bag wondering what she would find.

"Shoe trees? He left his collection of treasured diamonds and other precious stones, but only the shoe trees are to be mine."

Six weeks after the funeral, Camile phoned Sara.

"I didn't notice when you were at the house, but I guess you took his camera."

"Mom, I never took a thing. I'd like to have some memento that was his, but only if you want me to have it. I'd never just take it."

"He left you one dollar, Sara."

"He left me more than you know, Mom, but it isn't something that shows."

Camile sniffed disdainfully.

"Sara, your sisters don't want to hear from you anymore. Don't send them Christmas cards or letters. They know you are not part of this family, so don't do it."

Sara ignored Camile's barb. "I'm here if you want me, Mom. I'll stand by whenever you need or want me. I love you whether you want me in the family or not. I care about you. God has given me this love."

CHAPTER THIRTY-SIX

The Case of the Bulging Notebook

THE ROOM WAS CROWDED when Sara arrived. She looked for Marie but didn't see her. Their favorite place to sit was in the third row, directly in front of the teacher, Dr. Edwards.

Two empty chairs were left in that section. She sat in one and placed the tape recorder on the other, saving it for Marie. After greeting a number of people sitting nearby, she picked up the recorder, replaced the batteries, and inserted a new cassette. Immediately the empty seat was occupied, not by Marie but by a tall, lanky blond with a bulging notebook. Methodically he opened it and flipped one of the many tabs, giving the appearance of a secretary about to take dictation.

"Hi. I'm Palmer Hamilton. Is it all right to sit here?" he asked now that he was settled.

"Certainly," Sara answered, a little amused by his businesslike manner. It didn't really matter if she and Marie sat together.

"You look familiar," Palmer told her, "but I don't believe we've met."

A voice from behind Sara answered for her.

"You're talking to a celebrity, Palm. Don't you watch the commercials you schedule? Meet Sara Page. She's been here before. Dr. Edwards told her unusual story last Sunday."

It was Ray Riley. Sara turned to greet him, remembering that he was the friendly fellow who had urged her to attend the class social.

"Missed you last week, Sara," Ray told her.

"So you're the Sara I've heard about! I was impressed by what Dr. Edwards related. I'd like to hear the whole story. Sorry I haven't met you before, but I'm a compulsive note-taker. You know the kind—don't want to miss a thing. But I certainly missed out on meeting you. What did Ray mean about your being on TV?"

Sara was embarrassed. She preferred not to be in the limelight.

"I'm just a schoolteacher, Palmer."

"Don't let her kid you, Palm. She's just being modest. I never had a schoolteacher who looked like that, have you?" It was Ray again.

Sara wanted to ask about Palmer's job with television commercials when the class began. She turned on her tape recorder and Palmer began his intensive note-taking. She decided when the class ended to ask him about borrowing his notes.

"Since I missed the lesson last week," she began after class, "would you consider lending me your notes? I'll be careful with them, and I'll make sure you get them back."

"Of course, Sara. My notebook is so full that pages may fall out when I open it. We need a table. Why don't we have coffee together at a restaurant, and I'll go over them with you?"

"That would be nice, Palmer. But I have children waiting for me."

"That's okay. We can all go. My treat."

"I appreciate the invitation, but I don't think we should."

"Well, I suppose I can get them out for you here. I just thought they would mean more if I went over them with you. We're to put into practice what we get in class, so this could be like a lab session."

"You're very persuasive. Is that the price you require for borrowing your notes?" He laughed good-naturedly. Then she asked, "Are you sure you don't mind my two youngsters tagging along?"

"Sara, I miss my own kids. I'll enjoy being with yours."

Inside the restaurant the hostess asked, "How many in your party?"

"Four, but we'd like two booths, please." Then he turned to Sara.

"I hope that's all right. I probably should have asked you first. My kids like to have their own table and place their own orders—makes them feel grown-up. Is it okay?"

Chad and Stacy looked eagerly at Sara, hoping for her approval.

"You really know what children like," she told him, somewhat amused.

As they were being seated, Palmer discreetly leaned over toward the children. "Feel free to order whatever you like."

In their booth, next to the children's, he told Sara, "I thought it might be a treat for them, and we could talk. They're so well-behaved."

"Thank you. What about your children, Palmer? Do you see them?"

"Not often enough. I don't have custody of my three, but how I wish I did! The lack of discipline in our home brought our marriage to disaster. My wife was unable to set guidelines for them, and when I did . . . well, that's what gets me about their being with her now.

"I've learned so much from this class. I only wish I'd known these things before. It might have saved my home. You know, Sara, divorce is like losing an arm or a leg. It's not just severing a relationship. I'm sure God had that in mind when he said that a man and wife become one. When they separate, it's like ripping themselves into two parts. I don't care how casual some people act about divorce, something happens inside that leaves an indelible scar. But of course I don't need to tell you.

"Take a look at this!" Palmer opened his notebook to a special tab. There it was, meticulously spelled out in two columns on each page—a whole section. One column listed weaknesses and the other column listed strengths.

"I had to do both, Sara. If I only listed weaknesses, I would have gone under. I had to know what I did wrong so I could go on and not make the same mistakes. I asked God to show me about myself.

" 'I give you a search warrant, God,' I told Him. 'Show me what needs changing.' Then Ray Riley, at work, told me about this class on 'Who Are You?' I've been finding out what in my life needs altering."

He closed his notebook. Sara was glad. Even though she was vitally interested, she didn't want to appear nosy. It was like peeking inside someone's desk drawers.

"What an orderly, systematic person Palmer is," Sara thought. "He's a planner and a thinker, and I like that quality in a person."

In their class they were encouraged to share their griefs and mistakes. "It leads to finding solutions and brings healing," Palmer added.

"I have a hard time, Palmer," Sara told him, "opening up to others about my problems. Do you think it really helps? It seems so personal."

"I know what you mean. We don't want people to know we have weaknesses or faults, so we cover them up from ourselves . . . and others. It isn't just talking about problems that's important, Sara. I didn't understand that before. Now I know why they encourage this. The sharing together helped glue me back together again. It's therapeutic. And it's okay to share in this group because we aren't going to sit in condemnation."

"Really? I've heard others say that, but therapy sessions never helped me. Why do you think this works?" she asked.

"I wouldn't have believed it worked. It was so painful to do. But guess what happened! After I talked about it and didn't feel threatened anymore, I began to see how it was helping me. Those listening didn't think of it as. hauling out your garbage for them to look at. Their being nonjudgmental made it possible to share. You can't do that with just anyone. We encourage helping one another this way.

"I've learned that if I hide from myself, or keep it inside, well, I prevent healing. Those listening don't do the healing, but they make it possible."

"Why do you think it works, Palmer?"

"I'm not sure, but the Bible says, 'Admit your faults to one another and pray for each other so that you might be healed.'[10] I think it means to do what we're doing. If you decide you really want to remove the debris from your life, then confess it to a caring, praying person who doesn't condemn you. Then healing can begin. While it remains inside, it festers, eating away at you even though you may not be aware of it. It's getting it out into the open, and not allowing it back in, that I believe God had in mind when He encouraged confessing in order to be healed."

"Oh, I like that, Palmer."

"I seem to have gotten carried away by all this, Sara. I didn't mean to monopolize the conversation."

"I asked, and I'm glad you insisted and were willing to share. I hate to break this up, but I live 30 miles away. It's time to go home."

Palmer opened his notebook and removed the notes Sara wanted.

"We never did get around to talking about these. Maybe next week. I hope we'll get together again."

"This has helped me a lot, Palmer. I'd like to continue it."

"You know, Sara, I like your idea of the tape recorder. I believe I'll do that instead of writing all the time. Let's sit together again. Whoever gets there first could save a seat."

[10]James 5:16.

One Sunday, Palmer suggested an outing for the next Saturday, including both his and her children.

"Would you like to go to Farmer's Market for lunch? Have you been there?" When Sara shook her head, he continued.

"My kids can never get enough of that place. At the different stands they have every kind of food imaginable. It's not the same as a cafeteria. It's more like a progressive dinner. I think your kids will love it.

"After lunch we could go across the street for a tour of the television studios. You know that's where I work. If we wanted to take in a broadcast while we're there, I could arrange it."

On Saturday, with the five children in the car with them, Sara was wondering what she was getting into.

"We're just on a pleasant outing," she reminded herself. I'm not opening myself up for an emotional involvement. I made a mess out of that part of my life and I mustn't allow it to happen again."

After an interesting lunch, Palmer led them across the street on the tour. When they came to his office, he unlocked the door. Sara noticed his name on the door, indicating that he was the executive producer of the advertising division. Inside, one wall was lined with books.

"What a wide range of subject material to choose from!"

"When I divorced I moved my library here. I try to read a book every other day on diversified subjects. Someday I hope to move them back into the house again. It's better to have them shelved than to have them get musty in boxes. My aim is to choose reading that will not only make me better-informed but also help me become the man God wants me to be."

Palmer's 13-year-old son, Jeff, pointed to a wall plaque.

"This is an award Dad got while he worked at the Naval Academy in Annapolis," he said proudly.

"How interesting. What kind of research was it?" Sara inquired.

"I was in communications," Palmer answered. "Now I'm in charge of placing commercials on network programs."

Sara noticed another plaque.

"No wonder you got a job here. You were graduated from M.I.T. I'm really impressed, Palmer."

They were both making light conversation. It wasn't the physical attraction that drew Sara to Palmer, even though he was very good-looking. It was his perception and openness that appealed to her, qualities missing in Gary, Steve, and Rex. "It's so nice just to be friends."

On Sunday, Marie mentioned that she noticed that Sara and Palmer were together more and more. Sara was quick to inform her, "We have meaningful discussions and it's really helped me. I'm definitely not romantically interested."

CHAPTER THIRTY-SEVEN

An Unexpected Answer

ONE EVENING SARA had the Worths over for dinner.

Before she began to prepare the meal, she checked the day's mail. On an envelope she saw the words "Attorney at Law." That old feeling returned. A brief letter accompanied a form.

When her signature, witnessed by a notary public, was affixed to the paper, the divorce from Rex would be final.

"So Rex is really following through. Well, it isn't what I wanted, but now I know that at least one of my letters reached him. I sent it registered mail, and the card with his signature was returned.

"There's both a miracle and a tragedy here. I've stopped blaming myself. That's the miracle. The tragedy is that our marriage couldn't be salvaged. I really thought it could."

At dinner she told Jack and Sue she was ready to buy a house.

"It's interesting that you should mention it this evening, Sara," Jack told her. "We have friends who are moving to another city and must sell their home right away. They live near us. In fact, it was only last night that he informed me."

"Oh, Jack. Do you suppose it's to be my house? I love that neighborhood. Maybe they haven't listed it yet. I could look first thing tomorrow, since it's Saturday. Could you call now to find out if they'll show it to me? Before you do, let's pray together about it."

Five days later Sara signed escrow papers and handed over her down payment. In 60 days she could move in.

"Can you believe it, Sue? I'm just five blocks from you and Mother. I wonder what she'll think when she knows."

"Sara, maybe your living near your mother is significant. She's lonely now that your father is gone."

"I know. But each time I reach out she pushes me away."

"Sara," Sue went on, "I believe it's a big bluff. It's possible that she's been putting on a front all these years because she got trapped into it. She may not know how to back out of it even if she wanted to."

"You know, Sue, I sometimes think the same thing. I'll reach out again. And thanks for encouraging me."

By now Palmer's phone calls were coming regularly. It was a good friendship which cautiously avoided any romantic suggestion. Since they lived nearly 20 miles apart, the phone became their frequent link.

"Celebrate my birthday with me on Friday, Sara. Get a baby-sitter. I'll pay. Let me take you to a really nice place."

While they were talking on the phone, Chad yelled out loud enough for Palmer to hear, "Why don't you marry him, Mom? We like him." Palmer laughed and told Sara to tell Chad it was a good idea. When they hung up, Sara frowned at Chad.

"Whatever got into you, Chad? I didn't appreciate it."

"Oh, Mom! Don't be angry. You know you like him. We do. Stacy and I talked it over. We think he should be our dad. He would be, too, only you won't let him."

On Friday, when Palmer arrived, he called the children. He had a little celebration gift for them to open after he and Sara left.

"I didn't want you to miss out on my birthday," he told them.

Palmer chose a dimly lit restaurant. "Maybe we ought to be holding hands . . . not wasting this intimate setting, Sara," he told her after they placed their orders.

"Palmer, I think you should understand that we're just good friends. Let's not spoil it by getting romantic. It's our common interests, problems, and solutions that brought us together. That, and our tape recorders." And they both laughed.

"You know, Sara, sometimes we don't plan our own futures. Who knows if this isn't God's design for us?"

"I don't believe it, Palmer. God disapproves of divorce. So how could He be for this?"

"Maybe so, Sara. But have you ever thought that we have the same goals in life?" And then he brought out his big notebook from under the seat.

"I brought this in to show you, but there's not enough light. I'm going to ask the waiter for another candle or two because I want you to see this. It's my thirty-sixth birthday, and I've been reviewing my goals for the future."

Sara found the whole scene a bit amusing and wanted to laugh when the extra candle was added. Palmer pointed to a page where he had carefully listed his goals in black and white, adding little boxes neatly drawn in front of each goal. Some had been checked off, indicating that they had already been reached.

"Here's one for my kids. I'm setting money aside for their education. And this page is for spiritual goals. Everything in my life used to revolve around one thing, Sara. But now I've made a committment not to live just for myself. I want God to be first. Then I can expect His favor on everything I do. I like living like that. It's satisfying to me and gives me a sense of achievement. I wasn't always like this. I've got some goals for marriage, too," he added. He closed the notebook without further comment.

"I agree with you about commitment, because I've done the same thing, Palmer. And you're right. I used to think I was living it up! But this new life makes my old one seem dull. It never had lasting joy."

Palmer didn't press the romance issue any further that evening.

One night at a church seminar, Sara got a surprise when she found out what a tremendously capable leader and public speaker Palmer was. She saw in him a new light and admired him more than ever.

Six months had passed since they had first met. One day he hinted at marriage again. Sara was adamant.

"No, Palmer. If that's what you have in mind, this is it! I'm not going that route again. I've been hurt that way for the last time. Besides, if you knew what I've done you wouldn't want me. I'm worldly-wise. I know about infatuation. It's nice, but not lasting. You've just become emotional. We're not 20-year-olds.

"I want what God wants for me and I don't see how this fits. Anyway, it's much too soon to think about. If you feel romantic about me, we'd be better off not seeing each other. It's not healthy because you'll get hurt. I'm independent now. At 35 I can support myself and my children."

Palmer let the subject drop.

One day Sara realized that she had postponed going back to the doctor to get the clearance statement she had asked for. She phoned for an appointment. When she arrived, the doctor ordered a new X ray and laboratory tests.

"That's fine, Dr. Baxter. I don't want you to miss anything. I'm expecting you to write a statement for me that you found no evidence of the earlier problem. I want you to be satisfied."

In a few days she returned for the results. This time the doctor announced, "Here you are, Sara. A clean bill of health. I'm happy to give it to you, though I don't understand how it came about."

"Thank you, Dr. Baxter. You don't know what this means! I want it to remind me how good God has been to me."

The next time Palmer came to see Sara, Stacy met him at the door.

"How's my favorite girl?" he asked, giving her a big hug.

"I thought Mommie was your girl, but I wish you were my daddy," she said shyly.

"Say, I'd like that. How did you know I wanted that too?"

Sara acted as though she hadn't heard their private conversation.

"You remember the miracle-healing I had, Palmer? I want you to see the good news I finally got from the doctor. It's documented," Sara told him, handing him the letter with Dr. Baxter's signature.

"Say, this is great news, Sara! But how did you ever get tuberculosis in the first place?"

"What do I say now?" Sara puzzled. She hadn't anticipated this situation, and floundered for a reply.

"It's something I haven't been able to talk about, Palmer. I guess it's one of those skeletons I still have to remove from the closet."

"That's okay, Sara. You don't ever have to tell me anything. I love you just as you are. You don't ever have to shed light on anything—not to me. I'd love you no matter what skeletons you're still hanging onto. You see, Sara, I'm in love with the new Sara, not the old one. We wouldn't have made a good pair the way we were, anyway."

It was the first time he had used the word "love."

"Well, people can love each other without being 'in love,'" she reasoned. "I hope he won't press the matter again. I don't want to lose his friendship." Hastily she changed the subject.

A few days later he phoned. Suddenly he got serious about the subject of marriage again.

"Before you interrupt me, Sara, and I know you were going to, I want you to hear me out. I've thought about this a long time. Prayed about it, too. I love you, Sara. I've tried to tell you this.

"I wish I hadn't failed in my first marriage. You know that. I may have regrets, but I've stopped blaming myself. I know I'm forgiven and I'm ready to make a commitment to you, Sara. A life commitment. God's not holding my past against me, and He doesn't remind me of it even though I sometimes remind myself.

"You told me when we first met that you had put God first in your life. Okay. I want you to ask Him what His plan is in this. Does the thought of marrying me terrify you, Sara? Don't answer. Ask God all about it. Promise me you'll do it."

"I've told you before, Palmer, I don't think we can consider marriage. Will you abide by what He shows me and not bring it up again if His answer is no?"

"Sara, I have every confidence that God will give the right answer. One more thing. Neither of us can go back to undo our past. We can't regain what was lost back there. It's only what's ahead that counts. Think about that when you pray, will you?"

The more Sara prayed, the clearer it became that her feelings about Palmer were no longer platonic. One day she admitted to God, "It looks like I've fallen in love with him in spite of myself. How could this be? Why didn't You help me keep by guard up? You know how hurt he'd be if Palmer knew about my prostitution. I don't think I could ever tell him. With my past, I'm not worthy of having a husband again. Palmer is such a fine man. He deserves someone better.

"If you really approve of this, Lord, you'll have to point it out very clearly to me. I'm going to ask You something that seems strange to me. But I need a yes or no answer that is so definite I can't miss it. Dr. Edwards could easily fit something into his lesson. Will you have him be so specific that I can't misinterpret, and I'll understand that it's for me? Will you have him use the Bible to back it up?"

One Sunday in class, Sara sat down, and in a moment Palmer joined her on the left. She almost wished he hadn't because she was afraid her eyes would betray her love. And she was still convinced that God's answer to her would be no. They set their tape recorders side-by-side and laughed about it. It broke the tension for her. When Dr. Edwards was ready to begin, Sara recalled her prayer.

"Oh, Lord, I'm reminding You that I'm tuned in for what You have for me. I don't want to misunderstand a thing, so make it very clear."

Near the end of the lesson, Dr. Edwards hesitated.

"Something just came to me that I believe fits in. It has to do with copping out. There's someone here who needs this right now.

"You've been telling yourself, 'I'm not worthy of a new start. I made a complete mess of my life. It's so bad that I can't tell anyone about it except God, and He already knows.'"

"He's buried it in the deepest sea. Since He's never going to take it out to look at again, why do you want to? Stop accusing yourself. God isn't accusing you. You put on a diving outfit and bring it to the surface to look at again and again, reminding yourself of what a crumb you are. You're defeating yourself by your past.

"Paul the Apostle said, '*Put those things behind you*' that keep you from running in the race. Let me read it to you.

"'I'm still not all I should be . . . ! Now listen to this! 'But I am bringing all my energies to bear on this one thing: *Forgetting the past and looking forward to what lies ahead*, I strain to reach the end of the race . . .'[11] It's time for you to get on with what's ahead. There's a race to be won.

"Don't expect to run if you're saying 'I'm not worthy' or 'I can't forgive myself.' That's a weight that's holding you down. Lay aside every weight and get on with the life that's before you. You've been completely pardoned!"

Dr. Edwards continued speaking, but Sara didn't hear another word.

"This is for me! This is my answer! And it isn't no!

"I put the past behind me! NOW! And I won't take it out to look at again. That's it! I never forgave myself before. It's the one unfinished matter in my life . . . the one postponed action left for me to settle."

Sara sighed, then silently mouthed the words to herself.

"I forgive myself!" A tear trickled down her cheek as the impact of these words sank in.

"It's as if a spare room inside vacated and I posted a sign 'SPACE AVAILABLE. IMMEDIATE OCCUPANCY.' I know there's a special place in me reserved for God. It's been filled. Now a new space had opened. It's where the skeleton in the closet has been. Now it's gone! But it's going to be replaced. And I know who is to fill it!"

Palmer, sensing something very personal was happening to Sara, and not wishing to interfere, simply reached for her hand. He squeezed it gently, but firmly. When her watery

[11]Philippians 3:13.

eyes met his, and held, he knew he was part of it. Sara returned his squeeze, smiled through her tears, then spoke softly.

"I've been running from myself all my life," she told him. "But that race is over! Finished! I've entered this new race. I'm in it all the way. Let's run it together, Palmer."

"You couldn't have given me any better news, Sara."

Neither of them realized class was dismissed and everyone had left.

ABOUT THE AUTHOR

LUCILLE SCHIRMAN was in the Women's Army Corps, Chaplains' Division, during WW-II. After the war she entered college administration as Registrar at Northwestern College, Minneapolis, of which Billy Graham was then president.

She later spent twenty years teaching social science, and took up public speaking at conventions and church and social functions. A crippling disease confined her to a wheelchair for some time, compelling her to go on leave, during which she began writing and turned out LADY ON THE RUN.

Now out of her wheelchair, she lives in Santa Barbara, California.